THE
INVISIBLE
HOUR

Center Point
Large Print

Also by Alice Hoffman and available from Center Point Large Print:

The World That We Knew
Magic Lessons
The Book of Magic

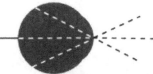

This Large Print Book carries the Seal of Approval of N.A.V.H.

THE
INVISIBLE
HOUR

ALICE HOFFMAN

CENTER POINT LARGE PRINT
THORNDIKE, MAINE

This Center Point Large Print edition
is published in the year 2023 by arrangement with
Atria Books, a division of Simon & Schuster, Inc.

The text of this Large Print edition is unabridged.
In other aspects, this book may vary
from the original edition.
Printed in the United States of America
on permanent paper.
Set in 16-point Times New Roman type.

ISBN: 978-1-63808-910-0

The Library of Congress has cataloged this record
under Library of Congress Control Number: 2023942184

I began my life for the second time on a June night in the year I turned fifteen. My name was still Mia Jacob, and I was still made of blood and bones, but when I stepped into the road on that night I walked into a different future. I left the way my mother had arrived, alone and in the dark.

The moon was yellow and the woods were pitch black. If you didn't know there were mountains and fields and that this was Western Massachusetts, you would think you had come to the end of the earth. In some ways that was true, at least for me. I could feel every breath that I took rattle inside my chest. Every heartbeat echoed. Freedom is not what you think it is. It's cold and hard and bright. That was what it felt like to change everything. To pick up the ashes and let them blow in the wind.

In the morning I was to be punished out in the cow field, in front of everyone, a cautionary tale so that one and all could see what happened to anyone who disobeyed. I was meant to beg and plead. I had asked to be forgiven in the past, but I was someone else now. I was the girl who knew how to escape, the one who could become invisible, who believed that a single dream was more powerful than a thousand realities.

They thought I only had a life that I lived here, but I had found other possibilities every time I read a book.

They locked me in the barn with the sheep. They told me I should think about what tomorrow would bring. But I had stolen a hammer from the men rebuilding a shed in the farthest field, and I'd left it underneath the hay in the barn. I'd always thought I might need to escape.

I worked on the lock for an hour or more, until my hands were blistering and bleeding. Nothing, and then, all at once, the lock came apart in my hands.

I was wearing gray overalls and my mother's red boots. I looked like a prisoner, and that was what I'd always believed I was, but not anymore. My long red hair had been cut as a punishment in the spring, when I would not leave my mother's grave site and had to be torn away, the ferns I'd held on to still in my hands. My hair was too beautiful anyway, that's what they said, nothing more than a vanity, the sort of attribute that would make me look in a mirror and think I was better than everyone else.

This time, the punishment was worse. They had hung a rope around my neck on which there was a badge announcing the rules I had broken. **A** for acts of wickedness. **A** for affront and for anarchy. **A** for avoidance and antisocial behavior. **A** for ambition. Tomorrow they would burn the letter **A** into my arm so I would never forget the reason for my punishment.

They had found books in my possession. Shakespeare's collected plays. *The Blue Book of Fairy Tales*, which had been my mother's favorite when she was a girl. Emily Dickinson's letters and poems. I am out with lanterns, looking for myself. Every time I had gone to town, I'd managed to sneak into the library. I knew there was magic there, and I knew they would do their best to destroy it. They'd burned my books tonight and I could still smell the sulfury scent of embers out in the field where they planned to punish me tomorrow. I had one more book, the one I loved best of all, hidden in the barn in a place where they'd failed to look. It was my treasure and my map. It was the book that had saved my life. Long ago, there had been other places where women were punished for being true to themselves. I kept *The Scarlet Letter* close to my heart when I left the barn and ran across the dark field. Sometimes when you read a book it's as if you were reading the story of your own life. That was what had happened to me. I woke up when I read the first page. I saw who I was and who I could be.

The only other thing I took with me was a tiny painting I had found in a cabinet in the office. Take it, Evangeline who ran the office and the school had said when she saw what I'd found.

No one wants that junk. It was a watercolor in shades of blue and green that I'd kept beneath my pillow. I looked at it every night and it always reminded me that the world was beautiful. It was beautiful even in the dark, with the soft green air all around me, and the fireflies drifting through the tall grass, and the white phlox growing wild in the woods.

The dogs all knew me, and they didn't stop me when I got to the gate; they didn't even bark. There were bats flickering through the trees. There were so many stars, but I didn't have time to look at them. I walked among the crowded thorns. I stood too close and bled. My mother didn't know how to unlock what kept us here, but I was different. I had the key in my hands, the book that was first published in 1850, the one that understood our story better than anyone who had ever known us. I left the badge that had been strung around my neck behind, making certain to tear it in two.

I went through the fields, then down the dirt road and past the old oak trees. In the distance there was Hightop Mountain, where bears still roamed. I knew what I had to do. Travel light. Don't look back. Take only what you need most of all. I slipped into the forest and headed toward town. I had been born here and had lived here all my life, but that was over now. I would remain invisible among the ferns and the pine trees, unseen by any passing traffic. Twigs and leaves crunched under my boots as I made my way through the dense greenery where the evergreens gave off a dark, earthy scent. It was the end of something and the beginning of something.

In every fairy tale the girl who is saved is the one who rescues herself.

When I came to town, I ran down the road. I ran faster than I ever had before. I went to the one place where I knew the door would be open. The place where I'd found the key. Long before the sun came up, before they went to the barn and found I was gone, before they began to search for me, I was at the library. That was when my life began.

PART ONE

THE HERE AND NOW

CHAPTER ONE

ACROSS THE UNIVERSE

Ivy Jacob came from Boston, and had lived her whole life on Beacon Hill, but whenever she was asked where she grew up, she would say, *West of the moon.* She laughed when she gave out that fairy-tale locale that had never existed in this world or any other, but anyone could tell from the look in her eyes how deeply she wished it were true. She had always felt like an outsider in Louisburg Square, an exclusive enclave of Greek Revival houses surrounding a small park and garden, all privately owned by the elite families in the city. Neighbors didn't necessarily speak to each other, but they respected one another, and they followed the rules. The other girls on the hill wore pleated skirts and blouses with Peter Pan collars, they did as they were told, and when they graduated from the Birch School, they went to Wellesley or Mount Holyoke. Ivy was different. She did as she pleased. Her parents didn't appreciate the way she sulked, or how she shamed herself with her short skirts, treating her beauty as if it were a curse, chopping off her hair one year and dying it blue another, storming out of the room whenever her parents tried to talk sense into her. All the same, she was an intelligent girl, and had always been a great reader, spending hours at the Boston Athenaeum; but despite her love of books, she ignored her schoolwork and was failing her classes, bored to death by her lessons. She loved Thoreau for his rebellious thoughts, and the Brontës for their dark and tragic tales of love, and Toni Morrison, whose novels made her cry and feel as if she didn't know the first thing about life.

What few treasures she had were stored in a small jewelry box she'd been given when she was a child. When the lid was opened, a dancer spun in a circle. Inside there were little more than trinkets, silver bangle bracelets, a ticket stub from a concert she'd gone to when her parents were away vacationing, the key to their maid Helen Connelly's house. Helen, who'd never had children and always regretted that decision, saw the family close-up, and she knew how unhappy Ivy was. She'd been with the Jacob family ever since Ivy was a toddler and thought of the girl as her own, even though she wasn't. If she had been, Ivy would have been pulled out of that private school, where she was so clearly failing; she'd know she was loved.

"For emergencies," Helen had said when she gave Ivy the key. "If you ever need me."

Ivy had thrown her arms around Helen to thank her. "Every day is an emergency," Ivy had whispered, and although she had smiled, it didn't feel like a joke.

"Don't forget," Helen had told the girl. "Day or night. I'm here."

Ivy was a true beauty, with black hair and gray eyes, but as she grew older, she became more unmanageable, at least in her parents' opinion. By the time she was sixteen her mother considered Ivy to be the bane of her existence. When she was a senior in high school, her grades were abysmal, she often slept past noon, and she'd become a vegetarian, a choice her parents were convinced she had made out of spite. Ivy had been picked up by police with a group that had vandalized the statue of John Harvard in Harvard Yard, painting his foot red. There had been one boy after another, and Ivy had recently been caught in her room in bed with a neighbor's son, a Harvard student named Noah Brinley, who was from a perfectly fine family; still, their actions were unacceptable. Noah's parents were not informed of the situation—boys would be boys after all—but Ivy was grounded for several weeks, although if her parents had been more observant, they would have seen damp footprints on the carpeting in the hall, left there on the cold

15

mornings when Ivy sneaked back into the house after nights spent in the Public Garden, or in Noah's dorm room, or wandering home along Beacon Street.

Ivy didn't realize what had happened until September, and by then three months had passed. She'd skipped her time of the month before, but one day she felt something move inside her. No one had discussed birth control with her, and she'd thought she could depend on Noah to take care of that, but he'd never been one to take responsibility. Now it was as if she had swallowed the sea, and there was a wave coursing through her, a quickening that felt as if another heart was beating against her own. Ivy had never thought about having a baby, children were of no interest to her, but now what was important in the world had changed.

Students were just returning to Harvard, and she found Noah in his dorm room, unpacking. He'd been away all summer, traveling with his parents in France, and somehow, he had not connected with Ivy after his return to the States. The truth was, there were other girls he found more interesting, ones who didn't have so much baggage and were more sophisticated in sexual matters. Noah was tall and handsome with thick red-blond hair. "Hey," he said uncertainly when he saw her in the doorway. Ivy looked heavier, and she had a strange, dreamy expression, almost as if she was in a trance. "What are you doing here?" Noah asked after a measured pause.

She was there to tell him that their lives were about to change, that they were meant to be together, that joy would be theirs, but when she announced that she was pregnant, Noah had no response. He appeared blank and fuzzy-headed, the way he did when he'd had too much to drink. Ivy told him she wanted them to run away together, and in response Noah slammed the door shut in case his roommate returned. "Lower your voice," he said, and at that moment, there in his Harvard dorm room, he sounded like Ivy's father.

Ivy had thought they were in love, that's what they had told each other, but now she saw the dark, sidelong look Noah gave her and she thought that she might have been wrong. She'd seen that look before, from her father as a matter of fact. Disappointment and distance. Noah was still in the room with her, but it was as if he'd already left.

"Do you think I would actually consider running away?" Noah said coldly, a scowl on his handsome face. "This is my sophomore year. This year matters. Don't screw it up for me."

Ivy felt like a little girl, abandoned to a world of chaos. The truth was, for all of her bad-girl attitude, Noah was the first boy she'd been intimate with. She couldn't go to her family doctor for help with birth control, he would have immediately told her mother, and the one time she'd gone to a clinic for help, there were protesters outside, and she'd been too nervous to walk past them. "I thought you wanted us to be together."

Noah depended on the goodwill of his parents, and this news of Ivy's would infuriate them. Who knew what price he'd have to pay? He would have never gotten into Harvard without his father's interference. "People change," he said with confident authority. He'd heard his father say so many times before.

Noah wasn't even certain how he felt about Ivy anymore. What did love mean, anyway? Ivy was beautiful, but what had made for amusing fun at the start—jumping into the Charles River, even though it was polluted and freezing, stealing from shops on Charles Street, having sex late at night in the Boston Public Garden—seemed childish to him now. Ivy could get rid of the baby or have it, that was her decision. What did he have to do with it?

"Hey," Noah told her. "What can I say? Do as you please."

"As *I* please?" Ivy was incredulous. "Isn't that what you're doing? Whatever *you* please?"

Noah took a step back. Ivy's gray eyes were like a cat's. You never knew what a girl like Ivy might do. She was so emotional. You never knew when she'd snap. She might ring up his parents or arrive at their front door, pleading for help. She might blackmail him or stalk him, lurking behind him in Harvard Yard, attempting to ambush him. He had his future to think of, and Ivy was already a part of his past. He would likely have difficulty remembering her in years to come.

"Look, I have a class," Noah said crossly, having no idea that he was behaving badly and not much caring. "Not everyone has all the time in the world."

Noah stalked away, resigned to the fact that not all liaisons ended well. Ivy wasn't the first girl he'd disappointed, and she likely wouldn't be the last. He had wanted to say, *It's your problem, not mine,* but it was easier to just disappear. Once he turned the corner, Ivy was already forgotten.

She waited a week, but waiting didn't make anything easier. Her dreams woke her in the middle of the night. Her clothes didn't fit her anymore. When she finally told her father about her situation, he slapped her, a gut response he forever regretted.

He wasn't ordinarily a violent man, but what was done was done and now Ivy stared at him as if he were a stranger. "What were you thinking?" he spat, agitated. He asked Ivy if she was trying to kill her mother, ruin his business, throw her life away.

"I'm having a baby," Ivy told him. "I thought you would help me."

She was sent to her room as if she were a child, and she heard her parents arguing down in the parlor. She sneaked out of her bedroom and perched on the stairs to hear what the adults were plotting. They had already decided her fate. Ivy would be sent to a school in Utah, a facility they referred to as a lockdown, and when the baby was born it would be placed for adoption. It was her body and her future they were discussing, but it seemed that it belonged to them, and they intended to take control of what they considered to be a disaster.

Ivy packed a suitcase and waited for them to go to bed, then she went down the three flights to the front door. She might have left a note for Helen, who had always been so kind to her, she might have taken the key from her jewelry box and ridden the T to South Boston, where Helen lived, but she wasn't thinking straight. Her impulse was to get away as fast as she could so that her parents couldn't rule her life. She would most certainly not allow them to take her baby. She didn't care that the front door was still propped open when she left. Her parents' belongings meant everything to them, and they were always careful to double-lock the front door. Let them see what it was like to have someone who didn't respect their desires or dreams. Let them know that she didn't intend to come back.

Ivy was shivering once she realized that her fate was in her own hands. All the same, she went to Harvard Square and sat cross-legged on the bricks near the T station, where young people gathered to hang out and buy drugs. Her back was against the wall, her suitcase stowed under her legs. Her long black hair hung loose down her back, and she was wearing jeans and a jacket that she now realized was too light for the season. It was chilly on September nights. Time was passing so quickly.

Ivy was hoping to spy Noah, yearning for him to change his mind, but he wasn't there, and if he had seen her there in the Square, he would have walked right past her. He'd already planned that should their paths ever cross again, he would not engage at any level, not even a conversation. He owed her nothing, after all. He'd simply avert his eyes and wish her away. He'd already done that as a matter of fact.

A girl with a heavy backpack sat down next to Ivy. "Hey, how are you doing?"

"How do you think?" Ivy was embarrassed when she realized there were tears in her eyes.

"I think the world can be cruel," the girl said.

Ivy wiped her tears away. What good would crying do? "Somebody must be happy somewhere," she muttered, although she didn't quite believe it.

"They are," the girl said. "And I know where."

Ivy's new companion was Kayla, or at least that was what she called herself now; she used to have another name, the one her parents had given her, but that didn't matter anymore. Kayla was on her way to Western Massachusetts. She'd heard about a community where people were respected for who they were and not expected to be who their families wanted them to be. They weren't judged and they shared all they had. She'd come to Harvard Square to panhandle and get enough cash together for the bus ticket.

As it turned out there was no need for begging. Ivy had her dad's credit card, and because her father had not yet canceled it, the girls went out and charged plates of fries at Charlie's Kitchen, then they each bought new shoes. After that, they went downtown, and Ivy used her father's card to withdraw enough cash for two bus tickets before tossing the American Express card in a trash bin at the Greyhound Bus Station. There in the station, Ivy froze for a minute. She knew everything was about to change.

"Don't be scared," Kayla said.

Ivy was shivering. The life she'd had seemed very far away, and she already regretted not calling Helen. "I'm not scared," she insisted.

"We'll find the place that will welcome us," Kayla assured her.

Ivy was exhausted and she was grateful to fall

asleep on the bus, where it was warm and cozy and dark. When she woke up three hours later in Blackwell, Massachusetts, she looked out the window and saw the night sky swirling with stars and she thought it might be possible that she had stumbled into paradise.

Kenneth Jacob came down the staircase at a little past six in the morning, and he knew something was amiss. He got the message his daughter had sent when she left the door unlocked. It had blown wide open, and there were two pigeons doddering about on the black-and-white marble tiled floor. Ivy had disappeared so completely it was as if she had been swallowed whole by the earth. The private detective Ken hired couldn't find her until ten months later, when she was living out in rural Massachusetts, past Blackwell on some run-down farm where she'd already given birth to a baby girl. The detective brought the photographs he'd snapped to Ivy's father's office on Beacon Street. Kenneth Jacob sifted through them as the detective explained that Ivy had fallen in with a cultish community run by a crackpot whose rules included a code that compelled members to sever all ties with their families of origin, completely cutting off contact. As it turned out, the Jacob family had long ago lived in the Berkshires and their direct relatives had made their fortune in the apple orchards outside Blackwell before turning to real estate and banking in Boston. One of their ancestors was said to have had a child with John Chapman, the man known as Johnny Appleseed, so Ken Jacob liked to say that apples ran in their blood.

In the grainy photos the detective had taken, Ivy's hair was braided and covered with a scarf, and her beautiful face was serene as she picked what appeared to be blackberries. She wore a threadbare man's jacket and carried a wicker basket. There was a baby on a blanket, left to its own devices as Ivy concentrated on the low-growing fruit. The sunshine was bright, and, in the distance, there was a forest of dark pine trees. Nearby was an orchard, and if Ken had known anything about apples, he would have seen they were a variety called Look-No-Furthers, descendants of the ones Johnny Appleseed had planted.

"Is she with the high school boyfriend?" Ken Jacob asked. He'd been tormented ever since Ivy disappeared; he'd always assumed he could right whatever went wrong and he had assured his wife he would do so again, but he'd begun to have doubts.

"Noah Brinley? Nope. No way. He's at Harvard. She's with this Joel Davis character. The one that runs the Community. He says he studied at Harvard, but the only records I found for him were over at the Massachusetts Department of Corrections. He did time at Bay State

Correctional Center, there on assault charges."

"Well, she won't be with him for long." Ken Jacob had had just about enough. This was no longer teenage high jinks; it was the total ruination of a life.

"Ken," the detective said. He was an affable guy who had seen terrible things in his line of work. He only used a client's first name when delivering bad news. "She married him."

Ken Jacob nodded. "Okay," he said. He sounded calm, but the truth was, he was in a panic. He'd been trained to always think of a backup plan in his investment career and as a boy had learned not to allow his feelings to show by his mother and his nanny. Ivy had turned eighteen, but there were ways around things. "Can we get the child?" He had been so convinced the baby should be placed for adoption when he first learned Ivy was pregnant, but now he believed they could undo some of the damage. They'd have a granddaughter. One perfect child. They'd protect her and take care of her. He didn't dare think, the way they hadn't protected Ivy.

"Unlikely," the detective said bluntly. "Davis is listed on the birth certificate as the father. So, we'd have a fight, and it wouldn't be pretty. From what I've heard, he's a son of a bitch."

A fight meant articles in the *Boston Globe*. It meant lawyers and courthouses. Ken wasn't certain his wife could take going through that sort of battle.

"We could snatch the child," Ken said. A gang of men could swoop down in the middle of the night; they could leave a truck idling outside the Community's gates.

"If you want to acquire the child, I have the guys for it. It would cost thirty grand. But there's always the risk that something could go wrong," the detective informed Ken. "You're spending money, but you have no guarantees."

It wasn't the money that bothered Ken Jacob, it was the idea of leaving his wife on her own if he were to be caught and sentenced. And so, tormented by all he could not do, he wedged the photographs he'd been given into the top drawer of his desk. He paid for the detective's services, and he never mentioned his daughter's whereabouts to his wife, even though he heard Catherine crying late at night. He thought the truth of what had happened to their girl was worse than most of the things Catherine could imagine. He couldn't bear for his wife to see the photographs of their brilliant little girl dressed in austere gray clothing, as if she were a Puritan. Ken used to go skiing and snowshoeing in that vicinity when he was a young man, stopping at the rustic Jack Straw Tavern; he'd gone to see what local people call the Tree of Life, planted by Johnny Appleseed himself on his way out west.

One winter he discovered that the folklore about the tree was true, it really did bloom in winter. It was a wonder and a marvel, one that could make a person believe in magic, at least for a time.

He couldn't help but wonder if Ivy had even thought about them. He wondered if she'd known that after she left, he sat by the front door most nights, waiting for her to come home. Well, now he knew, she wouldn't be returning. She was married and she wasn't their girl anymore. There was no need for Catherine to be told anything. It wouldn't have mattered, anyway. Some things that had been done could not be undone, and Ken Jacob was convinced that their daughter was a lost soul. If he had gotten into his car and driven three hours, Ivy might have run to him with the baby in her arms, grateful beyond measure. She might have cried and told him she'd made a mistake. She might have forgiven him for slapping her and refusing to help her when it mattered most. They could have forgiven each other, and the future could have been something they shared, but instead Ken Jacob went into his study, and he locked the door, and he never said her name aloud again.

Western Massachusetts had once been wilderness, and there were times when it still appeared to be a wild land, especially in January, when the snow was so high it was impossible to walk down the road, or in October, when the mountains were ablaze, as if the whole world had caught fire. The Community owned two hundred acres of land just outside the town of Blackwell, which had been founded in 1750. Residents of Blackwell had been unhappy when a trickle of strangers began to appear ten years earlier. The first group pitched their tents not far from the edge of Band's Meadow, they bathed in the Last Look River, and ate fiddlehead ferns and corn meant for livestock. They were a ragtag bunch, and all newcomers were greeted with love and kindness, even though many owned nothing more than a backpack slung over one shoulder and had arrived in town straight off the Greyhound bus. Others had left established lives to become searchers for beauty or truth, often arriving in BMWs or Audis, which were soon enough sold off at the Car Mart near the highway to Lenox, since possessions were not valued among the group and personal wealth was shared.

The Community's first bleak winter was spent in a pure sort of poverty with months of back-breaking work that left dark circles under the recruits' eyes. Before long, fifteen small houses had been built, and then the Community Center and the dining hall went up, and finally the dormitories for the children, with their white iron beds and neat cubbies for shoes and clothes. The barns were all raised in a single day by forty men, most of whom knew nothing about farming and so little about building that several accidents occurred that afternoon, including a broken leg and a nail rammed through the palm of a young man's hand.

After ten years, the locals had to admit the Community people worked hard, and when the mayor had sent the entire police force of Blackwell, three men and a lone woman, out to the farm to search for evidence of criminal activity, they found none. The town had no choice but to accept the likelihood that the Community was there to stay, whether or not they agreed with Joel Davis's philosophy. Davis was thought to be cunning and shrewd, but even those who were dead set against the Community found themselves being won over, at least a little, when they came face-to-face with Davis at the hardware store, or at town meetings, which he attended to make certain his land was not encroached upon. He was handsome, with dark hair and even darker eyes, but it was more than his good looks that were so appealing; it was when he spoke to you it seemed as if you were the only person in the room. He was focused and intense. *Can I be honest with you?* he often said in that deep voice of his, which made you stop and listen and give him a chance, even if you were opposed to the whole concept of what he was doing out there on the farm. He had those impenetrable, watchful eyes and many of the local women looked at him in a way that made their husbands uncomfortable when he spoke up against pesticides or new road construction at town meetings.

Joel proclaimed that every individual had to free himself from the sins of his ancestors, and that the only cure for the damage birth families caused to the psyche was to escape traditional relationships and form a new sort of family. Children did not live with their parents or attend public school. The women were obliged to appear plain, no matter how good-looking they might be, with their hair in braids, outfitted with work boots and jackets that didn't seem quite warm enough in winter. *You should be judged by what is inside you, not on how you look,* Joel always proclaimed. *You are starting anew. You are leaving one world for the goodness of another.*

The men in the Community were earnest and somewhat glum, bursting with brittle new muscles arising from their labor, their heads often shaved as penance for one misdeed or another. As for the children, they were raised to respect their elders and were reticent to speak unless spoken to. They were schooled at the farm, helping to raise the sheep and tending the vast vegetable garden. *What we take from the earth, we must return,* Joel told those solemn little beings, who gathered around him as he taught them not only how to weed and to hoe but how to be responsible people. Although he was evasive about his own past, his lessons were the only ones that mattered. *Love is at the heart of everything,* he told them. *Own nothing, covet nothing, and forget no wrongs.*

The acreage had been owned by Carrie Oldenfield Starr, deceased for more than ten years, a beautiful young woman from a local family who had used her inheritance to support the dream of her husband. Joel Davis had vowed to build a realm that would welcome all who were in need and were willing to work to create a better world. Carrie's family had never forgiven her for giving the land away to a stranger, and although many of the Starrs still resided in the Berkshires, not one had ever come to visit the small fenced-in cemetery that faced the mountain where Carrie had been buried. Some of the women at the Community believed that she was an angel who watched over them, but there were others who said they could hear her spirit crying when the wind came up, and they covered their ears and turned away and hoped they were wrong to have doubts. To stay here a person had to accept Joel's philosophy wholeheartedly. He might have ambition, he might be ruthless when it came to getting what he wanted, but everyone else must resist the impulse to desire more. Life on the farm was austere and laden with rules that covered nearly every action and every hour of the day. Anyone who disobeyed was punished and all doubters were cast out. The rules were memorized and recited by the children twice a day, at dawn and at dusk.

No acts of wickedness. No anarchy or antisocial behavior. No contact with original families. No contact with the outside world and their judgments. No reading novels or attending public school. No betrayals or disloyalty. No greed. No personal possessions. No vanity. No selfish behavior. No idle hands. No immorality. No terminating pregnancies.

Children belong to everyone. Love is everywhere. There is only one family, and it is us.

If a person should break the rules, their shortcoming would be written on a chalkboard, left up for weeks. They would be made to wear placards strung around their necks with the first letters of their transgressions there for all to see. *S* for selfishness. *Q* for those who asked too many questions. *C* for those who coveted their neighbors' belongings. *J* for jealousy. **A** for anarchy and acts of wickedness.

For women who went directly against the principles of the Community, if they wore colorful clothes, for instance, or were found with a book among their possessions, the punishments would also include isolation and the letters branded onto the flesh of their upper arms. *You shall not be like Eve,* Davis told them tenderly, *and lead us to ruination.* Children and teens were whipped out in the field, a stroke for every rule broken. This was done out of love, Joel explained. If you were not taught, how could you be expected to know better? If you were not a student, how could you ever hope to teach your own children? Love was everything, he said, as a transgressor was locked in the barn without food or water. Love was all they had in the world that they were building, and it would remain when the world outside fell apart.

Joel noticed Ivy on the night she arrived. Usually he was unapproachable, and didn't bother with new arrivals, unless they were homeless men, which he had been himself before he changed his life, but this time his attention was riveted. Ivy and Kayla were brought into his office, where he was working late after they'd made their way to the farm by walking down Route 17 in the dark. Joel had raked his fingers through his black hair. He had a natural arrogance that irritated some people and drew others to him. Joel sat at his desk while Kayla went on about how her parents didn't understand her.

"That sounds like the story of everyone who comes here," he said dismissively.

He then turned to Ivy, who hadn't said a word. He looked at her as if she were the only person in the room and she could feel her heart jolt. At that moment Ivy felt as if he saw her, the real her, not the pretty rich girl, for he seemed to look more deeply. He saw the girl who had feelings and ideas and who was now so terribly lost. Joel didn't ask her any questions, instead he just pushed his chair back, then stood and came to embrace her. "You won't be hurt again," he said. "I promise you that."

Ivy leaned against Joel and wept and wished that Noah and her father had said that to her, but they hadn't.

"I'll take care of you," Joel said. He spoke softly, so no one else could hear.

Kayla was staring at Ivy, glassy-eyed and annoyed by all the attention she was receiving.

Ivy wiped her eyes with the back of her hand and nodded her gratitude. In the times to come, she would thank him a thousand times over and sometimes she would mean it, but more often she would not. She meant it on this night.

"If you stay here, I'll make certain you never regret it," Joel vowed.

"Great," Kayla said, even though Joel's eyes were on Ivy. "We're in."

A woman named Evangeline led them to a house that several young women occupied. They would share a room. It was plain, but comfortable. The beds were all made with clean, fresh linens.

"He liked you," Evangeline said to Ivy.

Evangeline had been a college classmate of Joel's first wife, Carrie, and had given up tenure at Tufts in the psychology department to come help Joel run the farm after Carrie's death. She was married to Tim Hardy, who Joel had thought would be a good match for her. Tim had been a pastor in the army and had come to the Community when he was drug-addicted and homeless. Joel had offered him more than charity; he'd offered him a way of belonging. Tim still wore secondhand clothes, as if to remind himself of the time when he was hopeless and avoid getting a swelled head, even though he was now the foreman of the building crew. Evangeline was in charge of the children's house and the office and just about everything in between. There were several married couples in the Community, but some were more respected than others, and Tim and Evangeline were closest to Joel.

"Joel's been hurt before," Evangeline told Ivy, for she'd seen the way Joel had looked at the girl and she knew what would likely come next. "He lost the love of his life to cancer. Don't hurt him again."

Ivy knew that he was focused on her all through the autumn as slashes of red and yellow appeared in the woods. She had felt his eyes on her as she raked heaps of fallen leaves or assisted with the children in the play yard. She noticed that the children were polite and well behaved; even the youngest ones weren't allowed to run riot. Sometimes she felt like telling them to act up, to race through the fields, to climb trees or tell jokes, but she never did. Evangeline's vigilant eyes were always on her.

Ivy's favorite job was to work in the orchards, where she felt safe and hidden among the trees, preoccupied by the fairy tales she had always turned to for solace. Now, as the dark late autumn approached, she felt as if she were a character who'd been lost in the woods.

Joel had recently taken in several homeless people from Northampton to work and live on the farm, and now they were calling to each other in joyful voices even though it was drudgery to comb through the orchard for fruit. Ivy had seen them on the night they arrived, after they'd been brought to the dining hall. Joel had been the one to bring them their dinners, and then he had sat down with the new people as if he had known them all their lives. He had been so kind to them that Ivy's heart had swelled up with an abiding devotion. Most people were intimidated by him, but he opened himself to these people who had nothing and welcomed them to the Community. He'd lifted his eyes to her, and when he did everyone else in the room had fallen away.

Ivy was four months along and showing now. It was a chilly morning, and she was out gathering fruit in a wicker basket. She knew her family had something to do with apples, and they had never been a favorite fruit of hers. She wore a scarf and gloves and a man's peacoat. When she turned, Joel was standing there watching. She'd heard other women say it would be unwise to betray him or anger him; you had to earn his trust, and if you dared to break it, there was a price to pay. She had seen men and women wearing badges when they had gone against the rules. She was told they had lied or stolen, that they had been vain or disrespectful. Joel was an honest man and expected honesty in return. That's what Evangeline always said.

"Wherever I look, I always see you," Joel told her when they encountered one another in the orchard. "I see true beauty."

Ivy felt so unattractive, her face was puffy, her body heavier than it had ever been, that she couldn't help being flattered. "You must be seeing apple trees, not me." Ivy laughed, flushed with embarrassment, but also with something more.

"You're far more beautiful." His eyes were so dark, almost black. "Some things are meant to be," he told her.

"Like apples." Ivy gave him a fleeting look. She felt out of her depth here. The basket was heavy in her hands, and she set it down in the grass, aware that he was watching her. For some reason her breath was shallow in her chest.

"Like us," Joel responded. "I'd wondered if I could ever love someone again."

When Joel came toward her, she didn't step away. Ivy couldn't imagine that he'd want someone like her, an insecure girl who hadn't even finished high school, who didn't know how to drive a car and was pregnant and didn't know the first thing about being a mother. She couldn't imagine that her life could be set right. He kissed her in a way she had never been kissed before. No wonder people did as he said and believed in him. He was stronger than most men; for one thing, he knew what he wanted, even though Ivy wondered how he could be so kind to someone who had arrived on a bus, owning nothing, with nothing to offer. When she told him so, he smiled and shook his head.

"You have everything I want," he told her. "You are the apple, you are the tree, you are the orchard."

He didn't wait for what he wanted. Ivy was impressed by that after being with a college boy who expected everything to be handed to him. Two days after they'd met in the orchard, Joel went on his bended knee before her; it was old-fashioned, and another woman might have laughed at how serious he was, but as soon as he did, Ivy was his. Just like that, on an October day. She was a tree in the forest, she was the love of his life, she was so young she was unable to see the future, and on that day, she went forward, hoping for the best. All she knew was that she was the woman who walked through an orchard knowing that she was valued and loved, something she had unfortunately never felt before.

That was the winter when the snow fell for days and storms became blizzards, when the Lost River froze and turned blue, it was the winter of love when they walked through the drifts to an abandoned cabin at the edge of the woods so they could be alone. Ivy's belly was huge; she was due that March. All the same, Joel swore that she was the most beautiful woman he had ever seen, and she nearly believed him. They were inside a snow globe, after all. They were in a world of their own. "What do you want more than anything?" Joel asked her.

"A daughter," she said. "Your daughter," she added when she saw that he looked crestfallen. She knew that she said things to please him, that in some corner of her soul there was a hidden self she never allowed to be seen. Nothing was perfect, but this was close. Nothing lasted forever, although Joel swore what was between them was for all eternity. The snow was deeper all the time, and the world Ivy had known was so far away. She might have been anywhere, but she was here, in his arms, only six miles from the nearest town, but so far away she might as well have been west of the moon.

On the day Mia was born, there was a false spring. The lilacs bloomed all at once and the bees emerged from their hives, only to freeze when the cold, blue night fell. Petals turned black. Bees were found on window ledges, having frozen as they tried their best to reach the warm rooms inside. The Tree of Life planted by Johnny Appleseed did not have a single leaf that year. Ivy knew nothing about childbirth, and she'd thought she might die during the worst of her labor. She asked the midwife to put her out of her misery, but they didn't use drugs of any sort. "I can't do this," Ivy had cried, but then Joel had leaned close to whisper in her ear. He didn't leave her for a minute. "You have to walk through hell to get to heaven," Joel told her. She listened to him and calmed down. In this way she was bound to him, no matter who she had been before. "Breathe," he had said and that was what she did. *Have faith in yourself,* she thought. *Have faith in him.*

When they handed Ivy her daughter, the heart of her heart, the true love of her life, all of the pain she'd experienced was immediately forgotten.

"Our girl," Joel said, and Ivy was grateful that the child would have a father, even though here at the Community, children were raised in the children's house, the babies cared for by the women who worked in the nursery. She called the baby Mia, for she'd read that the name meant mine, and no matter the rules, this child belonged to her. Ivy had seven days alone with her daughter before she had to bring her to the nursery. Seven days of love and patience and solitude and sweetness. A wash of love came over her whenever she held her daughter, but the time spun by, and then it was over. Ivy's heart broke when Evangeline took Mia from her arms. Ivy was still scheduled to feed her, and those were the most precious hours of her day. There was a rocking chair by the window in the nursery with a lovely view, but Ivy never looked outside. She held the world in her arms, and when her visit with Mia was over, Ivy stood outside the children's house crying.

Some women saw her and reported her, and she was summoned to Joel's office.

"You have to be an example," he told her. "You can't break the rules."

Children belong to everyone.

Another woman would have been punished, isolated, and kept from her baby, or, if she continued to break the rules, taken into the fields to be beaten, but Joel had Ivy come sit on his lap and he gently made her promise to accept that her child belonged to the Community. He reminded her that love was everywhere, and if Ivy ever felt like crying again when she left the children's house, she stopped herself, worried that someone might see her. It wasn't so hard not to show what you really felt if you practiced, if you closed your eyes and imagined that your daughter was with you even when she was somewhere else, if you let the wind rise all around you, if you only heard the songs of the sparrows in the forest, a place so dark it was easy to get lost even in broad daylight, even if your eyes were open.

Ivy wrote the letter ten days after Mia was born. Ten days was all it took for her to know she had made a mistake. She went to the office after hours, took a stamped envelope and a sheet of white paper, and sat down at Joel's desk. She had been assigned to working in the office, where she helped with bill payments. *I trust you,* Joel had told her when he handed her the key. Evangeline had looked on, displeased, and that was when Ivy realized that Evangeline wanted Joel for herself. *Take him,* Ivy wished she could say. *Take it all.*

She had been thinking about the letter all day, and it was now fully formed in her mind. For the first time she knew exactly what she wanted to say, whether or not she was allowed.

Dear Helen,
   Should my daughter ever come to you and wish to know what happened, please give her this letter. Maybe it's not too

late for her to understand that she always belonged to me.

When Ivy finished writing, she addressed the envelope and slipped it into the outbox, along with the bills. In the morning it would go out with the other mail, and no one would notice that it had no return address, and that the envelope was damp, as if someone had been crying, as if they'd put their heart and soul into a letter that might never reach its intended recipient, a child who was now asleep in her crib, watched over by the women who worked in the nursery while her mother went to stand outside to look through the window.

Once upon a time, Ivy whispered into the cold March air, *I loved you more than anything. I loved you more than life itself.*

The wedding was held in the field, on the first day of June. It was a simple affair, pure of spirit and of deed. People said Ivy was lucky, they said she was the chosen one. The entire community formed a circle in the grass during the ceremony and there was a canopy of oak leaves tacked to a newly made wooden arch for the bride and groom to stand beneath.

Ivy wore a dress made by the sewing circle. They'd crafted their own pattern, then had worked on the dress until their fingers bled. The other women envied her, for Ivy was so beautiful; it was said that she'd grown up spoiled and rich and then she had just waltzed in and snatched up Joel, when so many of them had longed to be his. All the same, a wedding was a joyous occasion, and the long-sleeved white shift the women had stitched would be worn for years afterward, altered to fit every bride to come.

Evangeline held baby Mia, who at the age of three months was wide-eyed and silent. There were torches set into the ground, and as the sky grew darker, the rustic lamps were lit, globes of light that shone like stars. The heavens were above them, the earth was below, but here on the farm, human virtue and love were all that mattered. Ivy carried a bouquet of pale roses tied with brown string. No photographs were taken, that would have been sheer vanity, but those in attendance remembered what a beautiful bride Ivy had been. On this day, she wore her hair unbraided, falling down her back. Joel was waiting for her at the altar, a broad smile on his face.

You have come here to leave your old family behind, and start anew, Joel always said at Sunday meetings. That's what they were doing now. The bride and groom held hands in the field where the grass was so tall some of the children who were quietly standing there couldn't even be seen. It was as if they had disappeared into the gray light of evening. It was as if magic was possible here.

Tim Hardy, Evangeline's husband, wore a black suit, a size too big, and he held one hand on his heart as he spoke. Ivy and Joel repeated the blessing he gave them. Joel's grasp was strong and tight, and he didn't take his eyes off her.

Be true and I will be true to you. Be loyal and you will have my loyalty forever more. A woman should always honor her husband, and he will protect her in return.

Ivy felt something hot behind her eyes. In a moment she was blinking back tears, but who wouldn't be emotional on her wedding day? Despite the joy of the occasion, she felt like tramping through the woods to hide behind the fallen trees covered with pale green lichen. She wondered if Helen had read the letter, and if someone would come and save her from her own impetuous decisions, but it was a silly thought, they didn't even know where she was, so she remained there beside Joel. The idea of moving on from here seemed too far-fetched to achieve. She had no education, no money, no friends on the outside, no family, no profession, no assistance, no faith, no suitcase, no bus ticket, no other home, no one to help with her baby.

Ivy realized the white dress was stained green at the hem from standing in the grass. It would have to be taken to the laundry and bleached.

She thought it was likely that nothing lasted. It occurred to her that everything that seemed good had indeed been too good to be true. Tonight, there would be fireflies in the meadow and before long she would be in Joel's bed. She would belong to someone who vowed he would never betray her. Wasn't that enough?

Joel kissed her beneath the canopy of leaves. Wedding rings were a vanity. Honeymoons were unheard of. This was more, this was everything, a commitment for all eternity. There was silence in the field as they pledged themselves to one another. The only sound was made by little Mia, who let out a cry. But Evangeline covered the baby's mouth with her hand to quiet her and when she did three birds flew across the pale sky. One for the present, one for the future, one for the past.

Ivy thought of the first day her father had taken her to the Athenaeum, only a few blocks from their house, one of the oldest private libraries in the country, whose members had included Ralph Waldo Emerson, Louisa May Alcott, John Quincy Adams, and Nathaniel Hawthorne. He told her she could go there any time she wanted, and she'd spent countless rainy afternoons there in an old armchair, engrossed in one of the novels she loved. She had started with fairy tales and then kept on going until she reached *Wuthering Heights. Reading is never wasted time,* Ivy's father had told her. She wished he were standing beside her now, but he would have ruined everything. *Wake up,* he would have said. *What are you doing here? What sort of world is a world without books? I'm looking for safety,* she would have told him. *I'm looking for stars in the night sky, hope where there is none.* She wished he hadn't slapped her when she told him the truth. She had always been a daddy's girl, and he'd put up with a lot of bad behavior, but she didn't have a father anymore. She was Joel's girl now.

Standing there, Ivy told herself it made sense that reading wasn't allowed. There was so much work to be done at the Community there was little time for anything else. She stopped her foolish thoughts that went against the rules. Life was different here. It had been ever since she'd gotten off the bus with Kayla and walked up to the farm, although Kayla had been unhappy all winter. One day they'd walked into town with a group of other young women to see the Tree of Life bloom, an apple tree that was thick with blossoms as snowflakes whirled through the sky. Afterward, Kayla had come up to Ivy in the fields and quietly said, "Do you think you're the only one? You don't even know him."

Kayla had walked away with a triumphant grin on her face, for she'd intended to hurt Ivy and make her wonder, and she'd been successful.

47

They stayed away from one another after that. Kayla had been in trouble, and the trouble grew worse. It was said she'd stolen food from the kitchen, that she disobeyed and sat idly by rather than work. Joel announced that she had been breaking the rules of morality. Kayla had an **M** branded onto her arm as part of her punishment, and she'd been placed in isolation, locked in the barn. When she was let out, she had a haunted look, especially when Ivy was around. "This place isn't any different than anywhere else," Kayla whispered when they worked together in the field. She didn't sound brash anymore; as a matter of fact, she appeared to be shattered. "He gets to do as he pleases, and I'm left with the burden."

"What burden?" Ivy said. She had felt a chill along the back of her neck.

"What do you think?" Kayla patted her stomach. "I can't have it, and I'm not allowed to get rid of it, so where does that leave me?"

There was a clinic outside Blackwell, where pregnancies could be terminated, but Joel believed such procedures to be crimes against nature; he believed that a woman's body belonged not to her but to the Community. One of the men from the farm was stationed outside the clinic in a pickup truck, but even if any of the Community women had dared to enter, they had no medical insurance and no personal savings, and they knew what would happen to them if they were caught.

Kayla had disappeared one night when the snow was coming down hard. She hadn't been found even though a group of men had gone off searching for her. The weather was too bad, and people were told she likely took the bus back to Boston. But when the ice melted in February, a body was discovered in the woods. It had never been identified, even after an autopsy. In town, people said there had been multiple organ failures when a woman tried to terminate a pregnancy by ingesting poisonous herbs, including henbane and rue.

Joel had told the Sunday gathering that Kayla didn't have the strength it took to build a new society. *A woman who is weak is not a woman worth helping,* he told them. *Not like you, not like your daughters. You are all beautiful, inside and out. You are queens who have no need of a crown.* He went up to each of the women and bowed down before her, and when he came to Ivy there were tears in his eyes. "You know you're the only one," he told her, as if he had read her mind, and was aware that she had doubts, even though she knew she should not.

She never told anyone that on the night Kayla disappeared, there had been a faint knocking at the door of the house Ivy shared with Joel.

"Joel?" Kayla had called. Her tone, which was usually indignant, was soft and earnest now.

She stood there as the snow fell down. "If you don't let me do it, I'll do it myself." Joel was at a meeting with the men on the construction team and so Ivy was alone. She had pressed herself against the wall and remained quiet, and eventually Kayla had stopped knocking.

For all she knew Kayla was a liar. She lied about being too sick to show up for work, and about needing to have her own room because she was a light sleeper. Still, Ivy reproached herself for not opening the door to her friend. She told herself she didn't do it because the Community had taken such good care of Ivy when she arrived, and Joel hadn't left her side during her three-day labor when she brought Mia into the world. But when she searched her soul, she knew that the real reason was that she was afraid to hear what Kayla had to say.

On the day they heard a body had been found in the woods, Joel had brought Ivy a special present, a pair of red boots she had admired at the General Store.

"Wouldn't this be vanity?" she had asked him.

"Try them on," Joel had told her, and when she had he'd smiled broadly. "It's not a vanity to please your husband," he insisted.

He'd wanted forgiveness, she could tell, or maybe what he'd really been asking for was forgetfulness; either way, Ivy had given it to him, and she had never mentioned Kayla again.

Nevertheless, she thought of her every day, every time she slipped on her red boots, she wondered what would have happened that night if she'd opened the door and listened to Kayla. She wondered what might have happened if they had gone to the nursery and taken Mia and run away together.

Ivy had begun to think that life was made up of a series of accidents and drastic errors. The unexpected became the expected, you made the right turn or the wrong turn, and all of it added up to the path you were on. Happiness was there and then gone, impossible to hold on to. And here she was, in Western Massachusetts, the wife of a man who said she was his world. But sometimes she heard knocking at their door. He would be fast asleep, and she would get out of their bed and go to open the door, but no one was ever there. There was only the dark night and the sound of crickets, and it was as if Kayla had never existed at all.

Whenever it was Ivy's turn to work at the stand that the Community set up at the farmers' market on the town green on Saturdays, she found herself drawn to the library. It was an old brick building with a mossy slate roof and a turret with windows fashioned of old, wavy glass. Occasionally, Ivy said she was going to the public restroom at town hall, but instead she sneaked over to gaze through the library windows, and she stood there crying. There were lilacs all around, she could say she'd come to pick a few blooms for the dining hall. She looked inside, longing for the books on the shelves, but she didn't dare go in. These were the rules she lived by now, and the vows members of the Community made were taken seriously. She wasn't dealing with selfish, spoiled boys like Noah Brinley or uncaring men like her father. If either of them cared about her, wouldn't they have looked for her? Not Noah, she had no expectations of him anymore, but her father, who had called her a princess, her father, who had slapped her in the hallway of their house, who had planned to send her away, who had never once listened to what she wanted, who must have heard her crying at night when he walked past her room but had merely continued down the hall.

But now it was her wedding day, and the time when she might have returned home was over, and she forced herself not to think about the life she once had. She would never see her room again, or the books on her bookshelf. She would never sit in the Athenaeum reading on a rainy day, full of hope for the future. She was a married woman with responsibilities now. Her heart belonged to her husband, and her life belonged to him as well.

At the end of the day, when the sky was turning pink, everyone finally sat down at the rough-hewn tables for the wedding feast. New marriages here had to be approved by Joel, and because they were rare, it was all the more reason to celebrate. The women had been cooking all day, and there were fresh loaves of bread and vegetable stews. Cake was a luxury, and usually forbidden, but some of the women had made a three-tiered vanilla cake, sweetened with the honey from the farm's hives. No alcohol was allowed, except for the hard cider made from their own apples, Look-No-Furthers, which had a kick that could get a person drunk in no time at all; this was the alcoholic beverage that was said to be favored by Johnny Appleseed himself.

Children were at last let loose, galloping into the fields to catch fireflies, directed not to disrespect their elders with unruly shouts of joy. Ivy went to find Evangeline. She had been overcome with the notion that her child had been stolen, as they often were in fairy tales, and that she'd never see her again, but there was Mia dozing in Evangeline's arms.

"I can take her," Ivy blurted. She was constantly caught off guard by how fiercely she could love someone. She knew that the children belonged to everyone here in the Community, but as far as Ivy was concerned, Mia was hers and hers alone. Her darling child, with red hair and dark eyes, quiet, yet full of life, an endearing changeling born in a forest.

Evangeline kept hold of the baby. "You're the bride. Go enjoy yourself."

Joel had noticed that Ivy was missing, and he waved his arms when he spied her, gesturing for her to come back to him. The cake was about to be served and he wanted to feed it to her. The shadows of the yew hedges behind him were so darkly green the leaves appeared black. Ivy couldn't tell whether or not he was smiling as he signaled to her.

"Bye, baby," Ivy said to Mia. She bit her lip and told herself it was her night, her celebration, the start of their future, but as she walked back to Joel, a chill settled over her and she felt hollow inside. She thought about Kayla alone in the woods, searching for a way to claim her fate and her own body. The darkness was falling in shifting patches of blue. Before long the forest and the meadows would turn pitch black. There were bunches of wild phlox, shining like stars, and the voices of the children rose up, filled with joy as they raced through the tall grass, even though tomorrow they would be denied dinner as punishment for being too wild at the celebration. It was a perfect night, a heavenly night, a night that could convince you that miracles were possible, if you still had faith, if you loved one person above all others, if you told yourself you hadn't made a terrible mistake.

CHAPTER TWO

ALL THAT I NEED

At fifteen, Mia Davis was tall, with long red hair and dark eyes and a wide mouth that was her best feature. She would be beautiful one day, but she would have never believed anyone who told her so, for she was awkward and shy, with a lost expression, and she had been taught that to think well of yourself was a vanity. She'd never been any farther than the town of Blackwell, six miles down the road, and then only on Saturdays to work at the Community's vegetable stand at the farmers' market.

When she was younger there was no reason for her to believe that life was different anywhere else than it was on the farm, but after working at the farmers' market, she noticed that people in town seemed to have more of everything. They had houses and cars and clothes that weren't so worn; they went to the public school and had soccer meets at the playing fields near the Last Look River on Saturdays while Mia began working at dawn. Was that the reason these people appeared to be happy, while Mia had a gnawing sense of melancholy? She'd always assumed the cause of her unhappiness was based on her own failures. Perhaps she wasn't working hard enough, so, she worked harder. Perhaps she was selfish, so, she gave all that she had away, including her portion of fruit after dinner, as sweets weren't allowed. She turned from greed and vanity and had worn the same boots for over a year, even though her feet had grown, and she hadn't asked for a new coat, though hers had holes in the pockets. The other girls her age didn't complain, and they didn't seem to wish for anything more than they had, so Mia tried to do the same, even though she felt the stone of unhappiness inside her, rattling around, keeping her awake at night in the girls' dormitory. She did what she could to be true to the rules they lived by, believing that she always would, until the day when everything changed, a day she'd been waiting for, even though she didn't know it, when at last her eyes were opened and she knew what she had been missing.

They were in town at the market, setting up the tables for their stand. Ivy and Mia were working side by side; that often happened, even though, according to the rules, you were not supposed to be closer to your biological parent than to any other adult. Mia had been raised by the Community and she owed her allegiance to every single member in equal measure, but that wasn't the way it was. Mia and Ivy acted as if they had nothing to do with one another, speaking only when no one would notice. But they were more to each other, and they knew it, even though they hid it every day.

Ivy's looks, combined with her cool disposition, might have been the reason she didn't have many friends, even though she was a member of the sewing circle and attended all Community meetings. Mia had heard other women say that Ivy set herself apart, that she thought she was special because she was married to Joel. The truth was, she was not like the other women, who berated you the moment you made a mistake and told you it was for your own good when they punished you. She often seemed like she was somewhere else, in a world of her own, a world where there was possibility and hope.

This morning Ivy and Mia were loading up the tables with boxes of tomatoes. Mia remembered Ivy had told her that in old folklore tomatoes were thought to be poisonous, for they belonged to the belladonna family. Some people believed that a tomato could make a person fall in love, a tale so widely believed that the French called a tomato *pomme d'amour*, apple of love. At the Community, people were instructed to live in the present; they were taught not to read nonsense or tell tall tales, and Mia couldn't help but wonder how her mother knew so much about folklore.

When she was younger and she'd walked through the woods with her mother looking for mushrooms, Ivy had recited folk tales and fairy tales that she knew by heart. *Ssh,* she would say, *don't tell anyone.* That was the way her stories always began. She said she had lived in stories, once upon a time, and read a book a day.

Mia had once overheard Joel scolding her mother, saying *Are you here with me, darling?* when Ivy appeared to be distracted as they headed to Sunday meeting. Mia had been following with a group of children, all of whom considered Joel to be their father, for it was his word that mattered and his values they lived by. Mia always felt cold when he was near, chilled to her bones. He was her father, but he didn't seem very interested in her. He acted as if he thought she was a bother. On this occasion, when she was eavesdropping, Ivy had taken his hand and said, *Of course I'm here. Where else would I be?*

Back there in the before, Joel had said, wary, his face filled with concern.

Ivy had laughed. She had a beautiful laugh that reminded Mia of birdsong. *That place doesn't even exist anymore,* Ivy had assured him. *It's gone.*

Now, as they worked at the farm stand, Mia found herself thinking about all of the books her mother had read. "I was just wondering," she blurted, but she quickly stopped herself from saying more.

Ivy looked up from a huge wicker basket filled with tomatoes. Some were yellow, others were green, or a coral color, or a deep maroon that appeared to be black. There were several varieties, Black Krim and Green Zebra, Early Girl and Better Boy. "What do you wonder?"

Mia shook her head and resumed setting up their display. They charged a ridiculous price, but people said they grew the best tomatoes in the Commonwealth, and they sold out every time. "Never mind," Mia said.

Her fingernails were rimmed with dirt and there were blisters on her hands. She wore her hair braided and pinned up, as all the girls at the farm did, and so the back of her neck was sunburned. Maybe that was why she felt flushed. Maybe that was why she had a nagging feeling that there was too much she didn't know. It was the best time of year, late summer, when the evenings lasted so long, and Mia and Ivy often sneaked off into the woods. Once, they'd gone swimming in the Last Look River with no clothes on. Luckily no one had noticed their hair was wet when they returned at suppertime, although Joel had called Ivy to him and had looked at her darkly until she leaned in to whisper to him; then he had laughed at whatever she told him. Ivy had looked back at Mia when no one was looking, and she'd stuck out her tongue, which had made Mia laugh out loud. But often there were times when Ivy couldn't work her magic, and Mia had seen the edge of a brand on her mother's arm, although she had never made out what letter it was because Ivy always wore long sleeves.

"Cat got your tongue?" Ivy asked now at the farmers' market when Mia clammed up.

"I was just wondering where you came from."

"West of the moon," Ivy answered. She should have said nothing, she should have changed the subject, but the response that Ivy always had before she came here spilled out. You had to search west of the moon and east of the sun if you wanted to find your true love. "It's a place in a fairy tale," she explained when Mia looked baffled. Mia could almost believe that Ivy had come from an enchanted place. She thought she remembered a line from a story her mother had told her. *You have traveled far, but the hardest part of a journey is always the next step.* "I grew up in Boston," Ivy admitted. "And it wasn't a fairy tale. At least not for me. Someone offered to help me, but instead, I came here. I thought the farm was west of the moon, but I don't know if there is such a place anymore."

They realized they were being watched by Evangeline, who was known to be a tattletale, so Ivy fell silent. But as soon as Evangeline looked away, Mia was emboldened to ask another question. Her mother had answered one, perhaps she would answer another. Mia had always been curious about the brick building with turrets and green windows on the far side of the green. "Is that a castle?" she asked.

Ivy laughed. "You are too funny." Then she realized Mia was serious. Ivy had believed the Community's position that keeping their children away from the rest of society was a way to protect them from the cruelties of the world, but on this day, she wasn't so certain. "It's a library, Mia." When Mia still looked blank, Ivy shook her head, distraught. "You know what a library is. You have one at school."

The Community School library was a closet where printed materials were stored. Evangeline vetted them all to ensure that nothing controversial was included. Some of the pamphlets concerned math, some focused on handwriting and spelling. There were guides about hunting and fishing and harvesting crops. The history pamphlets had entire paragraphs blocked out with black ink. Mia had read them all and she hadn't found anything interesting yet.

"The library that I went to was called the Athenaeum," Ivy said in a dreamy tone. "On rainy days I'd stay there all day long."

Mia had such a wistful expression on her face when she heard about the library that Ivy made a snap decision. She looked over her shoulder and saw that no one from the Community was paying any attention to them. The men were busy unloading the trucks and Evangeline had driven back to the farm for more supplies. "Go on if you want to see it," Ivy told her daughter. "This one time. If anyone asks, say you're there to use the restroom. But be quick about it, understand?"

Mia nodded, then ran across the green, and quick as she could she dodged inside the cool entrance of the library. She stopped right there, breathless. She would not have believed so many books could exist in the world. There were long tables, and easy chairs by the windows, and when Mia wandered a bit farther, she came upon a children's room decorated with a mural of a boy dressed in green and a girl who held his hand and seemed to be flying. Here were shelves of fairy tales and folk tales. Mia found *West of the Moon* and began to read it, her eyes hot and tearing.

"Look, that girl is crying," a little boy said to his mother.

Mia left the room, and when she turned the corner, she found herself in the section where novels were kept. She reached up and took the first book she found. It didn't look like much, an old, somewhat moth-eaten edition with a brown cover and gold letters. But when the book fell open, she spied an inscription scrawled in blue ink.

To Mia, If it was a dream, it was ours alone and you were mine.

Mia returned the book to the shelf. She could feel her heart beating hard. It must be a trick. Joel must have set a trap for her. Mia looked over her shoulder, to see if she'd been followed, but the only one there was the librarian, at work behind the desk. And yet it seemed someone had known she would be here. Mia raced off as fast as she could, breaking into a run, half expecting Joel to appear and grab her, not daring to draw a breath until she was once again outside. She looked across to the farm stand. She could feel her heart beating hard. There was her mother, who had come from beyond the moon with her beautiful silvery eyes. Was it possible that they had both been enchanted? Ivy caught sight of her daughter and lifted her hand to give Mia the okay to run back.

"What did you think?" Ivy asked in a whisper when Mia returned to stand beside her.

"There's magic inside," Mia said.

"You know better than that. There is no magic." Ivy scowled. "Would we be here if there was magic?"

"Are you sure?" Mia said. "I think I saw something in a book."

"What kind of something?"

"I think it was a book that was written for me."

"Magic is a made-up concept that gives you the

idea that you can control something you have no control over."

"Like our lives?" Mia said bitterly.

"Mia, I did what I could."

Mia was surprised to see that her mother was near tears. She might have asked why, but the truck had pulled up with more produce and Evangeline and Tim were getting out. There were boxes and boxes of heirloom tomatoes, some of which hadn't been cultivated in over a hundred years.

"Just remember," Ivy told her daughter before she went to help unload the truck. "You can't live in a castle."

But now that she'd been inside the library, Mia wondered whether or not that was true. Her mother didn't know everything. She didn't know how to be happy after all. Every night Mia dreamed she had run away, and each morning when she went to the window, she was disappointed to find that all she could see were the fields and the oak trees, and beyond them, Hightop Mountain, where at least once a year someone who'd gone out hiking became lost and was never seen again. Now, each time Mia went to town, she sneaked over to the library. She looked for the brown book with her name in it but couldn't quite remember where she'd found it. Maybe she'd read it wrong. Maybe she'd been mistaken. She'd read whatever she could manage to get her hands on then, and sneaked random volumes into her backpack. Having no frame of reference for what might be best, she went alphabetically, beginning with Alcott. She read *Little Women* in the barn, and that was it, she was hooked. Mia didn't stop until she was spotted by the librarian.

Sarah Mott, in her early forties, had come to Western Massachusetts after receiving her master's in library science at Simmons in Boston. Sarah wasn't a local, and she wasn't one to judge; she always tried to keep an open mind, but she had a bad feeling about the Community. There had been a little commune in Blackwell in the sixties that people talked about, but that had been about peace and love, a reaction to an unjust and unpopular war. The Community seemed far darker, run by secret rules. Sarah could tell that Mia lived up at the farm because of her braided hair and her clothing, modest gray garments and black work boots. She'd heard that books weren't allowed inside the farm, and didn't that say just about everything? In a place where books were banned there could be no personal freedom, no hope, and no dreams for the future. Sarah was glad the red-haired girl visited the library, even if she was stealing books. Turn someone into a reader and you turn the world around. But she was so obvious in her actions and so clueless that Sarah really felt she had no choice but to confront the girl in the best way she knew how, by welcoming her.

"Did you need some help choosing books?" Sarah Mott asked.

Once she'd been caught, Mia was panic-stricken; she probably should have run, but instead she was frozen in place. She would rather be sent to jail than have her father called and be publicly punished. "No," she managed to say. "I don't need help."

"Well, enjoy the ones you've chosen, just know that we love to have the books back so other people can read them." Sarah handed Mia a library card. "This makes you official. Take out as many as you'd like."

That was when the door opened, and Mia stepped through. She gratefully took the library card and thanked Mrs. Mott. When she got back to the farm, she went up to the barn. Most of the ewes stayed away, but Mia's favorite, Dottie, came to sit beside her as she hid the card behind a loose plank of wood, in the place where she would come to conceal her treasures.

"Are you doing what I think you're doing?" Ivy said when they encountered one another in the dining room a few weeks later. They happened to be standing next to one another in line; there was no reason for anyone to think that they'd planned to do so. Dinner that evening was macaroni and sweet potatoes and tomato salad. "Are you going there?"

"Going where?" Mia said as if she hadn't the faintest idea of what her mother was talking about

"You know." Ivy gave Mia a little nudge. "The castle?"

"You said there are no castles in real life," Mia said cheerfully.

Ivy gave her a look. "Be careful."

"I will be," Mia assured her.

"I mean it," Ivy said, before breaking away to speak to some of the women who always said she never gave them the time of day. She had to be careful, too, and she knew it.

From then on, all that Mia knew about the world, she learned from books. She knew what heather looked like and what damage a typhoon at sea might do. She memorized names of streets in Paris and San Francisco and New York. She discovered the Lost Boys and a world in the future in which firemen burned books and people memorized entire novels to make certain they would never die. She read Shakespeare's plays and came to understand that transformations were always possible. The person she was becoming could not be seen by anyone at the Community and she often thought of her favorite line from Henry IV, Part I. *We have the receipt of fern-seed, we walk invisible.* Her real self was hidden with the books she kept in the sheep barn. Whenever Mia could get away unnoticed, she hiked into the forest to read her most recent novel on the bank of the Last Look River. The birds took flight when she turned the pages, the leaves were shaken from the trees. *If there be magic,* Mia whispered there in the forest, *let it be mine.*

In the Community, students stopped attending school after the age of fifteen. There was no graduation and no ceremony, they simply traded one set of chores for another. Joel believed that work was more valuable to young minds and occasionally, Mia worked in the office alongside Ivy, filing and sending out the mail. That was how Evangeline had found them, mother and daughter together at the desk going over the figures from the farm stand.

"Is she supposed to be here?" Evangeline asked Ivy when she spied Mia. "Wouldn't it be better for her to be working outside, getting more exercise?"

Children belong to everyone. Love is everywhere. There is only one family, and it is us.

"Why don't you ask Joel?" Ivy was always civil to Evangeline, because she knew the older woman's opinion mattered. She took the risk of speaking up to her now only because Joel was in the doorway. From the look he'd given her, Ivy knew what he would want from her when they were alone, and so she felt she had some leverage. "Mia is learning some business skills," Ivy said to her husband.

"Good for her." Joel nodded his approval. "Be smart, but not too smart," he advised Mia. "No one likes a girl who's too smart for her own good."

Mia flinched and lowered her eyes as she always did when she was in her father's presence. He was said to have the ability to see right through a person. Members of the Community swore that he could tell who was a liar in five minutes flat, and who was a thief in under a minute. That was why Mia was nervous. She happened to be both.

"Mia is quite enterprising," Evangeline commented, as if it were a bad thing.

"She's dutiful," Ivy responded. She lifted her eyes to her husband. She knew him better than most. Better than Evangeline. After all, she spent every night in his bed. "As am I," she said, looking directly at him and no one else.

When Joel left, Evangeline went into the attached kitchenette to make a cup of tea. Mia was done for the day and about to close the file drawer when she spied something stuffed into the very back, clearly ignored for years. She pulled it out and when she unfolded the paper she discovered a small, delicate watercolor painting of Hightop Mountain. There were the yellow fields and the ferns in the marshlands near Last

Look River. It was a rendering of the land before the Community came to settle here. For the first time Mia saw how beautiful Berkshire County was. The little watercolor was a treasure, the first thing she had ever wanted for her own. There was some scrawled writing on the back of the paper, in red ink, likely made of mulberries, faded and pale. Mia could barely read it, and the words meant nothing to her. It was the beautiful little painting that held her attention. Art was not allowed in the Community, and Mia had never been to a museum; she could not recall ever seeing a painting or drawing.

Evangeline walked in with her steaming cup of English breakfast tea. She always said it was the one thing she couldn't live without, and she kept the tea leaves in a jar hidden in a cupboard in the little kitchen because Joel always said having to indulge in something every day was an addiction, whether it was heroin or coffee or tea.

"What's that?" she asked Mia when she saw the girl fumbling with some paper.

"Nothing," Mia said, even though she knew it was the wrong answer.

"It's a painting," Ivy said as Evangeline peered at it. It looked harmless enough to Ivy, and she didn't care for the way Evangeline bossed her daughter around. "Mia wants to create a mural for the little ones at the school and she's going to copy this."

Mia was grateful that her mother had stepped in. She quickly folded the artwork into her pocket. She didn't pay attention to the writing on the back, but she'd noticed the signature. Carrie Oldenfield Starr, the name of Joel's first wife. Carrie wasn't spoken of much, although every year a bouquet of wildflowers was left at her grave on the day she had died. Ivy had told her that all they had was due to Carrie, and Mia had always wondered why this woman who was their benefactor was never thanked at Sunday meetings. Now she thought perhaps it was because she had been a painter.

"Art?" Evangeline said. "Would Joel be pleased with that?"

"His first wife was an artist. I think he would approve," Ivy assured her. She was his second wife, after all, and should have some say in the matter.

Evangeline stared for a while before she broke the silence. "Fine. Take it," she said to Mia. Evangeline wasn't going to argue the point, and it was true that the school could use some brightening up. "Just make sure you paint land-scape. No vain depictions of human forms."

The mural wasn't perfect, and working on it ate up most of Mia's free time for the next few weeks, so that she had to skip reading, but she actually enjoyed herself. Tim, the building man-ager, allowed her some leftover paint, cans of blue and yellow and green, and if you were a small child and had never seen a mural before, you might stare at the painted wall in a state of awe when you recognized Hightop Mountain and the fields where the corn grew in neat rows. Even Evangeline had to admit that Mia had done a decent job. The little watercolor by Carrie Oldenfield Starr was forgotten by everyone but Mia, who kept it hidden in the barn along with her library card. She often took it out to look at it, imagining the land where they lived as the painter had presented it, back when there was only a single white farmhouse alongside a small barn, before the Community had been built. Mia wished she was in that place right now, in the field where sunflowers grew, where it might be possible to be who you wished to be and you could read books all day long and no one would say a word about it. A place where no one would punish you for being who you were.

Take one risk and you'll soon take more. It's an addiction or it's bravery, it's foolishness or it's desperation. Mia went beyond the confines of the gate at the end of their long dirt driveway more and more often. She wondered what would happen if she were to travel west on Route 17. Would she reach the moon? Would she find city streets where there were bookstores and coffee-houses where she could be invisible and do as she pleased?

The best time to break the rules was during contemplation hours, Saturdays between four and six, when people were supposed to meditate and look inward, then get down on their knees, wherever they were, and be thankful for all that they had and all the Community had given them. That was usually Mia's reading time, but after searching for the original book, the one with her name in it, she had become restless, and that was when the wandering began. She went down to the athletic fields and watched a soccer match played by local children, excited for the winning team, even though she didn't understand the rules. She went into the bakery and stared at the gorgeous three-tiered cakes named after the deadly sins, including Gluttony, Envy, and Wrath. She sat outside the police station on a wooden bench. "Everything okay?" an officer coming out of the building asked her, a puzzled look on his face. People in the Community never approached the police, not for any reason. "You have a good view from here," Mia said. The building was directly across the green from the library. "I guess we do," the officer said. Mia took off quickly, not wanting to draw any more attention to herself. *I need help,* she'd wanted to say. *I need to find a way out.*

One afternoon while out hiking Mia found herself at the Jack Straw Tavern. People from the Community were not allowed to frequent the bar; consuming alcohol and mingling with towns-people were both forbidden. Still, Mia found the nerve to peer through the window. A hand-some young man bringing out the trash spied her lingering there.

"I don't think you're old enough to drink," the bartender teased. He could tell Mia was one of the commune kids, they all had a wild, underfed look, and he pitied anyone who lived out on that run-down farm where he'd heard everything was regulated, what you ate, how many hours you slept, who you could speak to. "How about some French fries?" the bartender asked.

Mia had never heard of them, but she said, "Sure," and followed him inside. The tavern was dark and comforting, with booths that had leather seats.

"Coming right up," the bartender told Mia.

There was an old gentleman at the bar, having an afternoon beer. He was Max Starr, from an old Blackwell family, and he could never figure out why his cousin Carrie had given away such a large portion of their land. He gathered this young girl was one of the squatters who'd taken over the farm. She had her hair braided in an old-fashioned style and was dressed plainly. Still, she was a pretty girl, and she smiled at him when she caught him staring.

"My cousin owned land where you live," he told Mia. "It was in the family for close to three hundred years."

"Carrie Oldenfield," Mia said. "She was a painter."

The old man sat back in his chair, surprised by the girl's knowledge and charm. She didn't look blank the way most of the Community kids did. "That's right. She went to the Museum School in Boston, and she studied in Paris, for all the good it did her."

"Why didn't it do her any good?" Mia wanted to know.

Max Starr snorted, disgusted. "Because she married him."

"I'm sorry she died," Mia said, feeling guilty for reasons she didn't quite understand.

"Everybody dies," Max Starr said. "It was the way she wound up living that was the problem. Lovely girl," he said. "Second cousin once removed." He shook his head. "Just goes to show, one man can ruin a good woman's life."

Mia wondered what her mother's life might have been like if she hadn't married Joel Davis. She might be west of the moon, someplace where she didn't have to make herself so plain. At the last Sunday meeting, there had been a complaint about Ivy from the other women in the sewing circle and she had been made to apologize for her misdeeds. Ivy's crime was to have recited an

Emily Dickinson line while they were working on a quilt. *I am out with lanterns, looking for myself.* Ivy had to walk up to her husband, in front of a gathering of the entire Community, so he could tie a badge on a rope around her neck. It was the letter *V*, for vanity, to be worn for seven days. As far as Mia was concerned, it hadn't made Ivy any less beautiful. It just made her hate her father more than she already did.

When the bartender brought over a plate of fries, along with a bottle of catsup, Mia sat down and proceeded to eat like a starving person. The food was heaven.

"Slow down there," Max Starr said as he watched Mia wolfing down the fries. "Don't they let you eat at that farm?"

"Boiled potatoes," Mia said between ravenous bites. "We absolutely don't have this."

"Are they crazy out there?" the old man said.

"Maybe," Mia said. She'd never thought of the Community that way before, but now that Max Starr had suggested it, she stopped to consider the way they lived. "I think so."

"Well, you don't seem like one of them," Max decided, having taken a liking to the girl.

"What do I seem like?" Mia asked, truly interested in what his answer might be. This was the longest conversation she had ever had with an outsider.

Max carefully thought over her question before

answering. "You seem like a girl who likes French fries."

Mia grinned. That's what she was. An ordinary girl who asked for a second helping and was granted her wish on this one day when she broke the rules and was just like anyone else in town.

That was when Mia began to think about the other life she might have if she ran away. She thought about it while she weeded the gardens, and in the laundry, where she steam-ironed clothes; and at the preschool, where she worked in the afternoons; and in the office, when she filed bills. She thought about it in the vegetable garden and every time she collected Look-No-Furthers in the orchard. She had begun to plot her getaway, and every time she saw her mother, across a room or on the other side of the field, she would think, *Let's do it together. When the night is dark, when no one can hear us, we will run down the road, we will stop the first car we see, we will never even look back, not once, not for a minute, and before you know it we'll be west of the moon. Let us walk invisible and disappear.*

At the end of the summer, a group of women stumbled upon Mia in the garden. It was the sewing circle hour, and she'd thought she'd be safe, but as it turned out there was a huge crop of tomatoes that had to be picked, and the sewing circle had been canceled. Mia's heart dropped when she saw them. She had begun to write out an escape plan on a scrap of paper. *Go at night. Climb out the window. Travel light. Don't look back. Take only what you need most of all. Ask Sarah Mott the librarian for money for bus tickets. Meet Ivy in the woods. Run as fast as you can.*

The scent of the tomatoes was fiery and sharp, and the sun was beating down on Mia's shoulders. When the women from the sewing circle burst through the gate, Mia had already torn up the list to bury in the dark soil. Only one scrap was left, clutched tight in her hand. Mia felt sick to her stomach thinking of what would happen if she were to be found out. She had only faced her father's wrath once, when she was eight years old and had jumped into a muddy puddle, and she had never misbehaved again. She had been banished to a dark cellar where they kept canned fruits and jam. She'd pounded on the locked door and wailed so terribly for over an hour that at last Ivy had persuaded Joel to forgo any further punishment, vowing that Mia had learned her lesson. But she was older now, and what she'd done was far worse.

As the women came near, Ivy's cool gray eyes found Mia. She could tell as soon as she saw her daughter. Something was wrong.

"Look who's come to weed even when she isn't on the schedule," Evangeline said. Her voice was warm, but she looked at Mia through narrowed eyes. "I always said you were enterprising."

Mia did her best to appear calm. She sat with her hands behind her back as the women found their places between the rows of tomatoes, eager to begin harvesting the last of the ripening fruit. She was imagining her punishment when she was caught, the lashes in the field, the locked, dark isolation, the extra work hours, when something brushed against her back. Without glancing at Mia, Ivy took her daughter's hand and pried it open, then got hold of the last bit of Mia's list. *Run as fast as you can.* That was all that was left. Ivy and Mia looked at each other, and as they did, Ivy had a half smile on her face as she popped the scrap into her mouth and swallowed it. Mia had to stop herself from laughing out loud. It seemed that her desire to break the rules had come from somewhere.

"What's that?" Evangeline said, noticing that Ivy was chewing, suspicious.

The sky was cobalt blue; it was such a beautiful day, whether they were here or a thousand miles away.

"A fly," Ivy said smartly. "It must have taken me for a frog."

Sarah Mott taught Mia how to use the computer at the library. Usually, the young people showed her tricks, but Mia knew nothing about technology and Sarah began with the basics. Mia thanked her for the instruction, and then when Sarah had left her to her own devices, Mia began to look through Blackwell obituaries. She was searching for Carrie Oldenfield Starr, but there was no mention of Carrie. It was as if the painter had led an invisible life. In her search, Mia discovered that several people had drowned in both the Last Look River and the neighboring Eel River. The one that interested her most was a little girl who was said to haunt the river and was called the Apparition. Every August at the Blackwell's Founders' Day Festival a play was presented about her drowning and her reappearance as a ghostly being who haunted the Eel River. Mia had seen posters about Founders' Day, but she'd never attended. Now she decided that this summer she would see the play no matter what. Luckily, on that evening, most of the adults had gathered at the Community Center for a meeting concerning next year's crops. Mia sneaked out her window, ran to the gate, and made her way along Route 17. She watched the performance from the edge of the mossy woods.

It was the end of a day full of festivities celebrating the founding of the town by a few families who'd come from Boston into what was then the wilderness. Paper lanterns had been strung across the town green and there were stands selling hot dogs and ice cream and blueberry pie. The stage had been built that morning, and most of the town watched as if spellbound. Mia was entranced as well. This was magic, the whole world changing before your eyes. A boy and a girl held lanterns as they searched for their missing sister. Mia could feel her heart beating faster. She was transported, but before she knew it, the play was ending, the Apparition was calling out to her sister that it was too late for her to be rescued but she could forever be seen near the river where she had perished. When the actors left the stage, Mia felt as if she'd woken from a dream. She turned to walk back to the farm and there was Ivy watching her.

"Do you know what will happen if they catch you?" Ivy whispered. She'd seen her daughter dart across the field and had followed her to town. Ivy meant to grab her daughter and bring her home, but by the time she'd caught up to her the play had begun and Ivy became as engaged as Mia was, as if she, too, had fallen under a spell. Now they walked back together through the dark, quickly, a scrim of fear intensifying as they considered what would happen if they were caught. The mood was gloomy, but all at once Ivy had smiled. She thought of how lucky she was not to have lost her daughter, to have a real live girl before her and not an apparition. "You know what the best day is for me?" Prowling around in the night had caused Ivy to feel that she was free to speak more openly. She felt as if she was the person she used to be, who sneaked out her window at night. "March sixteenth."

Mia looked at her mother. She had no idea what that meant.

"That's your birthday," Ivy informed her. "In case you wanted to know."

Mia had very much wanted to know, but birthdays at the farm were thought to be a vanity and were never celebrated; children born into the Community were never told their birthday so that the day would be like any other and they wouldn't fall victim to pride. Knowing the date made Mia feel as if she could finally claim herself. The night itself was magic. She could feel it. Here they were, just like a mother and daughter, invisible to all others, free to do and say as they pleased. Mia wished they could go on walking all through the night. They wouldn't stop until they reached California, until they were anywhere that was west of the moon.

"It was a good play, wasn't it?" Ivy said.

Mia said, "It was." She had nothing to compare it with, having never seen one before, but she knew she couldn't look away from the stage once the play had begun. *Oh, sister,* the Apparition had said, *look for me on starless nights.*

"There are no such thing as ghosts," Ivy said with assurance. "You know that, right? It's all made up. There are no spirits and no heroes, and nothing is a fairy tale. The stories I told you were stories. Nothing more."

"I guess," Mia said, and then she added, "Maybe it would be better if those things existed."

"It wouldn't be," Ivy told her. "We make our own mistakes, and spirits and stories can't make it right."

"Stories might," Mia said.

"I thought you were smarter than that." Ivy stopped short so suddenly that Mia almost crashed into her. They were nearly to the gate and the Community loomed before them in the dark, the grass and fields all turned pitch black. Ivy would have to come up with a good excuse for why Joel hadn't found her in bed. She sometimes said she sleepwalked and found herself in the meadow, and he seemed to believe her, so all she could do was hope he would believe her again. Everyone else was asleep. Everyone was dreaming. But here she and Mia were, together. "At least I hope you are." Ivy spoke in a soft voice. It was the voice of a person who loved someone more than anything in the world. "I hope you're smarter than me."

They weren't punished then, but their luck soon turned. Not long afterward, a forbidden book was found in the barn. Mia had been reading, and, suddenly realizing she was late to work in the garden, she'd left the book under a pile of straw in Dottie's pen instead of hiding it away behind the wooden planks. It was *Pride and Prejudice*. Mia had chosen it from the library without knowing anything about Jane Austen; she'd never heard the author's name before, but the title had made her think of people in the Community. "You'll love that one," Sarah Mott had told her when she checked it out. "You'll want to read the five other novels she wrote."

At the Sunday evening meeting Joel held up the contraband book one of the men had found while pitching hay. There was a deep hush in the room. *Pride and Prejudice*.

"Who will admit their pride tonight?" Joel called out. When there was no answer, he began to pace, as he did when he was agitated. "There is a reason we have no books here. They will divide us. They'll make us think the world outside can teach you more than you can learn right here. Some writer doesn't know you better than I do. They can't tell you how to live your life."

Mia was in the back row on a hard wooden chair. Her heart was pounding against her chest, and she feared that Evangeline, who was sitting nearby, could hear its wild beat. She was afraid that if no one came forward, Joel might go to the library and question Mrs. Mott, maybe even threaten her, and then he would discover that Mia was a frequent visitor. Or maybe he'd already been there and had written Mia's name in random volumes to remind her that she belonged to him. She was in a panic, half thinking she might just run out the door into the woods, when Ivy suddenly stood up at the front of the room. Her mother looked small from where Mia sat.

"It's mine," Ivy said. "I found it in a trash bin in town on market day. I started reading it, but I didn't finish. It made no sense to me."

There was a low murmur as people wondered what would happen next. Ivy was Joel's wife, his favorite, yet the rules were the rules. You had to pay for breaking them, no matter who you were. Mia overheard bits and pieces of what people were saying to one another, that Ivy was spoiled and deserved whatever punishment she got, that she'd probably read the whole book and lied about it and she'd likely read others as well. Joel gestured for Ivy to come forward, as if they were the only two people in the room. She didn't look at anyone else as she walked up to the podium.

Let's run, Mia thought. *Let's be invisible. Let's do it right now.*

"Bow down," Joel told Ivy.

Ivy's eyes flicked over him, but she did as she was told. She did so in a manner that made people even more annoyed with her, for she kept her dignity, and she didn't seem the least bit apologetic.

Joel called for a pair of scissors, which were

quickly brought to him. Mia covered her eyes. She simply couldn't look at what was to come next, and when at last she lifted her eyes, she saw that all of Ivy's beautiful black hair had been shorn down to her scalp. Strands covered the floor like the feathers of a blackbird.

"This is for pride." Joel spoke softly, which made things worse. It was as if he was being generous to a sinner, and the person being punished should be grateful to him. Ivy was known for her beautiful black hair, and Joel had loved the look and feel of it. His expression was fervent, that of a believer put to the test of his own rules. "This hurts me more than you can know," he claimed.

Ivy went back to her chair and sat down as if nothing had happened. Her posture was straight, and her expression concealed her emotions. From where Mia sat, she saw pride in her mother's face. Ivy looked even more beautiful without her hair, like Joan of Arc or a witch in Salem who was about to be burned.

As soon as they were dismissed, Mia ran into the woods, vanishing among the trees. It was her fault that the wrong person had been made to pay for her pride. *One man can ruin a good woman's life,* she remembered Carrie Oldenfield's cousin saying at the bar of the Jack Straw Tavern. Mia yearned for dark magic, something to save them, a spell that would destroy this place so that every one of the houses would burn to ash. Shakespeare had conjured magic in his plays, and Mia wished she could recite words that would pierce through Joel Davis as if they were knives. *If it will feed nothing else, it will feed my revenge.* This was the hour that she decided she would never fall in love. Love tied you down, it made you pay, it demanded all you had to give and repaid you with despair. She would never get close to anyone and would remain invisible, a girl without a heart. She would be hidden even when she was in plain sight.

Mia was intending to cut her arm with a stick and let her blood sink into the ground, as if she were a witch herself, as if she had power, when in fact she had none. She held the stick and merely sobbed, like an ordinary girl. There, in the dark woods, someone had managed to spy her. A hand on her arm pulled her back. There was only moonlight, but Mia could see her mother quite clearly. Ivy looked fierce with her nearly bald head.

"Next time don't leave your book in the barn," Ivy said. "Understand me?"

Mia's eyes widened, and Ivy responded with a low, dark laugh.

"Do you think I don't know you've been going to the library?" she said. "I used to be a reader when I was your age. I took your punishment because I let you visit the library and you probably inherited the reading trait from me, so I take what you've done to be my fault. I read and read and what good did it do me?"

"It's not a trait, it's a choice," Mia said, not knowing how to feel. She was grateful and angry at the very same time.

"Whatever it is, be more careful," Ivy urged her.

"We could leave here," Mia said in a sure, quiet voice. "I have a plan."

When Ivy looked at her something passed between them. Mia didn't care about Joel's claim that children belonged to everyone. She knew who was there for her. She knew who she could depend on. They were whispering, standing near one another; they could almost read one another's thoughts. "Will your plan tell us where to go?"

"California?" Mia said. She'd seen photographs in the library of Monterey and Bolinas and San Francisco. All of those places were at the other end of the country, as distant as possible from here.

For a while, Ivy didn't say anything, and Mia thought she was angry, but then Ivy heaved a sigh and said, "Honey, that's so far."

"That's the point," Mia said.

Ivy shook her head. "We'd never make it."

"What about Boston?" Mia was crying, but she didn't know it.

"Go back to where I came from?" Ivy said sadly. "What would I do there? I didn't even finish high school. I wouldn't be able to support you."

"I'll get a job," Mia said stubbornly.

Ivy laughed, but again it was something darker than laughter. When Joel had noticed that Ivy was restless during that first year, he'd told her that if she ever thought of leaving, he would keep Mia. *Remember that,* he'd advised her, and she had. "My girl," Ivy said. "You can dream, but know that's all it is."

The light in the woods was so dim they felt as if they were nothing more than shadows. Almost invisible, but not quite. They could hear the voices of people leaving the Community Center.

"Be more careful," Ivy said. "So far, I've been able to calm him down when he gets angry, but I don't know what he'll do if he's pushed too far. He's not the person I first knew, and I don't know what he's capable of."

After Ivy walked away, Mia remained in the woods, listening to the night birds, owls and herons shifting in the trees. She realized that she had been so startled by her mother's sudden appearance she'd forgotten to thank her for taking the blame for possessing a book. She said it now, even though she was alone; she spoke into the empty night, hoping that somehow Ivy would know that she was grateful. Mia would never forget who was there for her, and who took the blame, and who had followed her into the woods to warn her that nothing stays the same.

CHAPTER THREE

THE FOREGONE CONCLUSION

September was a glorious month, when the whole world turned yellow. It was the season of the harvest, time to pick and sort apples. Look-No-Further was the only variety they grew, for it was said that if you ate nothing else for three days you would still never tire of the taste. At this time of year, work was unending, and members of the Community were in the fields twelve to fourteen hours a day. Even the youngest children worked in the orchards, given sturdy boots and small canvas gloves so they wouldn't prick their fingers on the branches as they reached for low-growing fruit.

This year the crop was so huge, outside laborers had been hired. The Community members were told not to speak to the help in the orchards and to ignore the transient children, who played games between the trees, singing songs in a language Mia didn't understand. When the day was through, she sneaked over to the far field, where the caravans were parked, and watched the families fixing their dinners on grills set over fires. Children called and parents answered. Boys played baseball and shouted at one another. Mia wondered where these people had been before coming to the Community and where they would go next. She wondered if on their travels they'd seen all the things she'd read about in books. One evening a woman with long dark hair left her family and walked over to Mia, concerned to see a girl out by herself as darkness fell, standing in the damp grass and watching them. "Do you need anything, honey?" she asked. "Something to eat?"

The food smelled wonderful, but Mia shook her head. It wasn't food she wanted, but information. "No thank you," she said, but then as the woman was walking away Mia called, "Have you been to California?"

The woman turned and smiled. "Not yet," she said. "Have you?"

"Not yet," Mia called, and they waved to one another before Mia walked back across the field. The crickets were calling like mad at this time of year, their last sweet song. Mia might have torn up her escape plan, but that didn't matter; she had it memorized. She hadn't left today, she hadn't begged that woman to take her along when the apples were all picked, but that didn't mean it wouldn't happen. It didn't mean she would never see San Francisco, and Paris, and New York.

In books, no one helped a girl who didn't help herself and every fairy tale ended with the same lessons. *Trick your enemy, do what you must, believe in enchantments, save yourself.*

It happened late in the day, at the end of the harvest. The occurrence that changes your life is never expected, it is sudden as rain pelting down from the sky, it is a flash of lightning, it is the moment you will never forget. Mia was at the school, out in the yard helping with the little children at recess, watching them glide away on the old wooden swings. She was alerted to the fact that something was wrong when she heard fierce shouts, then a deep quiet. The worst that can happen often happens in silence. It is not the explosion, but the aftermath, when you see through smoke and ash, that you know how much you have lost.

Usually, it was possible to hear people's voices drifting over from the orchards until dark; Mia had worked there this morning, side by side with Ivy, until Evangeline told her she was needed at the school. Now Mia noticed there were no trucks idling, no calling voices of the hired workers, not even any birdsongs. It was still warm as summer, and the countryside was dotted with pokeweed and tangles of Virginia creeper growing wild in the ditches. Mia froze when she saw the men running. Evangeline came and informed Mia that there had been an accident. The truck collecting the bushels of apples hadn't had the brake on correctly and had slipped backwards and crushed someone.

"All you can do is accept what has happened." Evangeline's voice was kinder than usual, but her face was pale.

Mia saw the men carrying the body of a woman. Blackbirds in the fields arose, calling to one another until none were left behind. Mia's fingers were wrapped around the chain-link fence of the play yard as she watched the men bring the body to the main house. It was the season of the bees, when they fled from their hives and arose in swarms in the last of the good weather. Two of the men in the field were stung. Neither one faltered, and not a single cry was heard.

"Mia, come away," Evangeline called as Mia stood looking out.

But Mia stayed where she was, transfixed. She recognized Ivy's gray shift and the red boots she always wore.

Let's do it tonight. Let's be invisible, Mia had said that morning as they were picking apples. They had climbed a tree together and they might as well have been alone in the world, hidden by branches. Ivy had smiled at her daughter's suggestion. Her hair had begun to grow back, and to Mia she looked like a princess in a fairy tale, one who might consider escape, but then Ivy shook her head. *He'd find us,* she said. *And, anyway, where would we go?* She said that once upon a time, a girl at the farm tried to leave and take control of her own body and her own life and that the rules had killed her. *We're not birds,* she told Mia. *We can't fly away.*

Now they were delivering her from the orchard. Ivy's hair looked like black feathers in the bright sunlight. Her boots fell off as they carried her to the Community Center. They lay there in the grass, and no one seemed to notice. This was what the end was like, quiet and aching. *We never got to run away,* Mia thought. *We might have been birds and flown so far we'd be west of the moon right now.*

The sun was beating down on Mia's back and she didn't even know she was crying until a sob escaped from her throat. She knew the men who were carrying the body, she knew their names, and their wives and children, but they looked like strangers to her now. Joel came out to meet them, rushing over to embrace the body of his wife. People said you could hear his howl of grief in the farthest field. He didn't care who saw him weeping. If he noticed Mia in the play yard, it didn't matter. He couldn't have cared less. What was over was over, what was done was done, this was a world of love, and those who had been here would be loved evermore. Joel wiped his eyes and stood tall. He would have the women bathe the body and then they would bury Ivy in the small fenced-in cemetery that faced Hightop Mountain.

The service was the following day, in the graveyard where Joel's first wife, Carrie, was buried. The mountain was shrouded in clouds, and only renegade bands of light came through. The women were all dressed in black or dark gray and wore scarves to cover their hair. The children were gathered in a circle, all holding late-blooming purple asters. The girls Mia's age sang a song Evangeline had taught them about a blackbird in honor of the departed soul.

Ivy was wrapped in a white sheet and lowered into the ground. Coffins weren't used, as the Community believed it was best for the departed to return to the earth from which they came. Everyone could hear Mia sobbing. She'd been sitting up all night outside the Community Center, where the body had been kept, and when the women tending to Ivy, washing her feet and readying her for the world to come, came to chase her away, Mia couldn't be driven off. Finally, Joel had said, "Leave her be."

But now, as the grave was being filled in with dark, rocky soil, Mia flung herself upon it, shouting out that her mother didn't belong there. She belonged in California, far away from here. She pointed a finger at Joel, as if calling down a curse. "You ruined her," Mia cried. "It's all because of you."

Joel instructed two of the men to take Mia away. "Do it now," he said, with disapproval. He had always warned that too much emotion was unhealthy, and wasn't the girl's behavior proof enough of that? He watched as the men struggled with Mia, for she wasn't in the least remorseful for her behavior and she held on to the ferns around the grave, doing her best not to leave. When the men managed to pull her away, she was still clutching on to the ferns, now torn from the earth. *We have the receipt of fern-seed, we walk invisible.*

Mia watched the rest of the service from the woods, her face hot and streaked with tears. The love she and her mother shared was invisible, and it always had been. No one else knew the truth. Mia did not belong to any of the rest of them, no matter what they said. After the service, Mia went to the barn, where she sank down beside her favorite of the sheep, old Dottie. This world was over, she knew that much. The world in which she had dreamed that her mother would come to her one night and whisper, *Let's run away. Let's do it together. Let's be invisible at last.*

A week after the funeral, Mia still refused to get out of bed. She could be found there even when suppertime neared, and she refused to get dressed or tend to her chores. The women from the sewing circle came to get her up and dress her, but she refused. Evangeline swore that Mia had tried to bite her. At last Joel came to speak to her, even though it was unheard of for him to go to the girls' dormitory. The other girls left as soon as they saw him, then they huddled around the door outside wondering what sort of punishment was in store for Mia.

"Stand up," Joel told Mia. When she defied him, he grabbed her arm roughly. She twisted away, but it did no good, and later an inky blue bruise would form on her arm. Joel's actions on this day were just proof of who he was. Mia couldn't bring herself to look at him, because if she did, she would be unable to resist the urge to curse him to his face. She wondered if other people felt the way that she did when confronted by their fathers, distant and fearful of punishment, never daring to speak the truth.

"You're mine, but I won't play favorites," Joel told her.

No, he wouldn't. He never had. *Children belong to everyone. Love is everywhere. There is only one family, and it is us.*

"There's a price to pay for staying in bed and not meeting your responsibilities."

He found the scissors on the girls' sewing table, where they worked in the evenings before bed, then he told Mia to unpin her braid, which fell to her waist. She kept her eyes closed as he cut the braid off at the base of her neck with quick, deliberate motions. She couldn't bear to have him stand so close. When he was done, she stood there, her neck shivery. The braid of hair was on the floor, coiled like a snake. Joel usually made certain that the hair of a girl who had misbehaved was shorn to the scalp, but in fact he did play favorites on this day.

"My daughter," he said sadly.

In honor of Ivy, Joel left Mia's hair cut to just above her chin. He thought he was offering her kindness, but Mia hated him more than ever, more than she had thought possible.

"Do you think I don't miss her?" Joel said in a softer tone. "Do you think I don't grieve every night and every day? I feel as you do, but that doesn't give you the right to be disobedient." He seemed done, but just when Mia thought he would leave her in peace, he spied something under her bed.

"What's that?" Joel asked in a harsh voice.

Mia had found her mother's boots on the trash pile after Ivy's belongings were cleared out. Everything else that had belonged to Ivy was gone. Her worn clothes, her jacket, her hairbrush. Possessions were evil, Joel had told them, and hiding them away warranted punishment, but Mia no longer cared about Joel's false philosophy or his rules.

"Are those hers?" Joel asked.

"They're just boots," Mia stammered.

Joel thought it over, then he bent down and took the boots and cradled them for a moment before handing them to Mia. His uncommon generosity caused her to be suspicious; all the same, Mia clutched the boots to her chest. She'd take what she could get. She had learned that by now. The boots smelled of grass and earth and of the woods where she and Ivy had walked in the evenings, often in the moonlight, as if they'd reached the place where they longed to go and had already escaped.

"We keep our grief to ourselves and go on," Joel told her. "I expect you to do as you're told from now on. Do you understand?"

Mia saw how dark his eyes were, how he looked inside you for his own benefit, how the lines on his face told a story he kept to himself. She didn't really know him, and she never would, but she understood what he was telling her. He wanted things done his way, and if they were not, someone would pay.

"I do," Mia told him. She understood that her mother should have left him a long time ago, and that he couldn't accept anyone who said no to him, and that he had created his own world in order to control it, and that she didn't want any part of it. Joel reached into his pocket and took out the leaf from an apple tree, green but edged with yellow. Mia recognized it as one of their own, from the orchard of Look-No-Furthers, and she vowed, then and there, that she would never eat an apple again.

Mia did as she was told, but that didn't mean she didn't have a plan in mind. It didn't mean that the farm was her home, or that Joel was her father, or that anyone knew her, or that she'd continue to follow the rules. Two weeks later, she was scheduled to work at the farm stand in town. It was exactly what she was waiting for, and Mia lowered her eyes when Evangeline told her the news, trying her best not to give herself away. This was her chance, and she knew it might not come again. Her mother was gone, and nothing was left. But even if Mia had nowhere to go, she did not intend to let Joel decide her fate. She would become invisible and disappear completely. Her life was in her own hands, to do with as she pleased, the one thing that belonged to her, the only thing she could claim for herself.

That day at the market, Mia was working alongside a new member of the Community, Tom Miller, and she considered being paired with him good luck. Tom was a plodding fellow who had never been able to keep a job out in the real world, and he was so new he didn't know the rules. When Mia told him she had to run over to the library because she was desperate to use the restroom, Tom nodded and waved her on.

"Go ahead," he said as he set out the baskets of squash and zucchini and the last of the tomatoes. "I'm not your keeper."

He was, but he didn't know it yet, and Mia ran across the town green. Her plan was to leave this earth and allow her spirit to rise up like a blackbird. She could escape by going out the back door of the library, which led directly into the woods. She didn't want to call attention to herself by going in and out of the library too quickly, so she did what she always did and made her way to the fiction department, where she tried her best to steady her nerves. She had decided this was to be her last day on earth, and everything seemed intensified. The whispers of patrons, the creaks of the old wooden floor. Mia grabbed a novel without bothering to look at the title or author. She planned to take the path into the woods after she checked out the book so that fool Tom wouldn't spy her.

"Your choice is excellent," Mrs. Mott said when Mia approached the desk. "Nathaniel Hawthorne is one of my favorites."

It was the book that had been inscribed to her, with the brown and gold cover. Mia's hands were shaking, and she hoped the librarian wouldn't notice, but, of course, Sarah did. She always worried about this girl, trekking back and forth on Route 17, where the traffic was tricky, and it was difficult to see around turns when dusk fell. The Community was miles from town, then up a dirt road that local people were barred from using. There used to be wild blueberries growing there, and banks of cinnamon-scented ferns. Sarah was so busy thinking about the Community that she didn't notice the book Mia was checking out was a first edition, which wasn't meant to be circulated, for it had been printed in Boston by Ticknor, Reed and Fields in 1850.

"Did you know Hawthorne lived in a place like your community called Brook Farm, which was a complete disaster. There was also a failed experiment called Fruitlands, started by Louisa May Alcott's father, a totally disastrous under-taking."

"I've read *Little Women*," Mia blurted, though she knew she really shouldn't say anything at all to an outsider.

"Well, Louisa might have never written it, and the Alcott children might have perished from a lack of nutrition out in Fruitlands if nearby neighbors had not brought them fruit and eggs. There's nothing like that going on where you are, is there?" Sarah Mott asked, concerned.

"We have eggs," Mia assured her.

Mia had tucked the book into her backpack and if Sarah wasn't mistaken, the girl's hands were shaking. "Would you like a ride back home?"

Sarah Mott said. "It would be no problem. I could drop you off at the gate."

"I'm fine," Mia insisted. "I'm good."

She certainly didn't sound it. On impulse, Sarah wrote down her phone number and passed the note to Mia. "In case you ever need anything."

Mia smiled faintly. "Thanks, but I don't have a phone. I couldn't call you."

Sarah opened the desk drawer, then handed Mia a key to the library. "Call me from here."

"You shouldn't trust me," Mia said. "You don't even know me."

"I know what you like to read." Sarah shrugged. "That's good enough for me."

Mia remembered that Ivy had once said she'd been given a key she'd never used and she seemed to regret it, so Mia took the key. She didn't wish to be rude, but she had to hurry. If someone from the Community thought to ask where she was, Tom Miller might figure out that he'd best come to look for her. "Thanks for the offer," Mia told Mrs. Mott.

When Mia slipped out the rear door, the sunlight was blinding, but as soon as she stepped into the woods it was dark. Instead of heading toward the dirt road that curved up into the mountain, as she usually did to reach the Community, Mia cut through a field rife with wild thimbleberry, low-growing plants filled with tiny snow-white blooms. There were two rivers nearby, the Eel

River, said to be haunted by the Apparition, and the Last Look River, which had taken the lives of several boys who leapt into the water without looking and were swept away by the rising spring flow. Mia was approaching the Last Look River. There were wild ox-eye daisies attracting masses of bees, and when Mia lay down in the grass, the sound of their droning filled her head. The Last Look River was running fast after a series of thunderstorms and the water was nearly overflowing its banks. Mia was a good swimmer, but she intended to load stones into her backpack, which she would then slip over her shoulders to weigh her down. If they had left the night before the accident, none of it would have happened. They might be in California right now, looking at the Pacific Ocean, three thousand miles from here.

Mia held up a hand to shield her eyes so she could look around one last time. Gazing down, she noticed that when she'd flung herself onto the ground, the library book had tumbled into the grass, and when it fell open, there was the inscription. She hadn't imagined it.

To Mia, If it was a dream,
it was ours alone and you were mine.

The cloth cover was frayed at the edges and the title was a tarnished gold. It looked like a book that mattered, one that might have belonged in the rare books collection. *The Scarlet Letter*. Was it meant for her, or for someone else? Mia thumbed through the pages.

> *She had not known the weight*
> *until she felt the freedom.*

Here was the story of a young woman who had a child out of wedlock, shamed and judged by those closest to her, married to a man who was evil, and in love with one who was weak, forced to wear a badge with the letter **A** for adultery. It was the story of a woman who loved her daughter more than anything, more than life itself.

Mia paged through the book, then stopped and read again.

> *We dream in our waking moments,*
> *and walk in our sleep.*

She felt her heart hitting against her chest. She had been a sleepwalker, and now, on this afternoon when she meant to do away with herself, she had awakened with a start. Whether or not the inscription was directed to her, she felt as if the author knew her, and was speaking directly to her, for the tale he told of the Puritans and the story of life in the Community were so alike. In that moment, she felt closer to him than she had ever felt to anyone. The lemon-colored afternoon light was filtering through the branches above her. The peepers in the shallows were calling, a soft watery song. The rocks were gray shale, an ancient mix of mud and clay, and it was possible to find plant fossils, along with fossils of tubeworms and primordial insects. Mia was a born reader, just as her mother had been, and once she had begun, she couldn't stop.

She lay on her stomach, propped up on one elbow, quickly turning the pages, falling in love with both the author and the book. By the time the lilac-colored dusk clouded the sky, Mia was halfway through the novel. She had forgotten about gathering rocks, and drowning seemed a foolish waste of a life. She'd thought her only choice was to leave this world, but now she had discovered how terribly alive she was. She'd had a tingling feeling, as if she'd been stung by bees. This was how it felt to want more than being invisible.

As the dark pitched down in splotches, Mia shoved on her boots and raced to the farm, where, luckily, no one had missed her. When she saw that newcomer Tom Miller unloading the truck, she explained that she'd had female problems and had to run home. "Please don't tell anyone," she begged, and because he was embarrassed by the topic of conversation, he was willing to oblige.

That night Mia left the book in the barn beneath

some old boards. She had books hidden all over the barn, nearly two dozen volumes that were extras Mrs. Mott had given her. She finished *The Scarlet Letter* when she returned the next day in the pale morning light, sitting in the musty barn, her back against the splintered wood. She felt the book inside her heart, for the story so reminded her of the life she and Ivy had been leading. When Mia was done reading, she hid the book in her special place alongside her beloved painting, up in the hayloft behind a board she had pried off the wall.

At the end of the day, Mia went up the hill to the cemetery. The last of the sunlight was so bright, the air was so soft, and her pulse created such a steady rhythm in her head. She began to weed around her mother's grave, leaving the ferns she had planted there. She had been reminded of all there was to look forward to—books, sunlight, stories, the scent of the ferns. She wished that Ivy could see the sky and the clouds over High-top Mountain. Oh, glorious world. Oh, day that would never come again. How could she have ever thought of leaving it behind?

It happened a week after Mia had decided she wanted to be alive. She often went to visit the cemetery and had sat there a few times, rereading *The Scarlet Letter*, wishing she could tell her mother about the book. *We should have gone off to live in the forest. We should have never bowed to Joel's vision of what life should be like.*

In the dining hall, there was vegetable stew and biscuits and a salad made with the last of their lettuce and kale for dinner. It seemed like another uneventful Thursday, until Mia noticed the girls were all looking at her as she went to get a dinner tray. Evangeline was standing by the door watching her as well, her mouth set in a harsh line. Mia went on to pick up her silverware, but she had begun to feel a chill. What did they know that she did not? Before Mia could get her food, Tim Hardy and another man came up to her.

"He's waiting," Tim said, and that only meant one thing. Mia had broken the rules. There was no one to protect her. Ivy couldn't dissuade him now, and Mia would have to pay for her actions. She was no one special anymore.

Mia's thoughts were racing as the two men took her out to the cow field. There were torches burning, and on the grass she spied a pile of her books. She hadn't realized she had so many that she hadn't yet returned to the library. By now, everyone had followed them out of the dining hall. Joel was waiting, wearing a white shirt and black trousers, a badge in his hand. **A** for acts of wickedness. He came to hang the badge around Mia's neck. The moon was already rising over the field, a thin, pale sliver of light.

"Is this how you repay my kindness?" Joel asked in his dark, quiet voice. It was the voice he used right before he punished someone, soft and dangerous. "With such shameful behavior?"

Mia stared at him with an unwavering gaze, even though she was terrified, her knees shaking. "What kindness?" she said, for she felt she had never known any.

The bonfire had been lit, the flames rising high, the night flickering with heat. They had used old wood, chopped from apple trees taken down in the wet gusts of a storm, good for burning. The books were flung into the blaze one by one as Mia watched, half dazed, her hands and feet feeling numb. Joel insisted that the children do it, and each boy and girl who came up to the fire was solemn as they tossed books into the pyre. Pages fluttered like doves aflame, the burned bits of paper soaring into the dark, silent night. In the morning, Mia would be branded with an iron in the shape of an **A**. She would carry it with her all her life.

"Think about that," Joel said, as she was led to the sheep barn and locked inside. She sat down in the dark and she thought about it. She listened to the hissing sound as the bonfire burned out, and she decided the time had come. Hidden beneath the hay was the hammer she'd taken from the men working in the field. *Just in case I ever need it,* she had thought then. That was how she broke the lock, and she had never in her life felt more alive.

There was still a sliver of the yellow moon in the sky on the morning Mia left. It was pitch dark, but she could see through the gloom; she was used to going out to the barn to do her chores before dawn, when the mist was rising. When she crossed the field, the dogs didn't bark; they were all used to Mia, who always tried to save some of her supper for them. One, a collie named Jester, followed her through the tall grass. He was a good dog, friendlier than the others, and she might have cried at the thought of leaving him behind if she'd been a different sort of person, but she wasn't. She was someone who knew that the only girls who survived were the ones who saved themselves.

"Hush," Mia told the collie when they reached the fence. "Go home."

She clapped her hands, and the echo startled the dog, who took off into the dark. When she walked on, there was nothing to weigh her down. She was camouflaged by the night, and she felt protected by the vast empty landscape. She didn't even own enough to pack a suitcase, but she had her backpack and she'd taken the painting and the book with her. She scrambled over the fence, then took off down the road, staying in the shadows in case anyone should drive by. There were the huge oak trees, and the gate to the cow pasture that always swung open and stuck. The crickets were calling so fast the echo made Mia's pulse race. As she walked to town, she did her best to forget everything about her past.

When she reached the back door of the library, Mia used the key Sarah Mott had given her. She didn't dare to turn on any lights but instead made her way to the desk in the dark. There was moonlight streaming through the window when she grasped the phone. She had memorized the number the librarian had given her.

It was late and Sarah was asleep when the phone rang.

"Can you come to the library?" Mia said. "I'm hiding behind the desk."

Sarah threw on her clothes and walked over. She lived in the cottage behind the town founder's house, where there was a garden that grew only red flowers and red vegetables, tomatoes and peppers and chard. The lights in the library were off, so Sarah walked to the desk in the dark. When she saw Mia sitting there, her legs pulled up to her chest, her backpack beside her, Sarah Mott sat down beside her. The library felt hushed and safe, but now they found themselves whispering.

"Are you all right?" Mrs. Mott asked.

Mia's brilliant hair had been cut choppily at

chin length, but she still looked as if she had walked out of another time and place in her gray overalls. Usually, Mia avoided eye contact, but on this day she seemed different. Her pulse was fast. It had been ever since she'd walked away from the Last Look River. If she was wrong, if she couldn't trust Mrs. Mott and the librarian told Joel where she was, Mia didn't want to think about what would happen. But Mrs. Mott was listening, and it might well be Mia's last chance. "I need to get out of Blackwell. They punish people for reading at the farm. They burned my books."

No one else from the community had ever visited the library. Sarah now thought of the other children she'd seen at the farm stand in their ill-fitting clothes. The women who shopped at the grocery for staples like flour and cornmeal with their hair braided and coiled into knots, and the men loitering outside the hardware store, grim and untalkative. Every time she saw anyone from the Community, Mrs. Mott saw trouble before her. She saw trouble right now set within the fear in Mia's eyes.

"What do they intend to do?" she asked.

"They intend to ruin my life."

Sarah looked at the girl closely, her dark eyes, her grim expression.

"What would you like me to do? Call over to the police?"

Mia looked even more panicky. "No. Please. Don't do that. They might send me back. Do you think you could find me someplace to live?" By now her voice was breaking. "I don't care where I go as long as it's far from Blackwell. Do you think you can help me?"

Sarah Mott knew what the consequences might be for helping a minor run away, she might even be charged with kidnapping. All the same, she was matter-of-fact, the sort of person who rarely used superlatives. "I'd bet my life on it," she said.

They stopped at a gas station on the Mass Pike so that Mia could use the restroom. Sarah had thought to bring her a change of clothes, jeans, a slate-blue shirt, and a pale yellow sweater. Once she'd slipped them on, Mia tossed her old clothes into the trash can. When she saw her reflection in the car window, she thought that she looked like someone brand new, with her chin-length hair and her store-bought clothing. There she was, a stranger. So much the better. That was the way it should be.

Mrs. Mott was waiting behind the wheel, drinking a coffee in a to-go cup. "All set?" she asked. It wasn't yet 5:00 a.m.

"Definitely," Mia answered. She had already decided. She would never be back.

The friend Mrs. Mott had alerted about Mia's situation was Constance Allen. She and Sarah had been involved since college and lived together in the summer and on holidays, waiting for the time when Sarah could retire and move in permanently. "I would trust her with my life," Sarah told Mia as they drove east toward Concord.

Sarah and Constance had been in love ever since they met, even though Sarah had been married once; that had been a mistake. Her love for Constance, however, was something she would never regret. As they headed east, Sarah thought of the first time they'd seen each other, outside the library at Simmons. Constance was an elegant blonde from a wealthy family in Glen Cove, Long Island, while Sarah hailed from a working-class family in New Hampshire, just outside of Nashua. They had nothing in common, and Sarah already had her group of friends, fun-loving, smart girls, but none of them interested her the way that Constance did.

One bright afternoon, Constance came up to her in the dining hall. "You keep staring at me," she said. "Is there something you wish to say?"

There was, but Sarah had been unable to say it, or, perhaps, she hadn't truly understood all she wanted to say to Constance until after she had been married and moved to Western Massachusetts. Constance had been one of the bridesmaids at Sarah's wedding, and the night before the ceremony she had suddenly taken Sarah's hand.

"You've talked about Josh so often, but you have never once said you loved him."

Sarah had laughed. What was her friend suggesting? That Sarah walk away? The tent was set up in Josh's parents' backyard and the caterers from the Jack Straw Tavern would soon be arriving, and Josh's friends had thrown a bachelor party the night before that had lasted till dawn. But all at once Sarah knew what she had wanted to say all those years ago in the dining hall at school, that she didn't think she could survive if Constance wasn't in her life. It took her several years of a doomed marriage until she could drive out to Concord one Sunday. When Constance had opened the door in the early morning light, surprised and still in her nightgown, Sarah had said, "I'm finally here," and that was all it took for everything to be settled between them.

Throughout the drive Mia had been terrified that they were being followed and that Joel would somehow find her and bring her back. He was the sort of man who didn't let things go. *Don't test him,* Ivy always said. *Don't pick a fight with him unless you're willing to lose.*

Mia looked out the rear window of the car even when there was no one else on the road.

"You'll be safe here," Mrs. Mott assured her when they arrived at Constance's house. The street jogged along the Concord River. In the fields there were dozens of bluebird houses, little wooden boxes painted by children at the local school.

When Mia got out of the car she inhaled deeply. The air was fresh and gleamed with green light. It was noon, and the day was bright. Constance Allen opened the door of her little white house and waved. There were purple asters growing along the brick walkway on tall, thin stems. Constance was forty-five; and although she seemed ancient to the children who came to story time at the library, today, in her wrap sweater and jeans, she looked young.

"What are you waiting for?" she called cheerfully, and because it made no sense to be standing on the sidewalk like strangers, they went inside, and Mia began her new life.

Miss Allen informed her friends and co-workers that an orphaned niece had come to stay. Tragedies happened, and when they did Miss Allen was a good person to have on your side. Mia was promptly enrolled at the public high school under the name Maria Allen. A birth certificate was drawn up by a friend of Constance's carpenter, who knew a place where it was possible to obtain false documents. Mia was a good student, always handing in work for extra credit. She loved the classes, but she stayed to herself, ill at ease with other people her age. She adored her room in Miss Allen's house, however, which was lined with bookshelves and had a huge window overlooking a willow tree. Beyond that was the Concord River, and in the morning geese on their way south would call and the peepers would sing their last songs of the year.

Miss Allen gave Mia time to settle in, and on weekends Mia would spend afternoons at the library, reading, while Miss Allen was at work. She visited the houses of the great writers who had lived in Concord, Emerson and the Alcotts and Thoreau, but most often she went to the Old Manse, where Nathaniel Hawthorne and his wife, Sophia Peabody, had lived after their marriage, paying a hundred dollars a year for rent. Mia had read up on their history and knew that Sophia had been a painter who'd spent most of her life bedridden until meeting Hawthorne. She had given up painting at the age of thirty-four, and soon after becoming a mother for the first time she had written in the window glass with her diamond ring as she gazed out at a world of snow and ice. *The trees were all glass chandeliers.*

Mia had spent hours standing in the grassy yard of the Old Manse, hidden behind the lilac bushes, reading the words both the bride and groom had etched into the glass with the diamond ring, a declaration of true love. She knew the message by heart and could recite it as if it were an incantation.

Man's accidents are God's purposes.

Sophia A Hawthorne 1843

Nath'l Hawthorne

This is his study

1843

The smallest twig

leans clear against the sky

Composed by my wife,

and written with her diamond.

Inscribed by my

husband at sunset

April 3d 1843

On the gold light   S A H

Sunlight splashed against the windows as Mia observed the study where Hawthorne had worked, and she could spy the green divan where he'd rested while imagining his stories. She had searched out his grave in the old cemetery, up on Authors Ridge, the burying place of Concord's great writers, where people often left tokens of respect, flowers and pencils and pens all set down to honor Hawthorne's memory. Once or twice, she'd seen a crumpled note left for the author, who had been gone for more than a hundred and fifty years. She understood that when a book spoke to you, you wanted to speak back. For all this time, she had been holding one-sided conversations with the author, although sometimes she imagined the words he said in return.

She dreamed of Hawthorne, and when she walked through the cemetery, she imagined that he walked beside her. She supposed she had fallen in love with him, he took up so much space inside her head. She was so focused on her vision of Hawthorne she didn't notice when funerals streamed by, with mourners doing their best to step around her. Once she fell asleep beside his grave, and when she woke with grass threaded through her hair, she could not shake off her dream that the author had come to her, and that they belonged to one another. She felt closer to him than she did to anyone else, and often took out the book she had stolen from the library to read the inscription. Other girls her age were dating, having mad crushes on boys at school, crying in the corridors when they were dumped, starting all over again with someone new, but

Mia had no interest in any of that nonsense. What she wanted was impossible, but she was convinced there was magic in the world and if she waited long enough, if she really wished for it, he would be hers. Love in the real world must exist, otherwise why would it be written about so often? But what it was, and how it felt, was a mystery to her; it could not be what she had witnessed growing up, hiding with her mother in the forest just so they could speak freely.

After Mia had left the farm, Joel Davis stormed into the police station to report that his daughter was an underage runaway. After a search of the town and the woods, the police informed him there was nothing more they could do. It was evident that they believed whoever ran away from the Community likely had good cause, and after so many antagonistic years, they didn't feel obliged to go out of their way to help Davis.

One morning, when Sarah was replacing books on the shelves, she looked up and there he was in the reading room. She kept working even when Joel Davis approached the desk. She told herself she had nothing to fear and there was no reason for her hands to shake as they did.

"Are you the one who gave her all those books?" Joel asked. He had a hard look on his face and he hadn't bothered to kick the mud off his boots. He'd walked in as if he owned the place. "I'll bet you did. I'll bet you like to have people think just like you and fill their minds with trash."

"Are you a member of this library?" Sarah said.

"It's open to the public, and that's me. I'm the public." There was no debate over that. "If you know where my daughter is, and you fail to tell me, you'll likely wind up in jail."

There was still a tremor in Sarah's hands, but she narrowed her eyes. She'd be damned if she would back down. "I don't know what you're talking about."

"But you don't deny giving her those books, do you?" When Sarah didn't answer, Joel nodded. "That's what I thought. I can always spot a liar." He put down a leaf on the desk. "Give her this and she'll know who she belongs to. Her mother didn't leave me, and she's not going to either."

He walked out without another word and Sarah immediately called to tell Constance. She didn't think she should visit Concord for a while, just in case Joel Davis got it into his head to follow her. Once she'd heard that Davis had confronted Sarah, Constance felt she owed it to Mia to tell her what had happened.

"What exactly did he say?" Mia wanted to know.

"All nonsense. And he left some sort of leaf."

An apple tree leaf to remind her of her mother, to let her know she had a father and he had rights to her. Although she appeared calm, that night Mia slept fitfully. She had never spoken about her life at the Community, but Sarah had explained to Constance that Mia had run off after the tragic death of her mother. Constance's own mother had died young, and she knew what it was like to feel alone when you were much too young to experience that sort of abandonment. She heard Mia get out of bed sometime past midnight, and when Constance came out of her room she found Mia in the parlor, staring into the dark yard, keeping watch. Constance would never understand if Mia told her that Joel knew what you were thinking. He could spot a liar and a thief. He knew what you would do before you yourself did.

"You don't have to worry about him. He doesn't know where you are and he is never getting you back," Constance assured Mia. "Sarah and I wouldn't allow it. If we need to, we'll hire a lawyer and have you declared an emancipated minor."

Mia was grateful, and after that she told Constance she was able to sleep, but it wasn't the truth. Sometimes, when she was in bed trying to fall asleep, she thought she heard him rattling the windows in her bedroom, a goblin from the past who wouldn't leave her alone. Once she went out to the garden, and there on the iron table was a perfect apple tree leaf. It might have been coincidence, it might have drifted over from a tree in a neighbor's yard, all the same, after that Mia always got out of bed to make sure the locks on the door were bolted.

Some things could break you once you brought them back to life. Some things were best forgotten. Mia did her best not to think of the past, but it did no good. The days were fine, but once night fell, she remembered it all. Her mother laughing in the dark woods. The cemetery ringed with ferns and the mountain beyond. The rocks in her backpack on the bank of the Last Look River. The smell of books when they were burned on a bonfire. The inscription in the book written in blue ink. Running past the dogs to the gate with her heart pounding. The promise she had made herself that she would never go back.

At school, they were studying the genealogy of several of the writers who had lived in Concord, with Mia's presentation on Nathaniel Hawthorne earning her an A+. She found herself more and more curious about her mother's past. What sort of life might have driven Ivy to a place like the Community? Did she not have another soul to turn to, someone who might have taken her in? Mia recalled hearing people gossip out in the fields and in the dining hall, saying that Ivy was a spoiled rich girl. When Mia began to research the Jacob family of Boston, she discovered the gossip hadn't been entirely wrong. One of the Jacobs had run for governor in the 1950s and another had been on the board of Massachusetts General Hospital. Her grandfather was a real estate banker from an old Massachusetts lineage, a descendant of a line of the family who had, oddly enough, settled in Berkshire County after arriving from Amsterdam. One of her relatives, John Jacob, had been the first pastor in the town of Blackwell. A cousin, Lucy Jacob, had been murdered on Route 17, the same road Mia had walked each time she'd gone into town. Her grandmother's people had come over on the *Mayflower* and had been among those who managed to survive the first deadly winter of the original settlement, one of the few who had seen the buds of spring in the colonists' first year.

One Saturday Mia took the train to Boston. She told Miss Allen she was visiting friends, not that she had any. Mia had been to Boston several times with Miss Allen and easily found her way to Beacon Hill. When she came to Louisburg Square, perhaps the most elegant address in the city, she stood outside the Jacobs' large brick townhouse. It was October by then and the air was spicy and smelled like smoke. The Jacobs' house was so big it reminded Mia of a library. She shivered and buttoned her sweater and was glad she was wearing her mother's boots, which always kept her feet warm. The girls at the Community had called them witch's boots, but Mia had never cared. She knew what was beautiful and what was not. She knew her mother would have wanted her to have them. Standing there, Mia closed her eyes and tried to envision Ivy when she lived here, but all she could imagine was a beautiful woman whose hair had been shorn, who wished she had lived west of the moon.

The brick sidewalks were slippery now, slick with fallen leaves. Mia went past the black wrought-iron gate and up the path. On the door was a brass knocker in the shape of a lion, which she used to rap three times, quietly at first and then more insistently. No one responded, but she noticed there was a rusty buzzer that rang a bell, and she tried that. She could feel the vibration of the ringing bell travel along her finger to her wrist. There was a moment when she might have changed her mind and run, but she stayed rooted to the ground, the leaves from a tall oak tree falling around her.

A maid answered the door, out of breath and surprised, having run down a flight of stairs when she heard the bell, for no one ever came to call. "Did you want something?" she asked. There had been three women on the housekeeping staff years ago, along with a cook who came in on the weekends, but things had changed.

Now that Mia was here, she was tongue-tied. "I'm here to see Mr. and Mrs. Jacob," she managed to say.

"When it comes to him, that will be difficult," the maid said. "He's dead."

"Is Mrs. Jacob here?"

The maid was Helen Connelly, and she saw something she recognized in Mia. Her heart softened when she realized who the girl was. She had been waiting for this day. "Mrs. Jacob is having tea. I'll bring you in."

Mia followed Helen through the hallway into the vast, chilly entrance hall. There was a black-and-white marble floor, and the walls were painted blue. The paint was cracking from water damage.

"Plumbing," Helen said when she noticed Mia staring. "There was a leak."

They went to a glass bubble of a room filled with plants, some alive, others wilting, with wintry brown leaves and spent flowers. Mia supposed such a room was called a conservatory. There was an older woman with silvery hair, still in her nightgown, there at the table reading the *Boston Globe*. The teapot was in the shape of a goose and tea poured from the goose's beak. The tea was always served weak, no sugar, no milk. That was the way she liked it.

"You have a visitor," Helen said.

"Do I?" Mrs. Jacob said. She gazed up, uninterested until she spied the slender girl in the

127

doorway. She knew right away. The shape of the girl's face and her pretty, wide mouth. And of course, there was that brilliant red hair falling straight to her chin, the same vivid color Mrs. Jacob's own mother had possessed. She had thought the day might come when somebody would arrive wanting something. There was no reason to make it easy. No one had made it easy on her.

"I think we might be related," Mia said.

"Go out and close the door," Mrs. Jacob told Helen. "Come back in ten minutes." Helen turned and went to leave the room, then stopped when Mrs. Jacob called out that she had changed her mind. "Make it five," she told Helen.

"Talk as long as you'd like," Helen told Mia before she closed the door.

Mia was studying her grandmother. She hadn't known what a heavy drinker looked like until today. Pale, ashen skin and runny eyes, a tremor in both hands, pursed lips. She couldn't for the life of her imagine Ivy in his house.

"How much were you intending to ask for?" Mrs. Jacob said, her voice dry with sarcasm.

Under the bitter scrutiny of her grandmother, Mia wilted and felt utterly out of place. Even though she was wearing the new sweater and jeans Constance had bought her, she knew she was underdressed.

"Or is Ivy the one who sent you? Unfortunately,

128

she's waited too long. There's not as much in the bank as there once was."

"This has nothing to do with her." Mia had a vision of her mother in her gray overalls, her hands muddy from working in the garden, the scent of apples in her black hair.

"I know all about that Community of hers," Mrs. Jacob spat, her eyes fixed on the girl before her. A stranger, really, nothing more. "I found the articles about them in my husband's study after he died. She destroyed our lives for that nonsense. And, by the way, she's not getting a dime. Tell her that."

"I can't tell her anything," Mia said. "She died."

That stopped Mrs. Jacob. Her face sank and she looked so old. She looked like a woman who had lost everything.

"It was an accident," Mia went on. "During apple season. A truck backed over her."

Mrs. Jacob turned her head away for a moment and made a sound in her throat that frightened Mia. It was the way a sob sounded when it was choked back and swallowed.

"I expected as much," Mrs. Jacob said when she had gained control of herself. She wasn't about to feel anything for this girl standing before her. She hadn't felt anything for years. "And now you're here. If you don't want money, what is it you want?"

Mia wanted to say, *What do you think I want? A family, a grandmother, someone, anyone who might be interested in me, anyone who might possibly love me, who might want to know what happened to me.* Instead, she lifted her chin. "Just to say hello."

"Well, now you've said it." They stared at one another. "Is there anything more?"

Mia didn't know if her grandmother had always been this cruel, or if losing her child and her husband had made her so. "I guess not," she said.

"When I think of it, it's really all your fault," Mrs. Jacob said, her eyes trained on Mia. "Ivy becoming pregnant with you started the whole journey down the road to hell."

"Where do you think I was?" Mia said, provoked. "West of the moon?" She was embarrassed when her voice broke with emotion, but she knew which of the two of them had been to hell.

"That moon nonsense Ivy used to talk about was the beginning of things going wrong. All those fairy tales she read. That's probably how she wound up with you."

"Didn't you worry about what had happened to me?" Mia asked.

When her grandmother looked blank, Mia realized Mrs. Jacob hadn't thought about her at all. She hadn't thought of Mia as anything other than a sin and a burden and the reason everyone's life had been destroyed.

"You ruined your mother's life." Mrs. Jacob's pinched face was flushed with emotions that she didn't even think she had anymore. She had lost a daughter and a husband and now she was old. She really didn't care whose feelings she hurt.

"Maybe you ruined her life," Mia said softly. "And mine." She was beginning to understand how Ivy might have wound up at the Community, with nowhere to turn and nowhere to run. "I came here to see you," Mia said. "And now I have."

Helen was standing in the doorway waiting for her. More than five minutes had passed, but time didn't really matter anymore. "Shall we?" Helen said to Mia, signaling for her to follow.

Mia trailed after Helen. "She's hateful," Mia said.

"Mrs. Jacob lost her husband and her child," Helen replied. "But yes, she can seem harsh. I wish she would have said how sorry she was about the loss of your mother." Mia looked at Helen closely. If she wasn't mistaken, the maid had tears in her eyes. Perhaps she'd overheard Mia speak of her mother's death. "I didn't know," Helen explained. Her gaze fell on Mia and she made a decision right then and there. Instead of escorting her to the door, Helen headed for the staircase, then looked back. When Mia hesitated, Helen urged, "I thought perhaps you'd like to see your mother's room."

Mia could feel her heart beating against her

ribs. She felt dizzy, the way she had after her mother's death, when she knew some things would never be possible. She knew that now she would never have a grandmother or be part of her mother's family, but all the same she nodded and followed Helen up to the third floor. It was dark and dusty in the narrow hallway and the window shades were drawn. Clearly, no one came up here anymore.

Helen pulled open the door to a bedroom. "They didn't change a thing." She gestured for Mia to go inside. "That should tell you something. They did love her, they just didn't know how to deal with her. They grew up in a different time."

Mia was reluctant to go farther, yet she was entranced to think she could finally have access to her mother's world. She stepped inside and caught her breath. Ivy's room was exactly as it had been on the night she left Louisburg Square, except that the bed had been made. That had been Helen's handiwork, otherwise the blanket would likely still be thrown upon the floor. Mr. Jacob had never again entered the room, but for many years, Mia was told, Mrs. Jacob would sit up here, in the pink and white chair in the corner. She would come here and cry.

There were posters of France on the wall, of Monet's garden and the Eiffel Tower.

"She had big plans," Helen said. "Once upon a time."

On the desk stood a framed photograph of Ivy at sixteen, a beautiful girl with masses of black hair, wearing jeans and sneakers, her eyes made up with black eyeliner, a grin flickering across her face.

Mia moved on to the bookshelf. She thought of her own books tossed on a bonfire in the cow field, how each page became a spark in the dark, open sky. Here on the shelf, Mia spied *Beloved*, along with *Wuthering Heights* and Thoreau's *Walden*. Helen went to the closet and opened the door so that Mia might have a look there as well. There were filmy dresses perfect for formal dances and cashmere sweaters, but also piles of raggedy jeans and T-shirts. There were Converse sneakers and high black boots, and on a wooden hanger there was a forest-green winter coat. Mia ran her hand over the sleeve.

"Looks like your size," Helen said. "It's cold out there today. You could use it."

Helen gestured for Mia to try on the coat. It was a perfect fit. Wearing it felt like a warm embrace. It reminded her of the nights in the woods when she and her mother were invisible and could do as they pleased, even for an hour or two.

Helen closed the closet door and a world closed along with it.

"Your mother was sweet and dear, and she knew how to have fun, but back then, things were different, and it was an especially different

133

time for women and girls. I fear that time is with us once again, and women don't have the right to make decisions about their own bodies. It was a disgrace to be pregnant and unmarried at such a young age, at least among those here on the hill. Especially in this house. They had a dream for her, and that wasn't it. But she had a dream, too."

"We should have run away from the farm," Mia said. If she'd had a daughter, she would have done exactly that.

"If your mother had told me about her situation, I would have had her come and live with me," Helen went on. "Then I'd be your grandmother of a sort. I've thought about that many times."

"But she didn't tell you?" Mia asked.

"No. And the truth of the matter is, I didn't ask."

"I wish you were my grandmother." Mia imagined going home with Helen, sitting at her kitchen table, having tea with sugar and cream. "But you're not."

"People make mistakes," Helen mused. "You hear that all the time, but it's very true. They can't guess the results of their actions. They don't mean to hurt you, but they do." There was a pink leather jewelry box on the bureau, and when Helen opened it, a ballerina danced in a circle surrounded by a jumble of necklaces and hoop earrings and a faded envelope that was addressed to Helen.

"She sent me a letter to give to you if you ever

came here. She wrote it after you were born."

The two went downstairs together, not speaking until they reached the front hall.

"Don't forget to read the letter," Helen urged her.

"Thank you for showing me her room," Mia said.

"She was only a girl," Helen said. "Remember that. But she should have had the choice to decide what to do with her own body and her own fate."

Helen threw her arms around Mia's shoulders, then quickly backed away.

After the door closed, Mia stood outside for a while wearing the green coat, eyes fixed on the house. She saw that the black paint on the window shutters was peeling. Pigeons were nesting on the rooftop, and no one had bothered to chase them off. She couldn't imagine what it might have been like to grow up here and what limits had been placed on her mother, she only knew that she was glad she had come, and even happier to be walking away with a message from her mother. She went to the Boston Common, sat on a bench, and watched the leaves fall and be carried away by the rising wind, and then she unfolded the letter.

Dearest Mia,
    If you are reading this letter you have left the Community, and for that I am

grateful. Perhaps I am about to tell you too much, but perhaps it is better than too little. Perhaps I should have told you while we were together, but I am hoping it's not too late. My parents thought they knew what was best, and because I was sixteen and had no legal rights, they made plans for me to give you away. They planned to steal everything I cared about. My freedom, my ability to make choices, and you. More than anything, you.

I let you grow up believing things that weren't true because I thought the outside world was dangerous. I let you believe that we were safe where we were, and that wasn't true either. But I want more for you than I wanted for myself.

Here is the truth: There was a boy I loved, who I thought loved me, but when I told him about my situation, he said it was my problem. But you were never my problem. You were my joy. He was at Harvard and had a bright future, and he cared what other people thought. He begged me to keep his secret and tell no one who the father was. I could have gone to his parents, I could have destroyed him in their eyes, but what good would that have done?

You were mine and mine alone. You

were the best thing that ever happened to me.

It was a time when unmarried girls were shamed for getting pregnant, as if pregnancy was a crime they had to pay for with their suffering. I pray that by the time you read this letter, the world will have changed, and girls can make their own choices about what they do with their bodies.

I went to Western Massachusetts, where the Community said that kindness was the only rule. That wasn't true, but I didn't know that evil can look like something it is not. I did not know that until I saw it right before me. I had a hole in my heart and Joel Davis filled it. I believed I had fallen in love. I gave my life over to him because I was too young and too exhausted to do anything else. To the untrue man, the whole universe is false, and he convinced me of that so that I could not trust a single person outside the gates of the farm. He was not your father, but he promised he would always be there for us. He told me that if I ever left him, he would keep you. He would find you and take you from me, and that wasn't a bargain I was willing to make. You were mine and mine alone.

I don't know what your future will be, but if you're reading this letter you need to know I stayed because of you. I stayed because I was afraid to lose you, and for that, and for a thousand other things, I am so sorry. I made one mistake after another, but I wanted you to know the truth.

Once upon a time, I loved you more than anything. I loved you more than life itself.

Mia celebrated her first Thanksgiving at Miss Allen's. She didn't know what to expect, for holidays were ignored at the Community. She had changed since she read the letter, which she kept in a shoebox beneath her bed, along with her copy of *The Scarlet Letter* and Carrie's painting. She understood what she and her mother had between them had never been invisible. It had been there all the time. From the very beginning she had been loved.

Sarah had finally come to visit. For several weeks Joel Davis had taken to sitting in his parked truck on the other side of the green, but that had stopped, and Sarah assumed he'd given up the thought that Mia was somehow hidden away in the library. She finally decided it safe to visit Concord. Sarah had never missed spending a holiday with Constance, and she left at four in the morning, when the streets were empty, and she was certain she'd know if she was being followed.

The weather was glorious and crisp, and they had a wonderful dinner, then walked around Walden Pond. It was there that Mia thought she saw the figure of a man beneath the trees. When she blinked, he disappeared, and she assumed it was likely the same vision she saw when she thought Joel was in the garden at night. She told herself that he was a nightmare and nothing more. But later that day, she found a red leaf on the table in the garden with a stone holding it in place. She picked it up. The leaves were not yet changing in Concord, but they always turned early in Blackwell, and Look-No-Furthers had a vein of red down the center of each leaf. Mia threw the rock toward the river and tore the leaf into shreds, her pulse thrumming too fast. After that she didn't go out by herself at night.

Mia had come to fear the dark, but it was a sunny afternoon when she saw him outside the library. He was not a goblin or a shadow, but a real live man. He'd followed Sarah Mott on Thanksgiving but had bided his time. He liked to do things his way. He liked to be in control and he liked the element of surprise. Just a hint of what he might do was all that was needed, a rule, a threat, a red leaf. It was the first weekend of December, and there was a thin coat of frost on the grass. Mia had slept in and was now coming to volunteer at the library as she did most Saturdays, and there he was waiting for her at the door. Inside the library, Miss Allen was reading Edward Eager's *Half Magic* at story time. Mia glanced through the glass door and saw Miss Allen and the ten or so children gathered around her. It was as if they existed in another world, one where children weren't locked into barns, and women weren't branded, and men didn't do whatever they were told to do.

"Let's go," Joel said. "Your antics have wasted enough of my time. When a man can't control his own daughter, people start to talk, and I can't have that."

"I'm not your daughter," Mia said. She was shaking, but she looked right at him.

Joel smiled at her then. "You're whatever I say you are," he told her. "You were then, and you still are now."

Mia was grateful that a group of teenage boys were tossing a football around on the lawn. Their sweaty, cheerful presence reminded her that she, too, lived in that different world now.

"I'm not going anywhere with you," Mia told Joel. Her voice sounded perfectly calm, except for the last word, which cracked as she spoke.

"That librarian of yours led me right here. She's not as smart as you think she is." Joel came to take Mia's arm.

Mia tried to pull away, but his grasp was tight.

She felt as if he would be willing to break her arm if she fought him too hard. She remembered those inky blue bruises.

"Just walk," Joel told her. One of the Community's old pickup trucks was parked nearby. "I'm taking you home and you're going to do as I say. I'm serious, Mia. I will break you if you fight me on this. You're setting a bad example for everyone else."

"What do you think you're doing?" Mia heard Constance shout. She had raced out of the library door as soon as she spied Mia with a man she didn't recognize. He wasn't tall, but he cast a shadow across the frozen lawn.

Joel pulled Mia along. "Don't give me any trouble," he told her.

"You there!" Mia heard Constance call. "You had better stop right now."

Joel turned and faced Constance. She was slight with a fair complexion, and now her face was blotchy and flushed. She hadn't even had time to put down her book, and she carried *Half Magic* before her as if it were her shield. "I don't know where you think you are, but this is Concord, Massachusetts," Constance said. "You can't just come here and abduct people in broad daylight."

"She doesn't belong to you," Joel told her. He had never liked to be thwarted, and when he was, there was a price to pay. He turned to Mia, his eyes burning with anger. "Your mother would have wanted you to come with me."

"My mother is the one who told me you weren't my father." Mia knew that going with him was nothing her mother would have wanted. "You never were. She left me a letter. You were her biggest regret."

Joel gazed directly into her face. "I have legal rights," he said. "Your mother and I were married."

"That doesn't mean you're anything to me. I could sue you for false imprisonment," Mia told him. "I could go to the police right now."

West of the moon, the only girls who were rescued were the ones who saved themselves.

Joel looked at her, dumbstruck. "Is this the way you speak to me? I created you," he said in a tight voice. "What I have created belongs to me, whether or not I'm your father."

"Call the police," Mia shouted over her shoulder to Constance. "I'm being kidnapped." From the look on Joel's face, Mia could tell that he knew she was serious.

"I'm getting out my phone," Constance shouted back. "I'm calling them now."

"You always were a little nothing," Joel told Mia. He was grinning even though his tone was laced with spite. "I should have gotten rid of you on the day you were born. I thought about it, and Ivy would have done it. She would have left you on the steps of town hall if I'd told her to."

"That's not true." Mia was trying her best not to care, but he was hurting her all the same, and he knew it.

"I knew her far better than you did. I knew her parents didn't want her, no one did, except for me."

"Call the police now," Mia shouted to Constance. "Tell them I'm in danger."

"You think you've won," Joel said, and she did, because for all his bluster, he had let her go and was walking back toward his truck. Constance came to stand beside Mia.

"That piece of shit," Constance said.

Mia couldn't help it. She'd been terrified, and now she laughed out loud, nearly doubling over.

"What?" Constance said, confused.

"I've never heard you say that word," Mia told her. "You don't curse."

"When I see a piece of shit, I call it like it is," Constance remarked. "Always have. Always will."

They stood there for a while, in the cold blue air. The truck had vanished, as if it had never been there, but there was black exhaust in the air.

"You do not belong to him," Constance said firmly. "You belong to yourself."

Sarah Mott resigned from her position at the library in Blackwell and moved in with

Constance on the day before Christmas. There had been an opening at the library in the Concord School, and Sarah was delighted that at last she and Constance would live together; they all were. It was a snowy day when Sarah arrived, and after they unpacked the car, they took a walk around Walden Pond, then had a festive supper with homemade cranberry sauce and macaroni and cheese rather than the traditional turkey dinner.

"Will you miss Blackwell?" Mia asked Sarah when Constance went into the kitchen to prepare their dessert, pecan pie with maple walnut ice cream. She had planned to end the dinner with an apple pie, but Mia confided that she despised apples and wouldn't ever eat them again, not even if they were baked in a pie.

"Not if I'm here with Constance," Sarah responded. "What about you? Do you miss it?"

Mia shook her head. "Not at all." But the truth was, Blackwell surfaced in Mia's dreams. At night she found herself dreaming about the rising waters of the Last Look River, and the clouds above Hightop Mountain, and the yellow fields of grass. Sometimes Joel was in her dreams, watching her and not saying a word, as if he were a ghost from the underworld. Sometimes she had her own daughter, one whom she made certain to bring west of the moon so that no one and nothing could ever hurt her.

"I've heard people are leaving the Community," Sarah said. "People say he's mistreating the children and should be in jail. They say he couldn't even keep his own daughter in line."

"That isn't me," Mia said.

"It most certainly isn't," Sarah assured her. "He's a liar."

"Who's a liar?" Constance asked cheerfully when she returned with dessert. Snippets of conversation had floated into the kitchen, and she loved the echo of Sarah's voice in her house.

"That man," Sarah said. None of them ever said his name aloud. "Maybe he'll disappear into thin air."

"He's gone as far as I'm concerned," Constance said as she set down gold-rimmed plates of pie topped with several spoonfuls of vanilla whipped cream.

Later, after Mia had said good night, she slipped out into the yard. In the dark, she could hear the river as the wind gusted and tree branches shifted above her. The night was filled with glittering stars. Mia felt the damage that the Community had done to her; all the same, she missed certain things. Reading in the barn, her favorite ewe, Dottie, the ferns in the woods, her mother's laughter across the garden as they weeded, Hightop Mountain, the crunch of twigs under her boots as she made her way back from the library, sitting by the river immersed in the book she loved most.

Mia might not be able to trust anyone else, but she trusted Mrs. Mott and Miss Allen. Even though she had done her best not to have any emotions, there it was, it had happened. Standing in the dark, she realized that her heart had opened because of Sarah and Constance. In the morning, when they sat around the small decorated tree in the parlor to open their presents, Mia was given a leather-bound journal and a cashmere scarf, her first Christmas gifts. In return, she presented each of her rescuers with a copy of the book that had saved her life, paperbacks of *The Scarlet Letter* bought at the Concord Bookshop and tied with blue ribbon, the color of good fortune and gratitude. Her other gift to them was that she never told them when she saw a leaf from an apple tree on the garden table, or on her desk at school, or on the path to the library.

In her last year of high school, Constance and Sarah often took Mia to visit libraries. It was a lark at first, but it soon became a mission to see as many as they could. Mia first chose the library her mother had told her about, the Athenaeum in Boston. Next, they went to Harvard's Houghton Library, which held the largest Emily Dickinson collection in the world, along with nine hand-sewn texts created by the Brontës when they were children. They visited the Salem Athenaeum, said to be haunted by certain patrons who so loved the library they never wished to leave. After Mia was accepted to NYU, they took a trip to Manhattan and visited the main branch of the New York Public Library. Mia was stunned by the beautiful Beaux Arts building, officially opened in 1911. It had been built between Fortieth and Forty-Second Streets where the Croton Reservoir had been, an enormous engineering project that took nearly sixteen years to complete. There were the lions standing guard on Fifth Avenue, Patience and Fortitude, originally named Leo Astor and Leo Lenox for the men who donated portions of their huge fortunes to assist in the library's building.

Walking into the New York Public Library was like entering another country. Mia felt as if she could not be farther away from the past she had known, the burning of books on bonfires, the fields worked twelve hours a day, the orchards that turned pink all at once.

Open the door, open the page, and there you are. You hold the fern-seed, and invisible you can slip into a thousand volumes.

In the rotunda, Mia felt moved to tears when she saw the murals *The Story of the Recorded Word*, four enormous paintings charting the progression of writing. When they entered the Rose Main Reading Room—which was nearly two city blocks long, with a fifty-two-foot ceiling painted with a mural that was surely meant to reflect heaven, with its perfect blue skies and flowing clouds—Mia stood in amazement, dizzy with emotion, then had to sit for a moment to collect herself.

Constance came up beside her. "Are you all right?"

"It's all so beautiful. I can't believe I'm here," Mia said. The best things that happened to you in life were often a complete surprise. "Thank you for everything," she added, something she had always wanted to say. She owed Sarah and Constance everything. She owed them the life she was living.

Sarah had come to join them. "How lucky we've been," she said.

"How lucky *I* am," Mia insisted, and for the very first time she believed it to be true, for standing in the library on Fifth Avenue, she knew where she belonged. This was the world she was made for.

It wasn't easy to walk away from the past, even when you locked it up in a box for which there was no key. Memories rattle around late at night, they claw at the latch, escaping when you least expect them to do so. Mia still wouldn't eat apples or tomatoes and her clothes were often simple outfits that might have been issued by the Community's storeroom. When asked, she said that apples and tomatoes disagreed with her digestion, and that she couldn't be bothered with fashion and preferred to look plain, except for the red boots, which she'd had resoled. She told herself she didn't remember standing in the woods in the dark, and in time she didn't remember begging her mother to leave. She slept easier, for it seemed impossible that Joel would find her in Manhattan, where it was possible to slip into crowds and become invisible, where not even your own neighbors knew your name.

She often thought about Hawthorne and the inscription in the book she'd found. *To Mia, If it was a dream, it was ours alone and you were mine.* Whenever she went back to Concord to visit, on weekends or holidays, Mia took out her copy of *The Scarlet Letter*. She had never returned this special edition to the library, nor had she dared to tell Sarah she had taken it. She supposed that made her a thief, just as Joel had always claimed she was. Still, it was the book that had kept her alive, the one that seemed to tell the story of her mother's life, the one she'd always imagined had been written for her.

By the time she was twenty-five, Mia had succeeded beyond all of Constance and Sarah's expectations. They shook their heads in wonder, congratulating Mia on all she had accomplished. After completing her undergraduate work, she'd received a degree in library science. Mia had applied for a job at the New York Public Library and was both amazed and delighted when she was hired for her dream job in special collections. Every time she walked into the building she was overwhelmed by its beauty; it felt like a sacred place to her. How lucky she was to be here, in one of the greatest libraries in the world.

There were times when she wondered if spending so much time with books had prevented her from having a proper life. Her co-workers had husbands and wives and children, they went off for summer vacations on Long Island or in Maine and owned condos in Brooklyn and Queens, and here Mia was in the same apartment in Chelsea she'd rented just after graduating from college. She was stuck in the past that she tried so hard to forget. She knew Joel couldn't find her, but still she suffered from panic attacks. She imagined people were following her when she walked home in the evenings. She didn't answer her phone. When she was asked out, by a library patron or a neighbor, she said she was busy and then went home to be alone.

Recently, Mia had found she was compelled to use the library database to search the obituaries posted in the Blackwell newspaper. Joel's name was never among them, and in truth, she still didn't feel safe, even though years had passed since he'd come to Concord. She supposed that she would never trust the world as long as he was in it.

Research came naturally to Mia and she had searched through the records of Harvard alumni to discover that Joel Davis had never been a student there. She had, however, found that he'd done time at Bay State Correctional Center. Some people are who you think they are. Some people hide the wolf inside of them, but you can hear them howl.

Once, after drinking half a bottle of wine in her kitchen on a dark night, Mia had phoned the office at the Community. Did she imagine that she could call back in time and Ivy would answer? When someone finally did pick up and say hello, Mia recognized Joel's voice and fell silent, her heart racing. After a few moments he said, "I know it's you. You can never get away from here. I know where you are right now."

Mia had quickly hung up. She thought about her mother kneeling before him, taking the blame for Mia's crime of reading. She thought of her last night in the barn. The past was with her, tied to her feet with black thread. She saw glimmers of it out of the corners of her eyes when she walked down Fifth Avenue or went grocery shopping or simply looked out her window. Because of this, and because she vowed never to have her fate and her rights taken from her, she had kept her promise to herself. She had never returned to Blackwell.

• • •

It was a tradition for Mia to meet with Constance and Sarah on March 16 at the bar of the Algonquin Hotel, where they would celebrate her birthday. This year a light, sparkly snow was falling on the evening of their get-together. They had taken a table by the window so they could watch as the soft flakes fell. The city was quiet and peaceful. Mia never knew what her birthday would bring, sunshine and greening trees, or ice and storms.

Sarah reached into her bag for Mia's birthday present and threw Constance a smile.

"You don't have to give me gifts anymore," Mia said. "I'm not a child." All the same, she was clearly delighted as she untied the ribbon. Constance and Sarah's birthday gift was a tradition.

"Of course we do," Constance scolded her. "And besides, we want to. What is a birthday without a gift?" This year it was a pair of small gold earrings. Mia had had her ears pierced, but she almost never wore jewelry. Despite herself, Mia thought of such ornaments as vanities, but Constance had always disagreed.

"How beautiful!" Mia was blinking back tears. This wasn't vanity; it was love. "They're perfect," she said as she slipped on the earrings.

There were hugs and kisses and joy all around. But at dinner, Constance barely touched her food, and she soon excused herself to take the winding steps that led down to the ladies' room. She'd seemed a bit dizzy when she stood up, which she claimed was caused by the strong martini she'd had, for they always drank martinis on Mia's birthday and on all other happy occasions. It was only when she was walking away that Mia realized how frail Constance looked.

"What is it?" Mia asked Sarah. She knew something was wrong, but she hadn't imagined just how wrong. Sarah told Mia that Constance had been diagnosed with an incurable form of lymphoma. She hadn't wished to share this news on Mia's birthday, but the truth was, there wasn't much time left.

"We should have told you earlier," Sarah said. "I suppose we were wishing it away, hoping beyond hope, but of course, that never works, does it?"

Mia burst into tears, then wiped her eyes with a napkin and did her best to pull herself together, apologizing for breaking down. She rarely showed her emotions, but now she couldn't hold them back.

"You have the right to cry." Sarah had always worried about the effects of those early years at the Community on such a sensitive girl who'd had to bottle up her true feelings and follow those unspeakable, ridiculous rules. "You're entitled to your grief, Mia."

When at last Constance returned, Mia realized she was wearing a wig. She hadn't noticed before; perhaps she hadn't wanted to see it. She understood wishing things away. Oh, that she had hold of the fern-seed and could make this sorrow invisible.

When Constance noticed Mia staring, she touched the bobbed hairdo. "What do you think of the style?" She did her best to grin. "Is it me?"

"You're you no matter what," Mia said. She had never said a truer thing in all her life. "You always will be the one and only Constance Allen."

They were standing together under the awning, waiting for a cab for Mia, when she thought she saw him. At the parking lot across the street a man was sheltered from the snow. She told herself not every stranger was Joel Davis.

"Here you go," Sarah said when the taxi pulled up.

It was snowing harder, there would be over a foot by morning, a rarity in New York City. They hugged and said their goodbyes, and when Mia turned all she saw was the snow falling. *West of the moon, when the snow falls it's made of sugar,* her mother had always told her. *That way it melts when the sun comes out and the only ones who know it's ever been there are the ones who have seen it before it disappears.*

• • •

Mia came back to Concord most weekends now, and on Saturday nights they often fixed a supper of tomato soup and grilled cheese sandwiches, Constance's favorite back when she was a girl. Unfortunately, Constance seldom ate; she seemed to be subsisting on mugs of pale tea. She was fading right before their eyes. There was no more treatment possible, and the painkillers Constance had been given upset her stomach. She was sleeping more and more, so that night and day no longer made a difference to her. Each time Mia visited, she thought about the day when Constance had greeted her at her front door, waving to Mia, welcoming her home. She remembered standing on the lawn of the library when Constance had called Joel a piece of shit. Mia couldn't stop herself from sobbing when she thought of her life here in Concord. Oh, how lucky she'd been to find herself here, in a place where she could grow up without fear. She wished Ivy could have lived this way, surrounded by people who loved her, surrounded by books. She often thought of the day when she'd seen the men carrying Ivy across the field, when her boots had fallen into the grass, when the whole world seemed silent.

On evenings when Sarah watched over Constance, Mia often left to walk through town. She had never lost her talent for seeing in the dark, and in the fading light she crossed the meadows where there were still bluebird houses tacked to the trees. No matter where Mia's route began, it always took her to Sleepy Hollow Cemetery. Hawthorne's grave was marked only with his last name, the spelling changed from the original Hathorne when he began to publish so that he could distance himself from his ancestors. His wife's and daughter's graves were just beside his; they had been buried in England, then disinterred and moved here to be with him. Yet he seemed alone. He seemed to be waiting for Mia. As always, his grave site was festooned with offerings. Flowers, rocks, pinecones, along with many pens and pencils, to honor his work. Mia had fallen in love with the book, and then she had fallen in love with its author. Perhaps that was why she was still alone, reluctant to have anything to do with a man who couldn't compare to the brilliant author. *You were mine.*

Mia walked through the garden at the Old Manse, planted by Thoreau as a wedding gift for Nathaniel and his wife. What would she not do for a love like theirs? Anything. Everything. She looked in through the cloudy glass windows, written upon with words of love, then she walked home through the sleeping town.

Soon, the days had grown warm enough for them to sit out in the garden in the evenings, beneath the flowering wisteria vines, where they could watch the soft violet light fold itself over the river. Constance had rallied, insisting that she would rather be awake and in pain than dragged down into a drugged coma. She wore a blanket around her shoulders, and sometimes she seemed to be drifting off; then she would startle awake. It was the pain that drove her deep inside herself. That and the idea that each day was a gift, and soon enough she would be gone.

When Sarah went inside to get some glasses and a pitcher of water, Constance took Mia's hand in her own. It might well be the last opportunity to have a moment alone to speak. "Will you look after her?" Constance asked, worried about leaving Sarah alone.

"Of course," Mia assured Constance. "I always will."

"And what about you? Who will look after you?"

"I'm fine on my own." It had always been true, and it always would be.

"Don't be afraid to love someone just because of that one horrible man," Constance told her.

"I'm in love with my favorite author." Mia smiled. "Doesn't that count?"

"If you're talking about one that's already dead and buried, it won't do you much good." Constance knew about Mia's visits to the grave-site, and she had come upon the first edition of

The Scarlet Letter while cleaning up Mia's room. The inscription had been especially curious, and she wondered if Mia had written it to herself, or if it was just a coincidence. Constance was in pain, and she was failing, but she was too concerned for Mia's future to hold back. "When you love someone, look what happens," she said.

"What happens?" Mia asked, hoping Constance wouldn't notice that she was crying.

"This." Constance gestured to all that was around them with a look of delight on her face. There was the river and the wisteria blooming in the falling dark. There was Sarah returning from the kitchen with a pitcher of water and three green glass tumblers. There were the birdhouses in the field, and the stone path they had put in one summer. There was all they had been to each other through the years. "You have a life," Constance said. She was the one who was crying now.

"Is there anything I can do for you?" Mia wanted to know. "Just name it." It seemed that she did have a heart, something she'd never wanted, for as it turned out, it was breaking.

"My dear girl, you gave me back a hundred times more than anything I would ever want," Constance told her. "We were a family. What could be better than that?"

A week later Sarah telephoned at six in the morning. It was a workday, and Mia was stealing a little more sleep before she dressed to leave for the library. Manhattan was quiet at such an early hour, with the birds in the yard next door singing in the tree that had been there for two hundred years. Right away, Mia panicked, and as soon as she answered she could tell that Sarah had been crying. Sarah had been up all through the night, until now, when it was a decent hour to phone Mia.

"Constance waited until I was out of the room," Sarah said. "I had just gone to get her old copy of *Walden*. I read it to her every night."

"I'll be there as soon as I can." Mia was already packing. She didn't need much, only her black dress, and her mother's red boots.

Mia took the early train to Boston in a dazed state, then caught the commuter train at North Station out to Concord. She walked past the library and headed toward the river, thinking about the first time she'd come to town, when they'd driven all that way from Blackwell, barely saying a word. When she reached the house, Mia found Sarah crying in the kitchen, stunned by grief.

"Don't look at me," Sarah said. "I'm a terrible sight."

"What can I do to help?"

"The funeral has been arranged. I did it this morning."

"I'll phone everyone who should be invited," Mia assured her.

They were both wrecks, but they hugged fiercely, and after a while they stopped crying and decided to have tea. English breakfast, Constance's favorite. No sugar, no milk.

"I didn't actually think she would die," Mia found herself saying.

"Nobody ever thinks it will happen," Sarah replied. "Real life is unbelievable. Souls are snatched away from us, flesh and blood turn to dust, people you love betray you, men go to war over nothing. It's all preposterous. That's why we have novels. To make sense of things."

They chose some of Constance's favorite passages from Thoreau for Sarah to read at the service. *It's not what you look at that matters, it's what you see.* They skipped dinner, for neither had an appetite, and instead sat outside at the small wrought-iron table overlooking the river. They drank martinis, in Constance's honor, for a martini was always her cocktail of choice.

The lilacs had begun to bloom and there was a scrim of hazy purple all through the neighboring backyards and gardens. The hedge beside the back door was wreathed with flowers in shades of dark and light violet. The peepers were going mad, and, because it was dusk, clouds of mosquitoes and mayflies arose, birds swooped over the river, the verdant field beyond the far bank turned from green to an inky black.

Sarah was watching the bluebirds soar across the field, their last flight before night fell. The stars were already beginning to prick through the darkening sky. Soon the owls would hoot in the tree-tops.

"I always think of Constance standing at the door, waiting for us to arrive," Mia said. "She had the guest room ready for me, and she never questioned me the way someone else might have. She just took me in." Mia laughed then, remembering how fierce Constance had been when Joel Davis had shown up at the library, and they both recalled how brave she was, even though she was tiny, not more than five two. "I think she would have hit him with a book if she had to," Mia said. "And it was a paperback."

"I heard that he's having trouble with the government. I didn't know whether or not I should tell you."

Mia glanced at Sarah. "I should know."

"They're finally investigating him," Sarah told her. "It took them long enough."

"Good." Mia felt a burning in her chest. "I hope they put him in jail, where he belongs."

"He claimed the Community was a religion, and never paid a cent in taxes, and now the town council has asked him to prove that the land is really his, and he seems to have a problem doing that. His people are losing faith, and so many have left, especially the younger ones."

"I'm glad to hear that," Mia said. "I hope they all leave."

"There are a few holdovers, farming and tending the orchards, but I've heard that the buildings have all been neglected. People say the Community won't be there much longer."

Mia wondered what would happen to the cemetery if the Community land was taken over by the town. She thought of Ivy there, resting among the ferns. Mia could feel her heart opening and she thought of all the nights she had spent here listening to the river, and all the love Sarah and Constance had given her when they certainly didn't have to. She wished somehow Ivy could have known she had wound up in a family after all.

"I owe you and Constance everything," Mia said. "What would I have ever done without you?"

"My dear girl, I thought you understood," Sarah responded. "You rescued yourself."

Constance's funeral was held on an unusually warm day in May when the sky was cobalt blue. It was well attended, with guests that included colleagues from the library, neighbors and shop-keepers, children from the story time hours. Sarah and Constance also had a loyal circle of friends in Boston and Cambridge, many of them Wellesley alumnae, and they all were there as well. In the chapel of the big white church, Mia sat in the second row, behind Sarah, who was between Constance's two sisters, both of whom wept for all the years they'd lost when they weren't close.

It was a perfect day as they walked to the cemetery, following the hearse. There weren't many spaces left in the wooded section of Sleepy Hollow, and Miss Allen had been lucky to purchase a plot in a shady glen, where the crowd now gathered in a quiet and respectful manner, although Sarah could be heard weeping and Constance's sisters cried as well. People whispered that Constance had changed countless lives, as librarians often did, and it was true there were several people who had come to pay their respects that she likely would not have recognized, grown men and women who had found help and consolation in the library when they were small. *I have just the right book for you,* Miss Allen would always say, and she always did.

All around the grave were the flowers sent by those who were in attendance and those who were too far away to be in Concord. There was a wreath of white roses from a cousin, and a large display of lilacs from some of Constance's and Sarah's friends at Simmons. In the rear, behind all of the other bouquets, there was a glass jar of leaves. Mia felt something cold inside her chest, and she asked the funeral director's assistant if he might take that offering away.

"I don't care what you do with it," Mia said. She hadn't looked closely at the leaves, but she knew who'd delivered them. "Just get rid of it."

At the end of the service, Mia remained at the edge of the assembled mourners who circled Sarah to offer condolences. There was to be a gathering at the inn, with martinis served along with pimento and grilled cheese canapes on crustless white bread and dishes of macaroni and cheese. As Sarah guided Constance's sisters toward the inn, Mia remained beside the last of the rhododendron, still in bloom, with their huge purple flowers and dark, leathery leaves. She couldn't yet bring herself to have polite conversation with people she barely knew. She was cast back to the day of her mother's funeral, when Joel wore a black suit in the sudden stifling heat and Mia refused to leave the burying ground.

The day was growing even hotter, and Mia was wearing her long black dress and Ivy's boots. It occurred to her that she would never have had this second life if she hadn't run away from the Community, if Sarah hadn't given her the key to the library and Constance hadn't opened her heart to her, and she would be damned if she brought her bad fortune to them in the form of Joel Davis. She shivered to think that if she hadn't found *The*

Scarlet Letter, none of the rest of her life would have happened.

Mia opted to walk on, to find some solitude and shade, passing Cat's Pond, simply and artfully designed by Thoreau, where the calm surface was filled with water lilies. Thoreau had written about the garden cemetery, *In the midst of death we are in life*. She came upon the surprisingly grand grave of Emerson, a huge boulder up on the hill, but she went on, past Thoreau's modest grave, engraved with a simple *Henry,* walking until she reached Hawthorne's headstone. She sank down in the grass and listened to the birds in the trees. She had brought her copy of *The Scarlet Letter* with her, to remind herself that life was still worth living, even on this dark day. She placed the book on Hawthorne's grave. All that she was and ever would be was because of him. Without him she would not exist. She would be nothing at all, another drowned girl in a river where all the stones were black.

All around the cemetery paths there were wild plants, woodbine, raspberry, goldenrod, moss. Mia made a wish that she could go to the author who had saved her and know him, as she knew his book. Then she felt foolish, and much too grown-up for such nonsense, a woman sitting in a cemetery who still believed there might be magic in this world. She held the book to her chest. She could almost feel the words inside, as if each page had a beating heart. *If it was a dream it was ours alone.*

She could feel something go through her, as if there was lightning in the air, as if dreams could happen in the waking world. She curled up and gazed at the sky, and it changed from blue to starry black, as a sweep of crows went by. It seemed the world spun faster than it ever had before. All at once the birds were singing in the hedges, and morning was rising, and everything Mia had ever wanted had finally come to be.

PART TWO
1837

CHAPTER FOUR

THE MAN WHO DISAPPEARED

He was the man who people thought had everything, and yet, he'd always been convinced he had nothing at all. He was prone to black moods, even though he was doted upon by his mother and two sisters, and was highly intelligent, as well as so extremely handsome that when he walked through the town of Salem women grew faint. It was said that Lord Byron had the same effect on women, but Byron was most assuredly aware of his good looks and Nathaniel Hawthorne never looked in a mirror. He had no vanity and feared that all he would see in a mirror was the family guilt he carried, the poisonous remnants of all the dread and horror his ancestors had been responsible for, a burden that rested squarely on his shoulders. The dark history of his family led him to write about sin and redemption and do his best to make amends for crimes he didn't commit. He would change his name as soon as he was able, adding the *w* to distinguish himself from his predecessors, for his background was an embarrassment he wished to keep secret. His great-great-grandfather had been the cruelest judge at the witchcraft trials in 1692 and the only one to never repent; he and all his children had been cursed by the women of Salem, and now Nathaniel felt he was the one who must atone for the family's sins.

He'd begun to feel different from other people when he was a boy of nine, after injuring his leg. Such small occurrences could change a life and leave a person with a completely different fate, a path they would never have imagined they might take. One moment he was a part of the pulse of the world, and the next he could only watch, looking past the shady elm trees, prevented from joining in by a pane of glass, divided from all others. The cause of his injury had been a game of bat and ball, and the result of that game was that he needed to use crutches and was housebound for close to two years. Nathaniel had spent nearly all that time reading, and sometimes he felt as if each book was a raft and he was out at sea, as his father the sea captain had been before his early death when Nathaniel was only four.

His childhood affliction caused him to be moody, with a dark cast to his thoughts, but he had also become a keen observer during his recovery, able to see what others might not. His observations of cruelty went beyond those of most boys his age, whether it be a butterfly caught in a spider's web, or a homeless man on the street, or a stray dog set to howling. He began to invent stories then, written down in milk, what he called invisible ink, for he was interested in the telling and imagining, not in sharing the tales he concocted. No matter what anyone said, no matter what they believed, he was convinced that there was magic in the world.

Perhaps his fortune was set in place when he was born on July 4, an auspicious day. His mother, Elizabeth Manning Hathorne, known as Betsy to her neighbors, and Eta to her children, told her brothers that her boy would be exceptional, independent, and unique, and would grow to be a man like no other. She was soon enough a recluse, living in the grief of her widowhood, so enamored of books she taught her children to read nearly at the same time they learned to walk. The family had very little money following Nathaniel's father's death at sea after he had contracted yellow fever in the Dutch Suriname in 1808. They depended upon the kindness of two generous uncles who treated Nathaniel like a son, taking on all the family's financial burdens. Betsy and the children lived with the uncles in Salem, then, when it was deemed that Maine would be a more healthful place for all, they boarded on a farm until the uncles built them their own house. Nathaniel set to work creating a newspaper of his writings called *The Spectator*, distributed to relations and friends. It was then that Nathaniel truly began to appreciate the years he had spent alone in his room, the distance from other people that had given him the ability to observe and to feel what another might had also made him a writer.

While other boys had been skating and playing ball, Nathaniel had been considering the state of humankind. He came from people who tended to be gloomy, and his mother often was not to be found, having taken to her bed, avoiding the world in a way Nathaniel understood, for Betsy had never quite recovered after losing her husband. He felt for those who ached from loss. When a couple in Maine froze to death while they were in search of each other during a storm, and his uncle Richard had adopted one of their orphans, Nathaniel wrote an ode to the couple's love and faithfulness. He didn't sleep all night as he worked, and both his sisters knew then and there that, whether it was fortunate or not, Nathaniel's future was clear. Their brother would be a writer.

At Bowdoin College, Nathaniel had close friends, men who were fated to become famous and rich. Longfellow, who entered school at fifteen, a few years behind Nathaniel, was not known to go out to taverns and enjoy himself, but there were many others who were more than willing to savor their time at Bowdoin. They included Horatio Bridge, who Nathaniel joined for fishing and swimming in the ice-cold lakes and ponds, and Franklin Pierce, to whom Nathaniel was perhaps closest, and who would later become president. Still, Nathaniel wasn't swayed by his friends' craving for power and influence, even though he was the one who had endless potential, which included a brilliant mind and those good looks he always tried to deny. No matter what they said, he wanted nothing more than to be a writer. It had been his dream since he'd begun to read, and it was all he wanted even though his friends told him he didn't use his abilities to their full extent. Did he wish to waste his gifts on a life spent alone with paper and pen, locked away from all others?

Do you not see how you affect women? You could have them all if you so wanted. You could possess a future that would cause us all to suffer from jealousy. You are unique, and we all know it. One of a kind. Our dear friend who doesn't see himself as he truly is.

Nathaniel laughed at such nonsense, and he never told his friends about the curious things that happened to him, for it appeared that he was fated to have an appointment with the forces of magic. Twice he had seen ghosts, a matter he kept to himself. The first time was at the Athenaeum in Salem, where he'd spied an old man sitting in one of the library's armchairs who suddenly vanished into thin air. Nathaniel soon discovered that one of the library's wealthy patrons had, indeed, passed on in that chair, a spirit who was said to refuse to leave the place he had loved so well.

Another time, when he was about to go fishing, a woman in a blue dress stood in the grass soaking wet, as if she'd been swimming, but as he watched the blue of her dress became the open air and she disappeared bit by bit, watching him all the while. Later his uncle informed him there had been a drowning, a woman in a blue dress, a spirit called the Mermaid by locals. Nathaniel wrote a poem in her honor and continued to dream of women who were water nymphs, mythological creatures with lilies braided through their hair; he often awoke from these dreams aroused and in great physical need. Once, while walking through the remote woods in Maine, he had come upon a fortune-teller gathering sticks for a fire outside her wagon. He thought it best to avoid her, but the woman fell to her knees when she saw him, then lifted her eyes, staring as if bewitched. *Are you a man or an angel?* she had asked him, and he'd replied, *Only a man. And one who is often lost,* he thought. *One who couldn't seem to find his way in the world.*

Nathaniel often felt like a man talking to himself in a dark place. He was a loner, and he walked the streets at night, in the grips of what he called his *cursed solitude.* He locked himself away for days on end and accepted that this darkness of spirit was a family trait. His younger sister, Louisa, was also reclusive, known for her kind heart and her willingness to help her family, but he was closest to his older sister, Elizabeth, called Ebe, a pet name given to her by Nathaniel when he was too young to properly pronounce her given name. Elizabeth, too, had been a brilliant child, said to walk and talk at the age of nine months. She had a fine mind of her own, reading Shakespeare at twelve, and was well known to detest work of any kind that didn't have to do with writing and reading, though she had little choice, for someone had to see to the chores. Nathaniel, on the other hand, was the son, and he had a calling, and that saved him; he was a reader turned into a writer, as was often the case when people fell in love with stories and found themselves rescued by the pages of novels.

Nathaniel wrote a novel called *Fanshawe,* begun in fits and starts while he was at Bowdoin, and although it was true no one would publish it, he published the book himself for a hundred dollars when he was twenty-four. He was not surprised when very few people other than family and friends read this first attempt, one he was regretting as soon as it was set in type, seeing nothing but his mistakes when he glanced over the pages. He hoped that it would disappear from memory despite a few fine reviews trickling in from critics. He half believed that the writers who'd favorably reviewed his book were drunk or suffering from spells of guilt for the many wretched reviews they'd given to other writers.

The feeling that he was a failure settled upon him in his murky room, which he often didn't leave for days or weeks at a time, and then only to visit the Salem Athenaeum, the library where he read over a thousand books in twelve years, still writing as much as he could, endless pieces about literature and history, leaving Salem for the summers to travel with his uncles to the Saco River and the White Mountains and to Martha's Vineyard, for the heat made it impossible for him to write, and in truth, once begun, the writing seemed to possess him, as if it was real life, and the life he led at home was the dream.

Hawthorne seemed a different person in the summer months. It was in the forests where he found his inspiration, and his true appreciation of solitude grew stronger. *I lived in Maine like a bird of the air,* he later remembered, *so perfect was the freedom I enjoyed.* He didn't write in the summer, and he slipped off the skin of the boy at the window to become a man, with a man's desires. The shyness that usually plagued him evaporated during the summertime, and those who met him then saw an entirely different man than the haunted fellow in Salem. He was good at sports, an expert fisherman, and maintained long-term friendships that often led to rowdy nights at local taverns around Sebago Lake in Maine.

He grew more handsome each year, with his thick black hair and intense gray eyes, which could appear to be purple or blue depending on the light, and his striking features, the large, generous mouth that curled up when he was amused, his high cheekbones. He liked to talk, and he liked women, who were drawn to him as if he were an elixir for their souls, and because of this charm he didn't know he possessed, he nearly found himself engaged several times. He might have found himself unhappily wed if one of his uncles, Robert Manning, who was a surrogate father and had no family of his own, hadn't taken him aside and said, "Think before you act, boy, or you'll find yourself married to a stranger. Do you wish to wake beside this woman every morning of your life?"

Nathaniel resided in two worlds, the world of his writing and the world of his busy household, which he referred to as the owl's nest. His uncle Robert was a pomologist, a fruit expert known for the thousand varieties of pear trees he grew in his orchards. Robert was at work on his famed *Book of Fruits*, and he insisted that a writer could also have a life beyond books. Robert had big plans for his nephew, and worried that Nathaniel was ensconced in the world that existed inside his mind. One minute he would be present, deep in conversation, and the next he was behind glass, as he had been as a boy, even when there was nothing separating him from the rest of the world. He quarreled with his uncle about his future, insisting that no man could be both a bookkeeper and a poet, and that he intended to be the latter.

Robert wanted Nathaniel to wake from his dreams and fantasies so that he might walk into the dull, tired world of figures and numbers and people who had no patience for stories. No one noticed that Elizabeth was becoming more despondent by the day due to the restrictions that she faced as a young woman. She could not go to college, or even work as a librarian, or find love if she was not chosen, or make her own decisions about her fate. She wondered what it would be like to lie with a complete stranger in a rented room and not once worry what the consequences would be, whether an unwanted child or a ruined reputation or a life cast out from family and society.

I have dreams as well, she'd told her brother. *And they might as well be dust.*

Nathaniel was more fortunate than she, for he was allowed an education and a career, and it annoyed Elizabeth when he couldn't find any happiness. He'd sold a few hundred copies of his book before the publisher had ceased to be, but that was not enough to support his family, and his uncle sat him down and told him it was time for him to put away his dreams. On this the Manning brothers agreed; practicality was everything, and the cause for their wealth. When Richard had passed on, leaving nine children behind, Robert continued to act as Nathaniel's father and more, as a trusted friend Nathaniel often turned to.

"There comes a time to give up dreams," Robert had said. "I work because I must. We walk on earth, however we might stumble."

Elizabeth was Nathaniel's perfect audience, admiring her brother's work, yet unafraid to question it with her astute editorial opinions. She was his most severe critic and his biggest champion. Nathaniel had once declared *The only thing I fear is the ridicule of Elizabeth.* When he began a magazine, Elizabeth contributed, but the articles were published under his name, as such ventures were not thought to be proper for a woman. In his opinion, his sister was far more clever than he, which made him even more hopeless. "I can never find quite the right word," Nathaniel complained to her. One of his problems was that he was too quick to undo what he had written, finding the pages lacking in imagination. Elizabeth told him that judgment had ruined their family in the past, and he must not judge himself so harshly.

"It's not the words alone that will make your work great, it's your empathy," Elizabeth told him. "You feel what others do and see what others might. You are your characters, and they are you, whether they be men or women, young or old. This is more than a talent—it's a gift."

As he wrote feverishly, Nathaniel became the characters he imagined and was transformed into these imaginary persons entirely; it was as if their souls had slipped into his own. When he put down his pen, he felt hollow for several hours, brooding and at odds, until the person that he was came back to him, returning as if he himself was a spirit caught in the ether, a man who might disappear if he wasn't careful.

When Nathaniel's friend Franklin Pierce came to visit, they went to the harbor, a rough area where shiploads of tea and silk arrived from China and sailors drank Jamaican rum. The two young men drank as well, but Nathaniel always stopped them from doing anything completely foolhardy. No leaping off the pier into the stone-cold harbor. No smoking opium in back rooms. Women were often the ones to try to seduce him, even those who wanted to be paid offered him their favors. Nathaniel didn't know how other men behaved, but he couldn't deny himself every pleasure of the flesh, and often women begged for more. He was an angel and a devil both, one told him, exactly what a woman wanted most of all.

He and Franklin frequently went into the woods, where women of a certain character danced in very little clothing for a price, and men sat drinking until they found themselves either in the arms of one of these women or passed out cold. Pierce was nicknamed Handsome Frank, but he looked average when compared to Nathaniel. Franklin was a politician, and so he saw nothing unusual in the fact that most men were two-faced. There were nearly always women involved on their nights out, but mostly Nathaniel listened to their heartbreaking stories, the children they had been forced to give away, the parents who had nothing to do with their wayward daughters. It was nearly morning when they returned from such outings, and Nathaniel often would sleep in the yard so his sisters and mother didn't hear him come into the house and question him. He let Franklin sleep in the garden shed while he curled up beside the budding roses, strange blooms that were white at first, and then suddenly red.

Franklin had been elected to the New Hampshire legislature when he was twenty-four, was soon its speaker of the house, and was already planning a run for the U.S. Senate. He wanted to bring his friend along, and continued to suggest politics, but Nathaniel laughed. He was far too reserved and gloomy.

"Speak to crowds? I don't think so. It's best for me to stay in a single room."

"You don't see yourself," Franklin said. "It's quite the opposite. People are drawn to you. Men as well as women."

"The women don't know me. It's a momentary passion," Nathaniel said as they sprawled in the grass, hidden by the dark morning shadows, knowing the most sleep they'd get would be an hour or two.

"Nothing wrong with that, but no, it's more." Pierce considered his bighearted friend, who was naïve when it came to the shadier aspects of life. "You could be a fine politician if you'd give up your stories."

Nathaniel's uncle Robert had recently married, late in life, and Nathaniel had missed the wedding. He sent his regrets, not bold enough to mention that he was simply too busy writing to attend. There was no way for him to explain that a person didn't chose being a writer, writing chose you. Already, tonight's adventure was becoming a story in his mind of a young man's journey in the woods and the loss of his inno-cence. He began writing that night, not on paper but in his mind, and when at last he sat at his desk with pen in hand, the tale poured out of him, set in the Salem of his ancestors, for their cursed lives were behind many of his stories, and when he was called down to supper and Elizabeth asked why his shoes were so muddy and why there were brambles in his hair and why on earth

Franklin Pierce, soon to be a senator, had spent the entire day sleeping in the garden shed amid the bean seedlings and the burlap bags of loam, Nathaniel was not being dishonest when he said he really and truly did not know.

His stories and essays appeared in one magazine after another, and in the early spring of 1837, at the age of thirty-two, Nathaniel's second book, a collection of stories he called *Twice-Told Tales* was published to some very positive reviews, including one from his old school-mate Longfellow, now quite famous himself, who called it a work of genius. *Live ever, sweet, sweet book.* There were those who called the book remarkable and tagged Hawthorne as an American genius. Even Edgar Allan Poe, who rarely praised anyone other than himself, wrote *Mr Hawthorne is an original at all points.* This was when Nathaniel had added a *w* to the family name Hathorne for publication, hoping to distance himself from his family history and any possible effects of the curse that had been set on them during the witchcraft trials; yet the book had sold little more than six hundred copies and the publisher had gone out of business with few having read the book. It seemed another failure to Hawthorne's eyes. He was tormented by his writing now and sometimes imagined becoming a fisherman at Sebago Lake, for when he was a child, disappearing into the woods there was a pure pleasure.

The winter before his book of stories was published had been especially dark, with Nathaniel rarely leaving his room, writing as if the very act could erase the failures of his past. A deep gloom had set upon him so that he could barely see the light of day. Now at last, there had been a surge of spring and his tangled solitary time was over, but not in the way he had expected. In the month of May, when the lilacs in the garden bloomed in dark violet masses, Nathaniel's life changed, as it had on that day when he was nine and his future was dismantled. Only now he had come to believe that his life was on the other side of the glass, it was right there waiting for him and all he had to do was walk out the door.

It occurred after a night when Nathaniel dreamed he had died and was taken to his grave in a black carriage pulled by a single black horse. The dream was so real that he'd felt as if his heart had stopped beating. He had been in a coffin, surrounded by the dark, and though he had no voice, he'd done his best to cry out. When he woke suddenly, he could not hold back his yowls into the emptiness. He was breathing hard, and he was suddenly overcome with the conviction that he had best begin to live, and that time on earth was terribly limited; it passed in the blink of an eye. He had not lived his life, he merely existed.

Nathaniel's sisters had been awoken by his shouts and pounded on his door, worried that he'd become ill. It was early morning, not yet five and starless. Nathaniel was meant to go fishing with his uncle, they'd be after trout up in New Hampshire, but he could not imagine such worldly pursuits now. On this murky morning he felt too strongly as though he were a fish himself, caught in the net of some strange imaginings. He struggled to throw off his dream and managed at last to get out of bed, finding that he had fallen asleep while dressed.

"I'm fine," he mumbled. "Leave me be."

Nathaniel stumbled downstairs and reached for his black coat, then left the house, stepping into the dark morning, as he often did. There were hedges of lilacs in every garden he passed, and all of Salem seemed in bloom. When the city fell away, he began to trek into the forest, and soon he found himself in a woodland thick with unfolding ferns. Nathaniel felt intensely alive, his pulse was pounding in his head. He wrote about mysteries, wherein miraculous things could happen, whether redemption or damnation, and now he felt as if he had wandered into a tale from his own book.

The morning was humid and filled with bird-song as sparrows and swifts woke in the thickets. In the first shafts of pale light, the air was thin and sweet, and perhaps that was why he was so disoriented as he walked on a familiar path. He felt the world itself had altered and that he was merely a sleepwalker, caught in a dream. He had wandered in his sleep before, most memorably in Maine while camping with his uncle. Back then, he had been standing at the edge of a dark lake when he heard Robert calling his name.

"Do not take another step," his uncle had commanded, and those were the words that woke him. Nathaniel might have drowned, like the mermaid who was said to haunt the lake, if his uncle hadn't clutched at his shirt, pulling him back from the muddy shallows.

"Do you not see where you are, boy?" Robert said, all but shaking him. "You need to know the difference between a dreamworld and the world that belongs to us."

On this day, however, no one was calling for him to stop; no one grabbed his shirt and pulled him back, so he went forward. He had a tingling feeling in his fingers, as he sometimes did before he sat at his desk to write. To see what state he was in, he plucked a leaf from an oak tree. His fingers turned sticky and green with sap, and when he let the leaf go it floated down to the ground, as real as any other. This was no dream, that much was certain, and he was no sleepwalker.

There were midges flitting through the air that Nathaniel waved away, too real for his taste and extremely annoying as they swarmed around. His stories often occurred in a world where it was impossible to tell the difference between dreams and reality, and now it seemed he was watching his own writings come to life, as if he had entered a place where anything might happen, and the laws of nature didn't apply.

As he stood with his arms folded against his chest, he saw a strange tableau before him. A woman with long red hair was asleep in the grass. There was no sound except for the calling of the crows in the pine trees, no shadows but those of the clouds sweeping past in the brilliant sky. Nathaniel ran a hand over his brow as he squinted to see her more clearly. The light was sifting through the boughs of the trees and the air was so dense he felt dizzy. Some nameless longing drew him to this woman. She was a vision, and yet he didn't seem to be dreaming. To make certain he was in the real world he dug his nails into his skin, and indeed he felt the pain. He was alive and awake as he stood beneath the shade of a twisted pine tree, his heart pounding.

The woman was wearing a black dress and red boots and held a book in her arms, and Nathaniel couldn't help but wonder if he had invented her, as he did his characters, out of nothing more than words and raw emotion. Perhaps she would fall apart, in a stream of ink and paper, and he would have to gather the words that had made her from between the stalks of tall grass. Then she opened her eyes and Nathaniel knew the truth. This woman was real.

CHAPTER FIVE

WE WALK INVISIBLE

Mia saw the handsome man beneath a pine tree, his densely black hair too long, nearly reaching his shoulders, his face unshaven. She felt an instant attraction, as if she'd known him all her life. His eyes narrowed with mistrust as he observed her with suspicion, as if she were a changeling meant to do him harm. He wore a black coat, with the top buttons of his white shirt undone, for the day promised to be a fine one once the sun rose higher in the sky. May was the most beautiful time of the year in Salem, Massachusetts, especially after a harsh winter that consisted of endless weeks of snow and sleet with the north wind gusting off the sea. Now all the world was green again. In the woods, trout lilies and mayflowers were blooming, and the grass in the pastures was waist high. As she stood in the sweet-smelling field, with bees circling around her, Mia knew that she had done exactly what she had wished to do ever since she was a girl of fifteen. She had found the author of her beloved book.

"Are you lost?" Nathaniel called.

His voice at last, one she felt she already knew.

Nathaniel himself had felt lost on this morning, even though he walked here regularly. He tended to hike at dawn and dusk, so he would be less likely to run into anyone. He had never wanted idle conversation; he was usually caught up in a fictional world and didn't wish to be interrupted. Nathaniel had thought he'd known all the paths that led through the fields into the forest, he thought he'd be alone as he was every day, except for the presence of passing sparrows and crows, and occasionally, if he walked quietly, a deer. But today there seemed to be a scrim of magic over the landscape, for everything he knew looked different, as if the world itself had opened to allow him to see what he'd never seen before. He was here and nowhere else, not in the midst of a story he was planning, or in the grip of an article he was to write for a journal, or plotting out a novel. He was in this field, and he could hear the bees.

The woman stared at him wide-eyed, and he wondered if perhaps she didn't possess the ability to speak. All the same, she caught his gaze and held it and seemed unafraid. Was she one of the creatures he wrote about now come to life? Perhaps she was a ghost condemned to walk forevermore, or a woman who'd been abandoned by her husband or one who had attended a witches' festival, a mythological creature who walked the earth. In his writings, women were often principal characters, independent, with minds of their own, often truer to their emotions and to the natural world than the men around them.

Nathaniel noticed that the woman held a book. She carried it as though it was a treasure, which, in Nathaniel's opinion, books always were. Riches disappeared, but words lasted. "What do you have there?" he asked, always interested to discover what a person was reading, for he believed it was possible to see inside a person's soul once you knew which books mattered to them.

"It's my copy," Mia said defensively, as if he were accusing her of theft. She seemed both dreamy and panicked, as if he'd woken her from a deep sleep and she was now here, undefended, in a field.

Nathaniel didn't wish to challenge this woman in any way. "I don't mean to quarrel with you," he assured her.

For all he knew, she had come to curse him as his ancestors had been cursed. Perhaps her family had a history with his and a witch in her bloodline and she had intended to find him to make him pay for his great-great-grandfather's sins. Had she been lying in wait until he stumbled by so that she could work her dark magic upon him, or was it simply fate that had led him to this field? Nathaniel often searched for the resting places of witches on his daily walk, hoping to make amends on behalf of his family by saying a prayer, or placing wildflowers on a spot that seemed likely to be an unmarked grave. He wondered who he had stumbled upon, for this woman was wearing red boots, and local folklore cited red shoes as a mark of those who practiced witchery.

"Is it a story I might know?" he asked, always most comfortable when speaking about books, for literature, he had always found, held more for him than life, which seemed a dark tunnel from which he couldn't escape.

"You wrote it." Mia held up the volume with a brown cover and gold letters.

Nathaniel laughed and said, "Not likely. Not if it's any good."

"It was good enough to have changed my life."

"You're surely mistaken," Nathaniel said.

On this day, when he stood before Mia, Hawthorne was in his early thirties and he already considered himself to be a literary failure, having no idea of what he was to become. Now that she was before him, Mia wondered if it might be a mistake to tell him anything about his future. Once he learned what his work would be, it might somehow be forever changed. Mia was quiet and took the time to study him.

Nathaniel was tall and lanky with eyes that appeared to change color, from gray to violet, the sort of man who had no idea of how attractive he was or how his good looks might affect a woman.

It was a strange meeting, for Nathaniel knew nothing about Mia, and she knew him so well she could easily recite the facts of his life if called upon to do so. She knew how his family history had affected his sisters, who never married or had children, as it had his mother, who barely left her room, and how Nathaniel had locked himself away for nearly a decade before their meeting here today, writing like a man on fire in what he called his owl's nest, just as she knew that Melville would later come to idolize him, perhaps even fall in love with him, dedicating *Moby-Dick* to Nathaniel with extreme emotion: *In Token of My Admiration for His Genius*. She knew who Nathaniel would marry and the names and birth dates of his children, just as she knew the date that *The Scarlet Letter* would be published, March 16, her birthday, in the year 1850. Worst of all, she knew the date he would die. And now that she stood before him, she also knew she shouldn't be here. Already there was something between them, for he looked at her as if a star had plummeted to earth to light up the field that he walked through, a place known for little more than its nesting sparrows and wildflowers, not for such unusual meetings, the sort that had made him forget that he had planned to spend most of this day at his desk, in the clutter and darkness of the home he referred to as Castle Dismal.

Mia had read most of his novels while sitting outside the Old Manse in Concord on summer days, once daring to sneak into the house after hours, making herself so at home she took a nap on the green velvet settee in what had been Hawthorne's office. Now, she felt unbalanced in his presence, overwhelmed by all that he was and all that he would one day be, and what he would mean to her own life. His story of redemption and a mother's endless love for her child had caused Mia to rethink everything she planned to do and had woken her from her nightmare.

Time had now shifted, and Mia had been carried backward, as if she'd stepped into a storm. She appeared so startled that for a moment Nathaniel thought she might turn and run, but then he realized she was as curious as he, for she lingered in the shade of the tall trees, her eyes so dark they were almost black. She seemed to be staring directly into his soul, and he found he could not look away.

"Shall I walk you home?" he asked. He himself wished to never go home again, for he felt utterly intrigued by this stranger.

"You cannot," Mia quickly said. She had no home, and so perhaps the woods would have to do. Nathaniel was clearly taken aback by her response, so she added, "It's impossible for you to do so."

"How have you only just arrived here?" Nathaniel asked with a grin, attempting to put her at ease. "Did you arrive by magic?"

"I'm not sure. It's possible."

Nathaniel laughed, then saw she was serious. "Are you saying we're enchanted?"

"Would that be such a terrible thing?" Mia asked.

It was true that magic was in nearly everything Nathaniel wrote; ghosts and hauntings, sins and sacrifice had never frightened him. He'd always considered himself a defender of women who had been slandered, especially those said to be witches, so why would he fear one who might be real, with magic at her beck and call? And yet he felt something strange, not fear exactly, something more like longing, the way he felt when he wanted something he didn't expect he would ever have, the way he'd felt looking out through the window when he was a boy and all the world seemed beyond his grasp.

"Nathaniel, I wish I could tell you more," Mia said. "But I'm not certain that would be wise."

"You know me then?" he asked earnestly, for clearly, she knew him by name, which was odd. Surely, had they met before, he would not have forgotten her.

Mia's face was solemn. "I came from another time only to meet you."

"Did you?" Nathaniel said, wary and wondering if it might be best to say his goodbyes and leave. Perhaps his uncle had been correct when he told Nathaniel to find himself a proper job and join the family business and forget the nonsense of living inside his own imagination. *The world is waiting for you,* Robert had always told him. *And yet you lock yourself away.*

Was it possible that all those years spent dreaming and writing had in fact driven him mad, and now his mind was beyond his control, and he saw what was impossible to see and heard what was impossible to be true? If he wasn't careful, he might wind up like one of those pathetic creatures down on the wharf, sailors whose rough lives and bouts of drinking and carousing had made them lunatics incapable of doing anything more than wandering the streets, spouting nonsense, and begging for coins, unaware of what was real and what was mere fantasy. Nathaniel's heart had always gone out to such men, though he had always considered himself to be nothing like them; he had believed himself to be a rational man whose world opened when he began to write. Now he wondered if those worlds were no longer separate, and he had stepped into one of his own imaginings.

The woman still hadn't let go of that book of

hers, holding on to it as if it was a treasure she'd unearthed, which made her even more interesting to Nathaniel and made it less likely that he would turn and leave her there without knowing more. In his opinion, a woman who loved books was the best sort. He had faith in women's views of the world and their ability to feel compassion when men so often seemed aware only of their own needs. He truly wished that for the next thousand years all government could be in the hands of women, for men had made such a mess of the world, including his own ancestors, men who'd risen to power and fought to keep it, no matter who they might hurt or destroy. Nathaniel wished to be a different sort of man, if such a thing were possible, if who he was and what he would do weren't already fated to be. He had a large and wounded heart, and his sister Elizabeth always said he was overly emotional, but he wondered, could there be such a thing?

Despite the book the woman carried, and her obvious intelligence, he knew nothing about her. Usually speaking with strangers was uncomfortable for him, but this was not the case today. He felt as if a spell had been cast as they began to walk along together, and he felt transported. She was telling him some nonsense about herself, the colleges she'd gone to, when he knew it was impossible for women to enter universities or teach in one. He enjoyed talking with his sisters, especially the brilliant, combative Elizabeth, but conversing with Mia was like speaking with another man who knew as much of the world as he did, perhaps more, and yet possessed a woman's sensibilities and the ability to draw upon her emotions. She told him she was a librarian in the greatest public library in the world and seemed startled when he laughed, assuming she was teasing him. He knew of only one public library, up in New Hampshire, all the rest were private and had dues to be paid. As for women librarians, they simply didn't exist.

"They do where I come from," Mia told him.

"And where is that?" Nathaniel noticed that this woman didn't seem to care about her appearance. She ignored the burrs that stuck to the fabric of her skirt and the muddy ground they walked through. She hadn't bothered to pin up her hair nor did she wear a hat, as his sisters always did, to protect herself from the sun. She was not like any woman he had met before, not like the delicate Beacon Hill ladies he had seen on his trips to the city, or the farm women he'd met in Maine, or the women for hire in the taverns on the rowdy docks, a few of whom he'd gone to for comfort, though afterward he had been burdened by regret for using them for his own pleasure.

"New York," Mia told him. "That's where I live."

"Ah, New York." He'd been there with his

uncles and his sisters and had been amazed by the intensity of the city. If anything could happen there, and surely it did, perhaps there were women librarians as well. "I'll have to look for your library next time I'm there."

"You can't. It was built in 1911," Mia blurted.

"Nearly eighty years from now," Nathaniel said

Mia covered her eyes with her hand and looked up at him to see what his reaction might be.

"And how would you know what will come to be?" Nathaniel was caught up in his interest like a fish in a net. He didn't think he could look away from her now if he tried. This sort of magic happened in books, certainly it occurred in his own stories, but not in real life. He was under a spell; he was certain of it now. He saw details that he would never have normally noticed, as if everything had come into a sharper focus. That there were freckles across her nose and cheeks, that her eyelashes were the darkest brown, that her neck was long, and she wore pearls that glittered blue in the sunlight.

"In my time cities are lit up and you can reach the other side of the world in a matter of hours by flying across the sky."

"Like a sparrow?" Nathaniel should have been put off by such nonsense; instead he was intrigued. What if time was like water, and you could move through it at your will?

"Nothing like a sparrow," Mia said with a grin.

"So you haven't any wings?"

"Not any more than you."

They had stopped walking, and the sun was beating down, and perhaps that was why Mia's heart was pounding so. She, too, was under a spell, one she had created, and now it all seemed out of her control. She wasn't certain what would come next and was unsure of what to say and whether she should commit herself to the truth. And what would the truth do for either of them? And how would it change what was meant to be? She thought of a science class at school, and how she'd read about chaos theory, the notion that if a single butterfly moves its wings, it will affect everything on the other side of the world, changing all that was to happen into something brand new. One step, one bit of truth, and everything might be altered. Standing there in the bright sunlight, Mia wondered if she was that butterfly, and if with a single look, she could ruin his life.

"You're not an angel, are you?" Nathaniel asked as he studied her.

She could tell that his question was made only half in jest, for he had a serious expression and he frankly wondered if it might be true. He'd often thought he needed rescuing. If someone didn't save him, he sometimes believed he might lock himself inside his owl's nest and never come out again. He feared that on one dark night of the soul he might find himself walking out his window to sit on the roof, and that the darkness all around him might call to him in a way that daily life did not. He wondered about the time he had sleepwalked and his uncle pulled him back, if there was something inside him that wanted to dive into the cold water, if he had been drawn to darkness all along, and that it was only when he was at his desk, writing, that he managed to escape his own personal curse.

"What if I were an angel?" Mia asked him.

She had begun to worry about how little she'd thought out what it would mean to come here and how she might affect him and, by doing so, herself. She too was thinking of a dark place, the depths of the Last Look River, the shiny wet stones in her pockets, her wild imaginings that there was no other way to escape the Community, when as it turned out, all she'd had to do was unlock the door of the barn and run as fast as she could.

"If you were, I'd consider myself the most fortunate man to have come upon you," Nathaniel said. "But I would think so whether you were an angel or a woman."

They had come to a green pond. Both were broiling hot, and now they looked at one another and with a wordless exchange they realized they both had the same notion.

"Can you swim?" Nathaniel asked, for he knew that many ladies didn't.

"Of course." Mia knelt to remove her boots, which she left beside her book in the tall grass. Blackbirds swooped across the sky as she walked over the marshy ground, not seeming to mind the muck. Halfway there she called back over her shoulder, "Do you?"

Nathaniel removed his boots and shirt and followed her, naked to the waist. Mia was already standing in the reedy shallows. It was the most beautiful day, there could not be one finer, and she refused to think of how her presence might wreck both their lives. She would not think of herself as a butterfly, there to create chaos, but as a woman who had finally arrived exactly where she wanted to be. She looked up and counted the blackbirds overhead. Fifteen. The age she had been when she read his book.

"Won't you ruin your dress?" she heard Nathaniel ask. He stood with his feet in the mud and watched her wade deeper.

The water was ice, but she wouldn't think of going back to shore. "I don't mind." Mia made her way through the reeds until the pond was deep enough to plunge in. It was heavenly, though shockingly cold. Diving in woke every part of her and made her feel even more alive. Dragonflies skimmed over the surface of the water; the air was filled with them so that the sky turned a luminous blue. Mia faced the shore and saw that Nathaniel was staring. She looked like a nixie, a mythological creature surrounded by water flowers.

"Are you afraid of drowning?" Mia called.

In fact, he was. Up in Maine, he'd heard so many stories of people who had drowned, and had written the tales of some of them, and then had nearly drowned himself when he was sleepwalking. Now, though, despite his nagging fear, he dove into the green water and swam to her. Mia laughed and applauded his bravery, for it was so early in the season few would dare to swim here. The water lilies on their green pads were not yet blooming.

"Promise we won't drown," Nathaniel said, gasping in the cold.

"We won't," Mia vowed. She laughed to think of all she might have missed if she had left the black stones in her pockets, if she'd failed to read the book that had fallen open in the grass. If she only had a few hours here, it would be enough. It would be a dream that could last a lifetime.

They floated together past the reeds and Mia's dress spread out all around her like a black lily, and when she drifted too far, Nathaniel seized her arm. She could feel the heat from his touch go through her, right to the center of her chest.

"You're floating away," he said, concerned. It was so cold, it was freezing, and yet he was overheated.

His hand was at her waist, though she certainly

didn't need rescuing. "I've already told you," Mia said. "I can swim."

"What else can you do?" Nathaniel asked, puzzled by her every word and action. To say she came from another time, and knew what others did not, was madness, surely, and yet she seemed perfectly sane.

"I can tell you that you will be a great writer," Mia told him. "And your book will mean everything to me."

"I doubt that," Nathaniel said, embarrassed and flattered at the same time.

Mia thought of how one person could save another's life or ruin it without even meaning to. She had already said too much, and now she swam away from him, back to shore. She slipped on her boots and thought of the day when she went to the library and found his book. She'd grabbed the first volume she could reach so that Sarah would not be suspicious, for Mia always took out at least one book. She thought of standing at the river with the pile of black stones. She had read somewhere that every person who had tried to end their lives and had survived vowed they had regretted their attempt the moment they'd leapt from the bridge or swallowed the pills or dove into the rushing waters. She'd regretted it before she even tried, all because of him.

Nathaniel followed Mia through the mud. He was chilled to the bone, but he was also in a state of wonder. He felt as if he had wandered into one of his own tales. A woman arrives in a field and changes everything; she has secrets she won't tell, she has a history that is the heart of the story.

"Will I see you again?" Nathaniel asked as he came up behind Mia. She was wringing water out of her long red hair. There was a green puddle below her on the ground.

"If you find me," Mia said. Now that she was standing there, drenched, she knew that she had opened the door, and that she was about to walk through it.

"I will," Nathaniel said. "If you don't run away."

"Tomorrow then," Mia said. If she were wise, she would leave him and immediately go back before she changed the world without meaning to. Instead, she walked on. This was madness, she knew; she had no home, no food, no other clothes, yet she had no desire to leave. She wandered farther into the woods, thinking she would make a camp of some sort beneath a tree, but then she spied a low roof under the branches of an old oak. Thinking it was a cow barn, Mia went on to discover that it was a small ramshackle cottage. She pulled away the canopy of vines growing over the door and stepped inside. The place smelled like wet earth and had clearly been abandoned for some time, but inside there was a small bed and bureau and a spinning wheel. Someone had lived here once, and had cherished the place, and Mia gave her thanks to whoever the previous occupant might have been.

She spied a cradle in the back of the tiny house, covered by sumac that had grown up through the floor. There were cups, as well as two small bowls. She wished that Ivy could have lived in a cottage like this, that the vines would have covered the roof, that flowers would have grown up through the dirt floor, and they could have kept Dottie the sheep here and spun her wool on the tall wooden spinning wheel. Ivy had always insisted they had no choice, that Joel would find them wherever they went, but what if she had never gone to the Community and had made them a home in the forest as someone had clearly once done here? What if they had been invisible and had lived cut off from the rest of the world?

Exhausted, Mia climbed into the small iron bed. The mattress was stuffed with straw and still smelled sweet. She fell asleep in no time and dreamed she was in the apple orchard with her mother. In her dream, she grabbed on to Ivy's arm and made her run as fast as she could, and when the truck slipped down the hill the only damage it did was to knock down one of the old, twisted apple trees, a cutting from the one Johnny Appleseed had left behind on his travels through Blackwell.

There were holes in the roof of the cottage, and

when Mia's dream of the orchard woke her in the middle of the night, she could see the stars shining. It took her a moment to remember where she was, in a time before *The Scarlet Letter* had been written, in the year when Nathaniel was a man who thought he would fail at everything, on a night when he was already awake in his cluttered room on Herbert Street in Salem, waiting for the moment when he could see her again.

They met each morning at the pond. Nathaniel told no one, but the secret of where he went each day burned inside him, making it impossible to talk to his sisters, for he was not a liar and never had been, and at this stage of his life it was unlikely that he would have so radical a change in his character. A single untruth seared his tongue, and he began to avoid his family. A secret life is one that can only be shared by two, especially when love was involved, for that is what this seemed to be. He could not stop thinking of Mia. Whether she was an angel or a witch or simply a woman didn't matter, for she was all he thought of. He ignored his desk and had stopped writing. The real world called to him, perhaps for the first time since he was a boy and came alive in the Maine woods, connected to nature and to the secret life he had back then as well. A lone wanderer, someone who was more attached to trees and leaves and stars than he was to other human beings, a watcher in the window who had become a watcher in the woods.

He began to pilfer food from the kitchen to bring to Mia, and though he meant to keep his actions secret, he was no better a thief than he was a liar. In time his sisters noticed. Loaves of bread and cheese and leftover supper all disappeared.

"Perhaps he's feeding the poor down at the harbor," Louisa guessed.

"Perhaps," Elizabeth said, but she believed something else was at play. She knew her brother better than anyone, and she understood what it meant when he stopped writing. The cause was either a gloom that couldn't be lifted or a woman.

"Have you had a good day?" Elizabeth asked him when he returned that afternoon. His hair was wet, and he'd pushed it back; there was mud on his boots. She wondered where he'd been traipsing during the hours when he'd been gone. She noticed there was a smile on his face for no reason whatsoever. The weather was humid and he wasn't writing, and ordinarily these were factors that would make him miserable.

"Excellent," Nathaniel answered, which was not at all like him, for how does a writer have a good day when he hasn't written a word? And how does a man who has always believed himself to be cursed take the stairs two at a time so that he might sit upon the roof and study the stars?

When Mia brought Nathaniel to the cottage, he was surprised he'd never stumbled upon it before. "I think I overheard my sisters speak of such a place, but I've never seen it for myself. It has some history that no one speaks of."

Mia showed him the cradle and the flowers that grew by the gate, red roses that were about to bloom, and as she did he took note of all that she needed, blankets and some clothing, for she wore only the one black dress. They spent the day together climbing the hills all around Salem. He brought her to the harbor, where they watched the ships, and at the end of the day they swam in the pond, this time with neither of them speaking, as if the spell they were under was too strong for words. There were falling stars above them, and his hair was so long Mia held it back in one hand as she leaned in to kiss him. He was slow to kiss her back, for he didn't wish to ruin her in any way, or offend her, but then he did and he could hardly stop. He walked her to the cottage, and when they went to bed, they didn't leave, but instead they stayed there until morning. He never wanted to leave, but he went home and then later he returned with a basket in which there was a quilt and two dresses of Louisa's along with a loaf of bread and some cheese.

"Are you a runaway?" he asked. Nathaniel didn't imagine a criminal history, rather a husband or father who had treated her badly, for she had no belongings other than the book he had spied tucked under the mattress of the narrow iron bed, the one she said would change her life.

"Not exactly," Mia said. "Though I was once."

"So you wish to remain a mystery?" Nathaniel grinned. He had the oddest feeling that he was the person he had been before he was nine and had his injury and felt separated from the rest of the world.

"Isn't everyone a mystery?"

"Will you answer every question with a question?"

"Will you?" Mia asked, hoping to distract him, for she knew he wished to know her background and her history.

On the following day, Nathaniel arrived with a bunch of cut lilacs, and when he handed the blooms to Mia, she set them in a glass jar.

Nathaniel again noticed the book beneath the mattress. "Will you ever let me read it?" he asked.

"You don't need to read it. You'll write it."

She kissed him then. Every kiss was more than he expected. He had not known a lady to behave this way, but then again, Mia's character was so different than that of any woman he'd known; she appeared to have no idea of what the rules were, at least not here in Salem, where nearly everything that brought joy was considered a sin, as if their Puritan ancestors were still watching over them.

"I know we can't do as we please," he said to Mia, embarrassed by his own longings.

"How do you know that?" Mia asked. She stood and unbuttoned her borrowed dress. It was light wool, too heavy for the season, a deep rose color. He'd said his sister Louisa had bought the fabric in Boston.

"Mia," Nathaniel said, thinking of those women in the taverns, many of whom had unwanted children or who had harmed themselves trying to stop a pregnancy. "We can't be careless."

"We can be whatever we want to be," Mia assured him. "We can be invisible," she said.

But they weren't, for on the fifth day Elizabeth took the path through the woods. Her mistrust had begun when the food from the pantry began to disappear, and then Louisa complained that some of her garments were missing, and then there was the look on their brother's face, delight and wonder when he went out in the mornings, ignoring his work, whistling a sparrow's tune as he walked down their street.

In order to follow her brother and remain unnoticed, Elizabeth wore trousers she'd taken from the laundry and a scarf over her hair; she made certain to stay far enough behind so that Nathaniel wouldn't see her. She had the right to worry about him; as children they'd been on their own, for their mother could not cope with real life and the losses she'd been subjected to. Elizabeth acted as a mother would for Louisa and Nathaniel both; she was fierce, and she would not be tricked by nonsense and acts that would land her dear brother in trouble.

She saw them at the pond and then she knew. She wasn't surprised to find that a woman was at the bottom of Nathaniel's strange behavior. Their sentimental, emotional brother had fallen in love more times than Elizabeth could count. She shaded her eyes while she crouched behind some mulberry bushes. The woman held nothing back when she embraced Nathaniel. It was as if they had married themselves to one another without the benefit of any proper documents. Even a woman who could never hope for love for herself knew it when she saw it. Elizabeth turned and ran through the field. She was breathing hard, and she found that she was jealous of them both, of her brother for finding such passion, and of the woman for being so free with herself, as if she could do whatever she pleased without consequence.

The following day Nathaniel was called away to speak with his uncle. He asked his trusted sister Elizabeth to help him by taking a message to someone. He could not be in two places at one time, both with their uncles and with the woman with whom he had fallen in love.

"Love?" Elizabeth said, shaking her head. "Are you sure that's what it is?"

"You'll understand when you meet her," Nathaniel vowed. "Just go and tell her I will not be there till late afternoon. I don't wish to disappoint her. And I'm trusting you," he reminded his sister. "Don't let me down."

Elizabeth went with the intention of saying much more than her brother had instructed her to. She hoped to chase off this woman in order to ensure that Nathaniel would return to his work and not be tempted into ruining his life. All of the family's hopes rested on him, and if that burden was too much for him to bear, then Elizabeth would help him carry it as best she could.

Mia was at the pond, wearing one of Louisa's dresses. Her boots were muddy, and her hair was tangled, yet she was beautiful. She had shaded her eyes to get a good look as Elizabeth neared. Some might call Elizabeth plain, but she had her own sort of beauty, one she did her best to hide, with clear gray eyes not unlike Nathaniel's, and rather strong features. She also had a suspicious nature, heightened by her bright and inquisitive mind. The women approached one another with care.

"This explains my brother's state of confusion," Elizabeth said.

"Love is confusing," Mia said. She knew enough about Elizabeth to be cautious and not say too much. "Or so I've heard people say."

"Love?" Elizabeth nearly spat on the ground. "He's fallen in love a dozen times or more and then woken up to realize his mistake. If you're looking for a man with money or property, you have chosen wrongly. He has nothing."

"Ebe," Mia said. "Don't judge me so harshly. You don't know me."

"Do not call me by that name." That pet name was used only by family.

"I may not know you, but I know of your brother's affection for you. He often speaks of how unfair it is that you are limited because you are female, and he wishes you could have the rights he has."

"He can wish all he wants," Elizabeth said bitterly. "That will never come to be."

They walked along until they came to the cottage.

"You live here?" Elizabeth said, shocked.

"For the time being. Why? Do you know it?"

"It's a foul place, one filled with bad fortune. People say those roses grow in December, in the snow, in remembrance of all that never came to be. You shouldn't stay here." Elizabeth's expression had changed, and she appeared to be filled with emotion. "You should go home, Mia, if you know what's good for you."

Elizabeth revealed the story that not long ago, a woman named Lyddie had come to live here, not out of choice, but because her family had cast her out. She'd had a child and no husband, and she vowed she would manage to live on her own. She never said who the father of the child was, and he never helped her with her burden. Once or twice, Elizabeth had brought out jars of jam and tea. Nathaniel had known nothing of Lyddie's existence.

"Some things are best spoken about only among women," Elizabeth said.

The last time Elizabeth had come was after a snowstorm. She'd had a basket of blankets and food, but no one answered the door. There was eight feet of snow on the ground that winter, and the wind was bone chilling.

"I think I knew before I opened the door," Elizabeth went on. They were sitting outside in what was left of the garden Lyddie had planted. There was rosemary and parsley growing wild. That winter day, Elizabeth had found the woman and her baby frozen to death. She had left a note at the sheriff's office and had never spoken of it to anyone, not even to Louisa, until now.

"If you think you can do as you please you will surely suffer," Elizabeth told Mia. "What you do for love will come back to haunt you."

215

"That story can change," Mia said.

"It's not a story," Elizabeth said. "It's real life. Do you intend to marry my brother?"

Mia knew that Nathaniel Hawthorne was fated to marry Sophia Peabody, and they would have three children; it was history and fate, and if Mia dared to change it, everything else might change, including the book that saved her life. "I'm only here for a brief time."

"And then I will have to deal with the aftermath should he fall apart, and I can guarantee he will. He's a tender person."

"I knew that as soon as I read his novel."

"*Fanshawe*?" Elizabeth said with a worried look. Even her brother knew it was not the best work he was capable of. It was then that Elizabeth spied the book under the mattress. "What is that?" she said.

"Nothing but a book." Mia felt a fool not to have hidden the volume in a safer place. She, more than anyone, should know how to keep a book from sight.

Elizabeth recognized some letters on the spine and took up the volume before Mia could stop her. She looked at the brown cover with its gold letters. "Nathaniel Hawthorne?" Elizabeth said, her voice breaking.

Mia seized the book from her hands. "It's my personal belonging."

"Is it?" Elizabeth narrowed her eyes. She

wasn't certain she believed a word that Mia said. "It has his name on it so it appears that it belongs to my brother."

Mia sat beside Nathaniel's sister. She had little choice but to trust her. "It will be. When it's published in 1850."

"Don't tell me any more," Elizabeth said, distraught. "If I'm going mad, I prefer not to know. Once a woman lands in an asylum she never gets out. I'd leap from a window anyway."

"You're not mad, Elizabeth. I'm not from here."

"So you've been to 1850? Or do you just know what will come to be? Can you tell my fortune as well?" Elizabeth had never believed in witches; she assumed men had created such figures out of their twisted dreams and their fear of a woman's innate power.

"All I can say is that Nathaniel will write great novels, and this is one of them."

"Whatever you do, don't show it to him," Elizabeth warned. "It will influence him, and he'll change things, he'll rewrite and refigure. Whatever this is"—she nodded to the book—"it should be what he meant for it to be."

Mia swore she would not show him the book, but she herself didn't know if that was the truth, for inside was the inscription he'd written to her, the one she had first seen when she was fifteen. It was there still, and she was grateful that

Elizabeth had not opened the volume to see it.

"Eventually he'll find it unless you leave," Elizabeth warned. "And if you do come from another place or time, you surely must know any life with my brother cannot come to be. A fish and a sparrow cannot live in the same world. One will gasp for air and the other will drown."

"So I go back and I lose him?"

"Was he ever yours?"

Mia walked with Elizabeth through the forest and was surprised when Nathaniel's sister turned onto another path, one hidden by hedges. "There's something I want to show you," she said. "If you don't come from here, you should understand what we go through in our time."

It was close, with trees looming on either side. They ducked beneath the greenery and followed the path that had been trod often enough that the grass was beaten down. There was a hill shaded by huge trees, and all around were plants on bushy stems that would soon bloom with yellow flowers.

"My brother doesn't know about this place. None of the men in town have heard of it, but every woman is well aware of its existence. Some call it the Hill of Death, others call it Salvation Point. This is where women come to bury their babies, the ones they can't have for one reason or another, the ones that haven't yet quickened, and the ones who have. The herb you see all around is rue; it's dangerous but it's worth the risk for many, for it causes contractions and miscarriage. Women you would least expect to come here find their way to the hill, those who are too young, who are unmarried, or who have been taken by force, those that have made a single mistake never speak of it again."

"Have you come here?" Mia asked.

"Would I tell you if I had?"

"I doubt you would think it safe to do so."

"Tell me women get to make their own choices someday." They were both staring at the hill. Long ago this was where people came to bury the women who had been judged to be witches, and the women who came here now would be judged harshly as well, thrown out of society and left to fend for themselves. "Tell me there's a time when we can choose our own fate."

Mia thought of how much courage it took to go against the rules. She thought it was likely that such a hillside could be found outside every city. She could not say it would always be different in her own time.

"I suspect you can't tell me so," Elizabeth said.

"I can tell you that we try."

"Then go back to the time where you can try and leave him here to do what he must."

"I want him to write what he's meant to write. It matters to me in ways I can't express."

"Good," Elizabeth said, handing Mia a hand-kerchief but acting as if she didn't notice Mia's distress. "At least we can agree on that."

"He'll surprise you," Mia told her.

"I don't think so," Elizabeth said. "He's my brother. I expect a work of genius."

Nathaniel didn't arrive until just before dusk. He'd run most of the way, for he felt as if time was rushing by, a windstorm he couldn't prevent. He was annoyed with his uncle for keeping him so long to go over the finances of the carriage business, in which he had no interest but which he was still dependent upon. Mia was waiting for him at the pond.

"I can tell from the look on your face," Nathaniel said. "My sister was difficult. It's just her way and you'll become accustomed to it. You'll have no choice." He laughed. "For she'll never change."

"She wasn't difficult," Mia said.

Nathaniel narrowed his eyes. "Truly? That doesn't sound like Ebe. She's known for being difficult. Are you certain it wasn't Louisa who visited you?"

"Elizabeth was here, and she was logical, that's all."

Nathaniel shook his head, worried now. "Far worse if her logic affected you."

"You've affected me," Mia said.

This was the sixth day, and Mia would always think of what had happened between them as six days of love. She knew that had she stayed for the seventh day, she might never leave. Elizabeth was right. She didn't belong here.

"Let's go swimming," Nathaniel said.

"Now? It's almost dusk."

"That's the best time," Nathaniel said. "No one will see us."

All afternoon, Nathaniel had wasted his time talking about figures and fees and the coach business when he might have been here. Now he started to undress as if he couldn't wait to be himself once more. Naked to the waist, he knelt before Mia and slipped off the boots she wore. A firefly flitted through his dark hair and Mia waved it away, then rested her hand on his head. She would think of that firefly as the spirit that burned within him. She would close her eyes and see it on summer nights when she was walking through the streets in Manhattan.

"You first," Nathaniel said. He was close and whispered in her ear.

There was a last time for everything, and this was the time for them to be together. Mia stepped into the shallows and kept walking. For a fleeting moment, he thought she intended to drown herself, for it seemed she was so intent on going as far as she could. Nathaniel ran after Mia and seized her arm and held her to him.

"I still think this may be a dream," Mia said, leaning her face against his.

"If it is, then a single dream is more powerful than a thousand realities."

There was no reason for her to swim away, so she stayed where she was, her arms around him. She was no longer that girl with black rocks in her pockets; she wasn't invisible anymore. Right now, she had what she had always wanted, the man whose words had saved her, the story that let her know she could save herself.

Mia pulled her dress over her head, then slipped off her undergarments. She knew the stars were easier to spy in this sky, for Salem was so dark at this hour, and the air was cleaner. Each star seemed a thousand times more brilliant than the ones she'd known. Nathaniel reached to unclasp Mia's hair so that it fell down her back. It was so quiet it was as if they could hear the beating heart of the world. Crickets whirred and frogs called from the edge of the pond. It was the last time they would walk into the water, and the dark came falling down.

They stayed in the deep water, wrapped up with one another, remaining in an embrace until they were shivering. At last, they left the pond so they might be together in the tall grass. There was a full moon, glowing a deep red color. Some people called it the Strawberry Moon, others used the name the Rose Moon; it was a night when in folklore women revealed their love for their men by tying a thread around a tree, but that was not what happened in this field, not on this night. On this night, they thought not of words, but of deeds.

When they at last drew their clothes over their wet bodies, their hair was still soaking wet, their skin chilled. By now, it was fully dark.

"Let me stay with you," Nathaniel said.

"Not tonight." Mia sounded rushed, as if she had somewhere else to go.

"The moon will not be like this for another year," Nathaniel said, but still Mia could not be convinced to let him stay, even though the moon was bloodred, red as the roses that grew at the cottage.

"It's late," she told him, and it was. The air was so much colder now, and she couldn't stop shivering. She kissed him once, and then again, then finally pulled away to study him. She wanted to tell him everything, she wanted to thank him a thousand times, but instead she told him good night, and walked away through the tall grass. She left him as if this was not the last time, as if tomorrow would be waiting for them.

Nathaniel breathed in the night air. He watched her, for she'd stopped on her way to the cabin and was standing in the field. The dark was falling, ashy and soft, lilac at the edges. There was something he had planned to say, but Nathaniel had forgotten to do so. Now he remembered, and he nearly ran after her, but he could no longer see her anymore. *I would give you the moon if I could. I would give you anything you wanted.*

He didn't know that he already had given her what she wanted most of all, the book that she wished upon, as if it were a star. The grass was black in the night, but Mia had always been able to see in the dark. That was one of the lessons she'd learned as a girl. She'd had the habit of running away, she'd done it all her life, and now she remembered how much it hurt to do so. She remembered that you could never look back, because if you did, you would understand just how much you were about to lose.

CHAPTER SIX

BROTHER SPARROW

Nathaniel spent a day searching vainly for Mia, and when at last he stopped to rest, he slept all through the night. Now he awakened to find himself in a thicket of brambles just beyond Salem. The birds were rising into the trees in the early light, chattering with song, and he knew that she was gone. She had left the cabin as they'd found it, with his sister's dresses folded on the bed, and the quilt his mother had sewn there beside the clothing. Now that it was daylight, Nathaniel clambered to his feet. He spied the green pond, and the bank where they'd stood, and he knew he'd lost her. With no other choice, he began to walk, disoriented but following some interior map. After a while, he found himself at his own house. He stood on the pathway, so distressed he was sweating through his clothes even though he was chilled to the bone. How could you possess sheer happiness one moment, and lose it the next? He wore his white shirt open and went barefoot. He was himself, and yet he was completely changed.

Elizabeth was waiting for him on the porch. She'd told their mother and sister that he was off with his friend Franklin, though she knew he was likely with Mia. Now, she was stunned by his appearance when he came up the walk, for her brother was clearly devastated.

"Did she tell you what she planned to do?" Nathaniel asked, desperate for some information.

"Why would she tell me?" Elizabeth said, unable to meet his eyes. She knew what was best for him, but that didn't mean he would be grateful.

"She said you were logical," Nathaniel said.

"That's exactly what I am. She'd have to be a fool not to know that after speaking with me for five minutes."

"Was logic what I wanted?" He'd begun to think that sending his sister to Mia had been a bad idea.

"It's what we all must keep in mind."

"Is it? Logic is why I've lost her."

"You'll be fine," Elizabeth was quick to say, although she herself was not sure.

"Will I?" Nathaniel looked at his dear Ebe, the one person who had always known his heart; he felt sure she couldn't understand this inexpressible longing. His experience had the effect of a spell, taking him out of his ordinary relations with humanity, enclosing him in a sphere by himself, a place not even his beloved older sister could reach. "I doubt that I ever will be again."

Three months passed and there were no changes in Nathaniel's despair. He locked himself away and did not join his sisters for meals. He grew thin and grave, and he turned away invitations to see friends, refusing to go with his uncle to Maine. He was silent most days, and yet they heard him talking to himself at night, as if he was a madman trying to convince himself that logic did indeed matter in this world. Ebe sometimes stood outside his door; she felt responsible for his grief, but that didn't mean she believed herself to be in the wrong. She hoped she would hear him writing, but she never did, and then she worried that he had been permanently damaged. She had heard of writers who were so affected by loss, writing became a trap rather than a joy, and the words that once came so easily to them vanished, as if they were writing with invisible ink.

The family considered Nathaniel to be ill, for he went to bed and slept for days, a gaunt figure who refused food, barely managing sips of water, dehydrated and hallucinating, only beginning to recover when Louisa spooned broth into his mouth. He was in the grip of some spiritual agony, and he hoped his younger, more sensitive sister would understand his plight better than anyone else in the family. He told Louisa he had been in love with a woman who had come from another time, when women could be artists and painters and librarians as well as train conductors, when they went to universities alongside men, and wore trousers and cut their hair however they pleased, and married whomever they liked. In the houses there were lights that flickered on at a touch, on the streets there were carts that had no need to be drawn by horses; the buildings were as tall as the sky, with chambers that went up and down to deliver you up so high you could see Massachusetts from New York City. Louisa worried for his sanity and grew distressed thinking that they might have lost him to madness.

Elizabeth, his more practical sister, thought him mad to speak of such things to anyone else. "People will not understand and will think you've lost your mind," she told her brother. "If Mia has returned to where she came from, she has done so for a reason. Would you have her choose this time for herself, as well choosing to upend all the work you're meant to do? Should she dedicate her life to you and forget she is meant to have one of her own?"

Despite Elizabeth's warning, Nathaniel continued to express his feelings, as confused and wild as they were, and those around him worried more each day. He was livid when no one believed him, his moods turning absolutely black.

"Lock me up if you think I'm not in my right mind," Nathaniel said soberly to both of his sisters, his feelings deeply bruised. "I might as well be in a cage." His eyes flicked from one to the other, and he felt all the worse for how acutely they worried over him, Louisa's face swollen with fears, Elizabeth bleary-eyed, her expression grim.

Nathaniel only left his room to walk every evening at twilight, solitary journeys to Juniper Point, making his way past the eelgrass and the piles of salty kelp deposited along the shore, distracted and in despair, as if he were a man who'd recently been ill and now simply wished to be left alone. He spoke only to himself, muttering curses and regrets. He avoided the pond and the grassy fields and the cottage in thc forest. Instead, he kept to the isolation of the windswept banks, where the mudflats were teeming with shellfish. It was late summer, and there were some nights when the cold wind came off the ocean and froze hatchlings in their nests. On other evenings, when the tide was too high for him to follow the shore, Nathaniel went across the bridge into the hills north of Salem. He walked there in the gloom, and flocks of sparrows followed him as he wondered if he'd been deceived by his own powers of invention, and had imagined all he'd experienced.

The children who spied him in the falling

light called him the Bird Man, and said he was a ghost who could fly and that his black coat served as his wings. They said he'd been in love with a witch and had been enchanted, and that his family had been cursed and he could never escape bad fortune. Some women who saw him said he was an angel, one that had fallen to earth and needed saving, but when they tried to talk to him, he politely turned away, insisting he had nothing to say. On particularly dark, moody nights, Nathaniel often found himself down at the wharves, where he drank too much in the taverns. When he had so much that he could barely stand, he told stories about a woman he had loved who came from another time. He didn't seem to notice when people laughed at him as soon as his back was turned and joked that that was what came of being a writer, madness and delusion.

Nathaniel locked himself in his room and tried to write, but he met with no success. The writing he conjured added up to nothing at all. He felt as he had at the age of nine when he'd been separated from the rest of the world because of his injury. He knew he was meant to write the book that would mean so much to Mia, but words seemed as elusive as sparrows, flying out the open window as he tossed away crumpled pieces of failed work. He wished he'd begged Mia to allow him to read the book she carried with her, so that he might have memorized the words he now feared he'd never write. She had insisted it might ruin him to know too much, but wasn't he ruined anyway?

He gave up and put his pen away and concentrated on walking. He thought of the things people did for love, what fools they were, ruining their lives, giving up their homes and families, wanting someone so badly nothing else mattered. None of life made sense to him now, and he saw guilt and hurt everywhere. He searched the meadows and fields for the places it was said witches were buried for they had not been allowed to be interred in holy ground. Their last resting places were under beech trees and out by the high land overlooking the harbor. Nathaniel went down on his knees to beg for forgiveness. He'd begun to wonder if the magic he'd experienced was meant to make him suffer so that he would pay penance for his family's history of brutality and make amends for the deeds of his great-great-grandfather the judge. Nathaniel stripped off his clothing and stood naked under the moon and told the devil to take his soul if that would give him back the woman he wanted. But no evil spirit claimed him; there were only the bats fluttering in the trees in a nearby orchard and the mosquitoes rising in cyclones from the grass. Three months had passed, and Mia had not returned to him. He stood in the place where he had first spied her asleep in the tall grass, but all he saw were clouds of birds circling above him.

To write was to bleed, and since Mia had left, there was nothing inside him. He needed to prick himself to draw blood, to allow the hurt inside him to flow out. But writing was nothing to him now, mere fantasy and foolishness. Instead of sitting at his desk he continued to roam the hillsides with his arms stretched out, a scarecrow dressed in black, thinner and more angular than he used to be, his hair so long he tied it back with a leather band. He waited to lift into the sky, and yet he remained on earth, with his only escape to be found at the taverns. He had come to understand the men who slept in alleyways, the brokenhearted and the ruined. He cursed his own good fortune in finding Mia in the field, and he wished he'd never known what happiness was. Worse than never having had something was to have had it and then have it taken away.

There came a time when Nathaniel failed to return for two nights. When they had no word from him, the family could only imagine that the drink he was consuming had taken him over, as it did many men in Salem, rich and poor alike. Their mother took to her bed, besieged with worry that her son might do something rash. Men in his condition could easily harm themselves by accident or on purpose, stumble off the dock, pick a fight with the wrong antagonist, wind up murdered in an alley, robbed of what they had. When there was no other choice, Elizabeth donned a hooded black cape and went after her brother. She was intent on escorting Nathaniel home before some tragedy could befall him. She alone knew what tortured him, and because of this, she was willing to go where a woman of good standing was never seen.

Unlike Mia, who had understood what it would mean to herself and to Nathaniel if she stayed, it seemed to Elizabeth that her brother had lost the ability to tell fiction from fact. What Elizabeth feared most, more than alcohol or bad company or delusions, was that Nathaniel might ignore his great talent, and that was something she would not allow. Had she his opportunities, she would have written five books already, or perhaps ten, but since the world was closed to her, and the door was wide open for him, she would not stand by as he threw away the realm of possibilities which existed in the books he was destined to write.

Walking along the wharf, Elizabeth stopped to observe a ship that would soon be leaving for Barbados. How she wished she could hide away below deck and travel to a tropical land where no one knew her. Her imagination was considered far too large for a woman to possess, and she could well imagine what was out there somewhere. Blue skies, endless seas, a whitewashed house that was hers alone, shelves of books, dark rum, a bed with white cotton sheets, a place where she would not be forever known as Nathaniel's sister. Ebe wished she could dress as a boy, and sneak onto that ship, and live a life of freedom in the masquerade that a false identity would allow. She longed to do as she pleased, as her brother said his imaginary woman from another time had done. How she wished that she, too, could dress without care, walk the streets late at night, write and read as she pleased, and not be judged as a woman.

Elizabeth burned as she imagined her mirror life, a world which did not avoid passion and risk and possibility. She suspected that the colors of this life would consist of brilliant shades of blue. Her mouth was set in a grim line, for in Salem she only saw in black and white, and gray of course, the gray of the landscape and of the horizon, the dim shade of the Puritans' legacy, the monotone of the life she led.

Elizabeth peered in the windows of several taverns, at last locating her brother in a hovel. Women were not allowed in such establishments, unless they sold their services, but Elizabeth entered anyway. She went directly to Nathaniel to drag him from this disreputable place. The sailors drinking there hooted and clapped and raised their mugs in a toast when they saw a lady in their midst.

"That's right, girlie," one called in a rough voice. "Go ahead and teach that fellow how to behave. It looks like you know how to be a man, miss, better than he does."

"I know better than most of you, that much is obvious," Elizabeth replied, which quieted the crowd and made them glare at her. They didn't need a woman schooling them or talking back, certainly not one so plain in appearance and full of herself.

"I think you might get us killed," Nathaniel said, slurring his words, a frown on his handsome face.

"Then walk quickly and don't look back," Elizabeth suggested, linking her arm through his.

They hastily left the wharf and headed home, with Nathaniel stumbling beside his sister. All the while, he continued to apologize for not taking better care of her and the rest of the family until Elizabeth commanded him to hush.

"Stop blaming yourself," she insisted.

"What made me think I had the right to happiness? You surely don't expect that for yourself."

"But I do, dear brother," Elizabeth answered in a surprisingly gentle manner. "I just know I'll never get it."

It was no surprise that a woman was at the heart of the mess her brother had found himself in. Nathaniel's extreme good looks and charm had led him into entanglements he had later regretted, although, it was true, this situation seemed to be different. Still, Nathaniel had always been a true romantic, and Elizabeth envied him that trait. Had she not been forced to live within the constraints of a thousand rules, she might be much the same, falling head over heels with anyone she happened to meet. The very idea of something that would never happen made her wince.

"Do you think I can't see you are in the hold of some spiritual agony?" Elizabeth said to her brother. She felt duty bound to remind him that what he wrote was not the waking world in which they lived their lives. There was no magic here in Salem, Massachusetts, and no mysteries. Mia would ruin his life, Elizabeth vowed, and he would ruin hers in return. "She spoke to me of other times, but, Nathaniel, we are not living in a dream, as much as we might want to. Do you not think I don't wish for miracles and magic every time I look into a mirror and see who I am and what is expected of me?"

"And what is expected of me? To forget the woman I love?"

"You cannot have what is not meant to be and if you try, you will break your own heart, Brother, and you will break hers as well."

Nathaniel knew he was lucky to have such a wise sister and he responded after some thought. "You're correct, as usual."

"Of course I am," she said. "Just as I'm correct

when I speak about your greatness as a writer." Elizabeth was a pragmatist; had she not been, she would have leapt off the dock to dash herself upon the rocks. Instead, she told herself that each day must be a garden in which she grew whatever was possible given the season. "You're alive and well," she consoled her brother. "Think of all of those who are not."

Their home soon loomed before them, the closed shutters, the peeling paint, the heavy drapes concealing the gloom within. "We do not live in our house," Nathaniel said, so tipsy he could hardly stand. "We only vegetate."

Their garden was filled with twisted vines brought across the sea from the Barbary Coast a hundred years earlier by their sea captain ancestors, transplanted to each house where they had lived. It was nearly impossible to see the lilies that struggled to bloom in the shade, or the herbs Louisa did her best to cultivate, for all that they grew was overtaken by the stubborn vines that simply refused to die, even when pulled out by their roots.

"You never leave your den," Nathaniel said, referring to Elizabeth's small, cluttered chamber. "And I never leave the upper story of my owl's nest."

"You're on the ground now," Elizabeth said pointedly. Self-pity from a man was something she could not abide, not when she had a woman's issues to deal with. It was time for him to consider his good fortune and privilege. "You could easily walk away and leave that haunted room of yours."

Nathaniel understood that Mia had done the right thing. She had gone back to her proper life, the one in which she found his book in the library and was saved from the life she had been leading in some way he didn't quite understand. The question of whether or not he would ever write that book was a heavy burden when all of his words were sparrows, and each one flew away and couldn't be caught no matter how he might try.

After fetching Nathaniel from his drunken evening, Elizabeth convinced the family that something had to be done. True, she felt somewhat responsible for her brother's despair, but she kept that to herself, never mentioning Mia. She had done all she could, now it was time to meet with their uncle Robert so they might come together and set things right. They all agreed it was preposterous to imagine that Nathaniel's condition had been brought about by the family curse, that inheritance of guilt placed upon them by the witches their ancestor had sent to the gallows, and yet they wondered if they weren't meant to suffer more than other people. Louisa reminded them local folklore claimed that no one in their family would ever be happy.

"Who on earth is happy?" Elizabeth said, annoyed, her high-pitched voice breaking the spell of their shared despair. This was a practical matter, she declared, and Nathaniel had been ill before, after his accident when he was a boy. They were all well aware that his anguish often occurred in the dead of winter, when he couldn't stop writing and refused to leave his room, and now summer had become a season of despondency as well, and soon enough they would be headed into autumn, a time that affected him strangely as well.

It was decided that Nathaniel was suffering from nerves, as many young men and women did. No one would dare to speak of madness, for they would not allow such a fate to befall their dear Nathaniel. He was brilliant, and a dazzling mind was a challenging thing to possess.

The first step was to encourage him to return to the living. He agreed to join his Bowdoin friend Horatio Bridge in Augusta, Maine, where he celebrated his thirty-third birthday. But that night he was as drunk as he'd ever been and could scarcely remember what had transpired. Some men think too much of themselves, and some see only their flaws. Nathaniel had always been plagued by all that he should be and wasn't, but now he seemed truly haunted.

When he returned to Salem from Maine, he was more disheartened and miserable than ever.

Elizabeth stood outside his door and heard no sounds from within his chamber. No books lifted from the shelves, no pen on paper, nothing at all. For a writer not to write was the worst malady. Again, their uncle was consulted, and a plan was agreed upon. Robert Manning would convince Nathaniel to come back to life in the best way he knew how. Robert made his way upstairs and pulled up a chair close to his nephew's bed.

"We can make this right," Robert said.

"I swear she came from another time," Nathaniel told his beloved uncle. "And yet I was in love, and my love was returned, and now I've lost her and sometimes I wonder if she ever existed at all, or if I invented her as I would my characters." Nathaniel was glassy-eyed, his face racked with emotion as he sat up in bed to face his uncle. "Is it possible that we dream in our waking moments, and walk in our sleep?"

Robert was studying his nephew, a kind and weary expression across his face. "We can never know what is possible." Nathaniel's uncle was also burdened with a strain of desire and urges that he kept to himself. "Life is not always what we wish it to be."

Nathaniel leaned back, exhausted from his wild thoughts. "If she was a mythological creature that I invented, that would mean I was mad. That's what you think, isn't it?"

"I don't think anything of the sort. I think

you're a fisherman, a pursuit that would clear your mind. Come with me to Lenox."

Robert Manning had always considered fishing to be curative for the soul. The quiet hours spent in nature, the splashing echoes of rivers and streams, and, of course, the beauty of trout, every variety a wonder to behold, could calm a man's restless soul.

"Whatever has happened to you, you are still the man I know," Robert said. "Let's go for trout."

The men studied one another. It wasn't really a suggestion, but rather a decision that had already been made by all who loved Nathaniel as they'd clustered in a distraught group in the parlor not more than an hour earlier, worried for his future. They decided upon fishing then and there, convinced that a trip to the countryside might soothe his distress. Nathaniel was their shining star, and all their hopes rested in him. Let his life begin again, more simply at first, so that he could be healed each and every day. In Robert's eyes, fishing not only could lead Nathaniel to recovery but also remove him from the grasp of his worried family fluttering around him, making matters worse.

"What do you say, boy?" Robert asked, for even though Nathaniel was thirty-three, a man in every way, to Robert he would always be that boy who loved to visit his uncles in Maine, where he had freedom to wander through the woods and swim in every pond he came to.

Robert had looked upon Nathaniel and his sisters as his own children. He knew that all things begin with kindness and that all hope began with trust. Robert sat there with the worry evident in his large dark eyes, his nephew's champion as always.

"Remember when you were nine, and you thought you'd never be well again?" he said. "Let us see if healing can happen another time."

Nathaniel thought about all Mia had told him about the town of Blackwell, not far from Lenox, and he surprised both his uncle and himself by agreeing to the suggestion that fishing was the answer to his woes, if only to ease his family's worries.

"We will go," Nathaniel told his uncle. "Why wait another day?"

They found their way to the Jack Straw Tavern, a comfortable inn not far from Lenox, just outside the town of Blackwell. There were rooms to let on the second floor, plain, simple chambers that would allow them peace and privacy. The Jack Straw was a rural place, nearly six miles from town, and Robert had often stayed there while fishing in the streams and rivers nearby. He preferred the Eel River but often fished in the Last Look River as well. Their rooms were at the rear of the building, with windows that overlooked Hightop Mountain, a towering green peak where bears were said to be found in every cave.

Blackwell was a small, clannish town, filled with folklore. There were stories of eels that could turn into women, and a ghost who haunted the river, and of a garden where everything that grew turned red. It was a place that intrigued Nathaniel, for he knew it was here that Mia had found his book on a shelf in the library, and here that she had spent her early years. The surrounding area was beautiful, with vast green vistas and so many orchards that the air was scented with the aroma of apples, not yet ripe but fragrant all the same. Berkshire County was still untamed land, and a person could forget the foolish rules and regulations of polite society and wander freely here, in rough clothes and with an interest in nothing more than the natural world around him.

Nathaniel found he could breathe more easily once they'd arrived. The air was sweet and fresh, far cooler than it was in Salem, painted with a bluish tint when one gazed into the distance. He felt closer to Mia here and to what they had shared, for she'd often spoken of Blackwell and the farm where'd she'd grown up, with its rules and its heartless leader who had ruined her mother's life. Nathaniel had lost his appetite when she vanished, but now it returned to him, and he and Robert had a quick dinner at the bar. The area was famous for a dish called eel pie, but they ordered roasted salt potatoes along with a stew of barley and chicken instead and were easily satisfied by their simple meal. Along with the food, they had mugs of the local ale, called Love Me Twice, said to be an aphrodisiac for some, so sweet that swarming bees were drawn to it and were made drunk by the fumes rising from the barrels set out behind the inn. The beauty of the place was everywhere, in every leaf and hill, and though the food was simple it was tasty, and before he knew it Nathaniel had cleared his plate.

"You've begun to recover already," Robert said hopefully.

Nathaniel was certainly relieved to be gone from Salem. It was the city of his nightmares, one filled with misfortune; every street he walked in that city was a street his cursed ancestors had trod, never remorseful for their dreadful treatment of women declared to be witches. He much preferred to be a stranger in a strange land. Perhaps he should think of all that had happened as a dream, and not wish for more, other than to write the book that Mia would one day find.

Uncle and nephew said their good nights, having planned to meet at an extremely early hour in the morning, so they would arrive at the river when the fish were waking. They flipped a coin to decide where to fish, and Nathaniel's heart flipped as well when heads came up. The Last Look, the river Mia had said she had often visited. He wondered if when he approached the bank, he might walk back into that dream of his and somehow see her once more, and he had a surge of excitement, brought on by his desires and by the ale he'd been drinking.

Once Nathaniel was in his room, he unpacked the small bag he'd brought, placing his clothing in the bureau drawers and his old fishing boots beside the door. He'd worn his black coat for the journey, and now, in the overheated room, he removed it to hang upon the back of the chair. He fully intended to think of nothing but fish and mountains and pine trees and keep his mind preoccupied, but he couldn't stop himself from imagining Mia swimming in the pond, her black dress left in the grass. He sat on the narrow bed, his head in his hands. The hour was late, but summer light lasted long here in the mountains. Nathaniel heard the birds outside his window, swifts and swallows and sparrows, all nesting in the eaves of the Jack Straw Tavern. It was likely that his uncle was already asleep in his room, or perhaps he'd stayed at the bar for another ale or two. The birds' racket would be silenced once darkness fell. Love was cruel and unpredictable, and yet he wanted it more than words, more than anything. He was a madman, it was true, but wasn't every writer? He set out the paper he had brought with him, and the pen and ink. He sat at his desk, but he, who in the past could not stop writing, now did not put down a single word. He could not think of a single story, other than his own. Instead of writing he fell asleep, and all night long he dreamed of her.

It was not yet dawn when there was a knock upon his door. Robert stuck his head in, surprised to see Nathaniel asleep in a chair, his head on the desk. "Ready for the river?" his uncle said. "Wake up and join the living!"

Nathaniel was clearly not yet on the mend, for his bed had not been slept in, and when he came down from his room, he wore the wrinkled clothes he'd spent the night in. All the same, Robert clapped him on the back and pretended all was fine. Lovesickness was curable; it always had been if it was caught in time.

They would be headed for the Last Look River, where there was said to be a mysterious variety of blue trout, a catch prized by local fishermen, that could only be found in the rivers outside of Blackwell. Robert had brought the rods, along with flies that he'd crafted himself from sewing thread and blue jay feathers tied onto a single hook. If the problem was that Nathaniel could not write, well, that was more difficult to remedy. Still, fishing and writing had a good deal in common. You had to wait and be prepared to catch what came your way. You had to know the difference between a shadow and the real thing.

The violet-colored dawn would lead to a glorious late summer day, and the air was not yet suffused with heat. Though it was not officially autumn, there were already a few yellow leaves in the swampy areas. Nathaniel was in better spirits once they began to walk, although when they reached the river, he suggested he head out by himself to the far side of the bank, out beyond some bramble bushes full of berries. Robert wanted the day to be congenial and uplifting, and he protested at first, but Nathaniel convinced him such tactics were best.

"A lone fisherman always does better, as you well know," he told his uncle, clapping Robert on the back.

They both settled into their separate areas behind the bushes. But fishing did not interest Nathaniel on this day. He was too busy imagining Mia's last time at this river. Ever since, she had carried the book he was to write wherever she went. What tale did he have to tell that would impress her so? In the past, stories had come to him all on their own. Characters walked onto the page, in grief or in mourning or filled with delight. He picked up one of the flat black stones and flung it across the river so that it skipped, spooking some frogs in the reeds. It was his responsibility to write the novel that she'd found; he must think of it as an honor and not allow himself to be wrapped up in regret, which caused writers to go utterly blank.

Nathaniel stepped over the rocks until the water was waist high. The Last Look River was fast and treacherous. People said it was a siren that called to men who sat on the bank. They said that trout in this part of the Berkshires could turn themselves into women if they desired to do so and fall in love with mortal men. It never ended well, just as Elizabeth had said. Men cannot live with mythological creatures. Several people had drowned in the very spot where Nathaniel now found himself, and their last look at the world was of the cold green water that drew them down into a whirl, and the trout all around them and the rocks lining the riverbed.

Nathaniel understood the urge to leave the world behind, but when he looked upward, into the boughs of the trees, each leaf reminded him why he wished to be alive, even while he was aching with loss. By the end of the day, he was drenched and cold and happy. He was a writer, he would write the book for her, even though he had no idea what it might be about. He had managed to catch two trout, to prove he had truly been fishing, not only imagining. He had the trout in his bucket as he walked upriver, only to discover Robert asleep beneath one of the huge old oaks. In Robert's bucket there were six trout, three of them blue as the sky. Nathaniel waited for his uncle to wake, delighted to have more quiet time to himself. He thought of luck and love, how both came to you uninvited, and stayed only as long as they wished to, beyond anyone's command.

"I dreamed we were lost," Robert said when he opened his eyes. It was likely the name of the river that had influenced his dream. That was how mysterious the world was; standing alone in a river could make you feel as if you were the only person on earth, and nearly come to believe it, and wish for the company of those you loved best.

"We're not," Nathaniel said warmly. "We're right here where we belong."

"And you've not gone mad?" Robert asked.

Nathaniel laughed and some birds took flight, startled by the sound of his voice. "Not yet."

Nathaniel leaned his back against the tree and looked out at the river. His uncle had been right. Sitting by the river where so many had drowned, he'd remembered who he was meant to be. He had no story to tell, and yet he knew he was still a writer. He closed his eyes and saw a string of words, as if they were sparrows sitting in the tree. *Talisman, transformation, oracles, labyrinth, solace.* Words were magic. That was all he knew. Words were all they had. And if that was true, then anything was possible. He simply had to wait for the story to come to him, and then all he had to do was write to make it so.

PART THREE

TWO WORLDS

CHAPTER SEVEN

WHEN WE WERE HERE

The end of summer in New York was scorching, with days so brutal people waited anxiously for darkness to fall, even though the nights weren't much better, as heat continued to rise from the asphalt and cement. Ice melted as soon as it was taken out of the freezer; pigeons were unable to lift into the sky. People ran cold showers, and when out shopping, they lingered by the frozen food in the supermarkets; they took the subway to Coney Island or sat under trees in Central Park on wilted patches of grass. Still the world seemed to be burning.

It was possible to feel more alone in Manhattan than anywhere else no matter how many people surrounded you. This was especially true during the last few days of August, when the streets were crowded with everyone who didn't have the time or the funds to go on vacation. There was an emptiness, as if the city floated in the ether, as if it were a dream and everyone on the avenues, dressed in the lightest clothes they could find, undershirts and shorts or summer dresses, hadn't yet woken from sleep. Mia had been back for more than three months, and she still didn't feel as though she belonged in her own world. At night she dreamed she slept beside Nathaniel in the cottage bed. There were stacks of paper and written out on every page was the book that had saved her, the one she could recite word for word. *Love, whether newly born or aroused from a deathlike slumber, must always create sunshine, filling the heart so full of radiance, that it overflows upon the outward world.*

What was most important was for the book to be written and for her presence not to disturb Nathaniel's life and work. And yet, it was as if she were still in that field of grass where she'd first seen him. Here in the city, she couldn't see a single star. She avoided people and didn't answer the phone, which often rang in the middle of the night. When she walked to the grocery store or the coffee shop she often had the sense that she was being followed. She felt nervous and ill at ease, and recently, she had stopped showing up for work.

In the mornings, she was sick to her stomach, exhausted before she even got out of bed. She spent her days staring at her neighbor's yard, not even wanting to read. She waited for the night, when she could dream of Nathaniel. In her most recent dream, he had climbed a tree and was high above the earth. He was calling her name and saying, *You can come back. I'm here waiting for you.* But as she awoke, it was Elizabeth's voice she heard ringing inside her head. *A fish cannot live in the world of a sparrow. One will gasp for air and the other will drown.*

On the last day of August Mia found the leaf on the stoop outside her building. Leaves in Blackwell were already beginning to turn yellow at this time of year, as this one had. Mia told herself it was a coincidence, but the very next day she found another, this time inside the hallway of the building, which could be entered only if someone had a key or managed to convince one of the neighbors to let him in.

That night she answered the phone when it rang. She didn't say a word; she merely listened to the emptiness on the other end of the line. And then he spoke. "I always knew you were a thief. I just didn't know what you were trying to steal from me."

Mia hung up, her hands shaking. She had no clue as to what he was talking about, but she knew that once Joel Davis had an idea in his head, it was nearly impossible to convince him otherwise. All she knew was that he had found her, and so she phoned Sarah and the very next morning she took the first train to Boston, then the commuter train to what had always seemed like home. Mia intended to walk to the little house by the river and was surprised to find Sarah waiting for her at the station.

"You didn't have to meet me here," Mia said.

"I'm afraid I did." Sarah looked grim. "He's shown up again."

Mia tried to remain calm, but she could feel her heart pounding against her ribs. She had a sudden memory of the girls in her dormitory at the Community, all rushing out to avoid Joel when they'd heard he was coming upstairs to talk to Mia after her mother's death. She recalled the look on his face when he said, *I will break you.* She knew that he would. *I don't know what he's capable of.* That was the reason Ivy had stayed, that was why she could never run away and why she said they could never be invisible as long as Joel was watching over them.

"Here in Concord? How could that be? He was in New York yesterday."

"He must have known you would come here. I looked up this morning when it was still dark, and there he was in the driveway."

"*Your* driveway?" Mia couldn't help but sound panicked.

They had left the train station to walk to the library, which had always been a safe place. Sarah no longer worked at the Concord School and instead she volunteered here most days. Occasionally, she found herself looking up from her work, half expecting to see Constance; then she remembered that she was alone. It was easy to trick yourself sometimes, if only for a moment or two.

"That's why I met you at the train station," Sarah said. "You can't come to the house. For all I know he could still be lurking there. He could be waiting under the lilacs."

"Maybe it wasn't him," Mia said, desperately wanting that to be true.

"Mia, I talked to him."

The first thing Sarah had noticed was the movement of the heart-shaped leaves that Constance always said were as beautiful as any flower. She thought perhaps the wind had picked up, as it sometimes did off the river, but then she spied a shadow cast across the driveway. She wondered if there were crows in the hedges, as there sometimes were, birds so intelligent she could call to them to eat crusts of bread from her hand, but then he stepped out of the greenery. He appeared as if he belonged there, as if this was his house rather than hers, for Constance had made certain that everything that had belonged to her would go directly to Sarah.

Sarah opened the front door but kept the screen latched. "This is private property, sir."

"I know all about private property," Joel Davis said. Sarah didn't like the look on his face, or his tone. But she acted as if it was perfectly normal to have a man station himself in her driveway.

"The government is trying to take my land away. The deed is missing and guess who has it?"

"It's really none of my business," Sarah told him.

"You made it your business when you stole the girl."

Sarah then made the mistake of looking into his eyes. He had a way of looking into you and making you feel as if there was nowhere to go, as if he had you in his grasp and you had best not try to oppose him.

"Mia has the deed and I want it," Joel Davis announced.

Sarah forced herself to meet his gaze. She thought of all the harm he'd done and all the lives he'd set off course and suddenly she didn't feel the least bit afraid. A man like Joel fed off fear and insecurity. "For your information, Mia doesn't live here anymore, so you've come to the wrong place."

"I know where she lives in New York, and I know she'll come back here to visit you. Maybe I'll just stay for a while. I'm sure you wouldn't mind, Sarah."

It was the fact that he said her name, as if he knew her, and had power over her, that set her off. There was no way she would allow herself to be at his mercy.

"I'm calling the police," she announced. Sarah had already taken her phone out of the pocket of her skirt, and behind her back she had already punched in 911. There was a crackle as the police dispatcher answered. "I'm being robbed," Sarah said loudly before announcing her address. "Come right away."

"I'm the one who's been robbed," Joel said in response. All the same, now that the police were on their way, he had no choice but to leave. "You tell Mia I want it back and I intend to get it. I'll find her here, or in New York, or wherever the hell she goes." He gave Sarah a long look before he got into his truck and took off.

Sarah had been so rattled that she didn't think to take down the license plate number. Afterward, she'd had a talk with the police, and they had contacted the authorities in Blackwell. That was how she'd discovered there had indeed been a court case, and Joel had lost. The police had come to claim the land and arrest him for setting fire to several of the buildings, but right before they arrived, Joel Davis disappeared into the woods. He would rather have the buildings burn than have the town take them, and on the night of the burning there was so much smoke that deer were seen racing down Route 17, and a bear was found on the town green, hidden behind the bushes.

"The Blackwell authorities said the farm is mostly deserted now," Sarah told Mia. "Most of the younger people have left, and Joel is angry about that. Nobody listens to him anymore."

The story hour that Constance used to lead now let out and children ran across the lawn carrying copies of *Magic by the Lake*.

"They questioned a woman who said she'd been the schoolteacher," Sarah added.

Evangeline.

"Did they?" Mia nodded, not at all surprised that Evangeline would be among those who had stayed on the farm. The tattletale, always so jealous of Ivy, who always had to be second in command, the one they had fooled when Ivy took the slip of paper from Mia and had eaten it rather than let Evangeline have proof that rules had been broken.

"She said you stole the deed that proves he owns the property. She said she was there in the office when you did it, and that you were always sneaky."

"I was," Mia admitted.

"No, you weren't." Sarah was firm on this. "You were a survivor." Sarah handed over a leather satchel she'd brought along. "I think it would be wise if you relocated from your apartment for a while. I wish you could stay here, but it's the first place he'll look. He could still be in Concord waiting for you to show up. I should have come to New York, but there was something here I knew you would want."

Inside the bag Sarah had brought was Mia's copy of *The Scarlet Letter*. Ivy's letter was folded inside, along with the watercolor she'd found in the Community files and the pearls that had belonged to Constance, and the gold earrings that had been a birthday gift. All of her treasures.

"Evangeline was right about me. I stole this book from the library in Blackwell." Mia was admitting this for the first time.

"I know. I found your keepsake box years ago." Sarah patted Mia's arm with affection. "If not returning a book to the library is the worst you ever do, dear girl, then you're an angel. 'Time hides no treasures; we want not its then, but its now'," she said, quoting Thoreau. "This is your now. A treasure is a treasure if you think it is. The book is your treasure, and Joel thinks you have his treasure as well."

Mia recalled the day she had worked in the office and found Carrie's painting, hidden in the back of the file cabinet. She now turned the painting over to read the inscription. *I leave my husband everything, all of my land as far as the eye can see.*

"I never knew what this meant, but I do now," Mia told Sarah. "It's the deed. It's what he's been looking for all this time."

Sarah brought a small paper grocery sack out of her purse. "He left this in the driveway." Inside the bag were a dozen Look-No-Further apples, not yet ripe.

There was one place where he would never

find Mia, and that was the place she'd always wanted to be. Now that she considered it, she thought Elizabeth was wrong, and that a fish could live with a sparrow after all. They would be in different elements yet remain close, as far away as a leaf, or a whisper, or a kiss. If she could have Nathaniel for her own, Mia didn't care if she remained at the edges of his life, in a cottage in the woods, hidden away and invisible. She would not freeze during a cold winter as the previous tenant had; she would not care if no one from town ever spoke to her. As for Nathaniel, he could still live as he was meant to, be married, have children, write his books, but every now and then he could be hers. She could tell Nathaniel all he must do to make certain he would live the life he was meant to have and write the books he would have written if she'd never returned. She would show him lines and chapters if need be; she would recite his own words to him.

Sarah clasped the pearls around Mia's throat, and they embraced, but they didn't prolong their farewell. Goodbyes were too final, and so they said nothing at all, as they had when they drove to Concord all those years ago, when they both knew that Mia would never return to Blackwell. They understood there were things that a person must forsake when she was running away.

Mia walked across town. It was still hot, but the

season would soon change, and purple September asters were already blooming in the fields and yards. In a few brief weeks, summer would be over, the air would be crisp and cool, and out in Blackwell the leaves would turn red. Mia quickly made her way to the north side of town, where there was a bus stop outside Crosby's market. She didn't dare return to the cemetery for fear that Joel was still in town, but if she had reached Nathaniel in the place where he'd been buried, she believed she could reach him again at the house where he'd been born, and that was her destination now. She was going to Salem.

When the bus arrived, Mia stepped on and paid her fare, then made her way to the rear. Only a few other passengers followed her on, a woman with a baby, a boy of sixteen or so, a man who buried his face in his copy of the *Boston Globe*, two girls chatting about school. Mia sat down, and as the bus set off, she began to read Nathaniel's book for comfort. She was reminded that nothing was written in stone, and that fate could change, and that not everyone who filled her pockets with river rocks drowned. After a while, Mia stowed the book in the leather satchel and looked out at the road. Concord already seemed like a dream to her, and her apartment in New York might as well have been on the moon. She would go as far as she needed and she would never be found. She would walk invisible into a world in which impossible things had happened and would most certainly happen again.

In Salem, Mia exited at Bridge Street. She heard the shrill cry of a child being comforted in his mother's arms and a teenage boy calling out to the friends who were meeting him, but all she thought of was her own destination as she made her way along the twisting streets, turning onto Williams Street. Finally, there was Washington Square, framed by eighteenth-century mansions. The route then took her to the House of the Seven Gables at Derby Street. Mia had visited the museum with Constance when she was in school, but now as she approached, she felt a wave of fear. It was what she'd always felt when Joel was near, and she didn't understand until she looked over her shoulder.

There was the man who had been reading the newspaper on the bus following a block behind her. She hadn't bothered to look at him before, but now she recognized Joel. She was instantly chilled, as if he had arisen from the underworld and brought winter with him. She might be walking through drifts of snow, or skating on the blue ice of the river with Ivy, nearly invisible, but not quite. Joel hadn't aged well, he looked shrunken and bitter, but she knew him all the same. That was when she took off running. Her breath was shallow in her chest as she raced on, desperate to keep as much distance between herself and Joel as possible.

The grand sea captain's house at the front of the museum had been built in 1668 and was purchased in 1782 by Samuel Ingersoll, a wealthy, well-known sea captain himself. His daughter Susanna, a second cousin of Hawthorne's, inherited the property, which was said to be haunted. Mia knew that Nathaniel had visited Miss Susanna frequently and that the stories she'd told of his ancestors' greed when some members of his family did their best to take the house from her would later inspire his novel *The House of the Seven Gables*.

Nathaniel's birthplace was modest by comparison; originally built in 1750 on Union Street, it had been moved in 1958 to what was now a museum campus. Nathaniel had been born in a room above the parlor, and had lived there for four years, until his father died at sea. The gardens outside the houses were comparatively new, having been laid out in 1909 in the Jacobean style, with four centuries of garden varieties, gray-green in tone, planted with herbs used for healing, and masses of flowers, including lavender, artemisia, tarragon, bee balm, and thyme. There were snapdragons and impatiens, coral bells and delphinium, hollyhocks, Canterbury bells, and an extraordinary arbor of twisting wisteria of a variety introduced to Massachusetts during the nineteenth-century China trade. Visiting hours were over, but Mia saw a young man readying the museum for closing and she urgently signaled to him.

"Hello!" Mia called. Her hands were wrapped around the gate posts. She thought of the day when her mother's body was carried across the field and then of how Joel had locked her in the barn. Her heart was beating too fast. "I've lost something. Please! Hurry!"

Mia gestured for the employee to come closer, and he did, curious, for she was a stunning figure with her red hair loose, nearly reaching her waist, and her old-fashioned black dress. The summer intern was a college student who had written a paper on *The House of the Seven Gables*.

"I was here earlier, and I lost an earring in the garden," Mia told him as he drew near. She sounded so distressed. "May I look? Please, I'm in a terrible rush."

The intern glanced over his shoulder. He was meant to set the alarms and lock the doors, then set the bolt on the gate after he'd left. It was his first time closing up alone. According to the rules, no one was allowed on the grounds after hours, but he found himself moved by this woman's plight.

"They were a gift from a dear friend," Mia confided. "She's passed on and they're all I have left of her."

Joel was on the property now. She spied him on the corner, coming towards them.

"Can you open the gate?" Mia sounded truly desperate now.

"Sure," the young man said, won over when he saw tears brimming in her black liquid eyes. He leaned in to unlock the latch. "Can you do it quickly?"

"Absolutely," Mia assured him. She ran into the garden. The trellis was abloom with the last of the fading roses, climbing New Dawn, a delicate pink variety of small rose that did well in salty soil. Mia knelt down. She would not let one man ruin her life. She would not be bound by history or fate.

"Stop right now," she heard Joel shout.

Mia thought of her mother kneeling before him, she thought of the days when women had to confess their sins. Finally, she held the fern-seed and was at last invisible. A haze descended, and the young employee of the Seven Gables disappeared in that murky light, as if a fog had rolled in from the sea and nothing was as it had appeared to be. She heard the gate slam open, and her name shouted out, but she didn't have to obey Joel anymore. The young man who worked at the museum shouted *Hello! Are you still there?* but by then Mia was curled up beside the hedges outside Nathaniel's house, there in the bright sunlight in the summer of 1837.

THE SALEM OBSERVER was being delivered by a young boy who nearly tripped over Mia. He hadn't noticed her on the brick walkway, where she now sat cross-legged, her head aching, over-heated and starving. She felt as if she'd traveled halfway around the world. The air was lazy and yellow and thick, and it wasn't easy to breathe.

"Miss," the newsboy said, unnerved in her presence. "Should I direct you to the Seamen's Widow and Orphan Association?"

"No, thank you," Mia said, rising and brushing off the rose petals that clung to the fabric of her black dress. It was the last burst of summer, and the day would be blistering. Mia wished she had thought to wear lighter clothing. It occurred to her that she hadn't properly prepared, just as when she had run away from the Community, for she'd taken nothing with her but the painting, the book, and her mother's letter tucked inside a canvas bag worn over her shoulder. *Travel light. Don't look back. Take only what you need most of all.*

The newsboy helped Mia to her feet, then awkwardly bowed, as if he stood before a queen. He found the stranger extraordinary, with her loose red hair and strange crimson-colored boots. The boy thought perhaps he'd found a fairy who lived beneath the hedge, and perhaps he'd have three wishes granted, but he wasn't bold enough to stay. "Good luck to you, miss," he declared, before he took off running.

Nathaniel's sister Louisa watched the encounter between the newsboy and the stranger from the window; curious and nervous, she called her sister to her. Elizabeth always knew what to do. But when Elizabeth came into the room and looked out the window, she said, "Oh, damn!" She crossed her arms in front of her chest and studied the scene on the path leading to their house. Of course, Mia couldn't leave well enough alone. People in love were such fools, they made up excuses, they wound up doing as they pleased no matter how much good advice they'd been given. A small part of Elizabeth was impressed by Mia's recklessness. If she had some of that herself, perhaps she'd be in Barbados right now.

"Do you know who she might be?" Louisa asked of the woman in the black dress.

There'd been good reason not to inform Louisa about Mia's existence; Elizabeth's younger sister was too softhearted, and if given free rein, she would have likely invited the stranger to move in with them. She pursed her lips, as she always did when she was thinking deeply, which was much of the time. She wore a plain muslin dress and a quilted jacket, having planned to do nothing but read all afternoon. Obviously, those plans had now been interrupted, but she'd gotten rid of Mia once, so it was likely that she could do so again.

"You stay here," Elizabeth told Louisa. "Keep Eta up in her room," she added, using their nickname for their sensitive mother. "She doesn't need to be involved in this." As so often happened, the children had become the caretakers of their fragile parent. Frankly they had been ever since the death of their father at sea, and Elizabeth, for one, resented her position in the family, not that she would ever shirk her duties as Nathaniel often did, forgiven by one and all, including his older sister.

Elizabeth went outside and shook her head as she glared at Mia. "You did the right thing, yet now you've seen fit to return and do damage. Did we not discuss applying logic to the situation?"

Mia felt quite dizzy standing in the sun in her long black dress. "I'm not here to do damage," she said. "And I had no choice, Ebe."

"There's always a choice," Elizabeth said briskly, grateful that her brother was not at home. He was a romantic and a fool and a genius and the person she loved best in the world, and he needed absolute concentration so he might focus on his great gift. She had thought she and Mia had agreed upon that.

"Really?" Mia said. "Do you have the choice to attend Harvard?"

"No more than you would if you stay here," Elizabeth shot back. "I thought you understood you needed to go back. He was ill for weeks after you left, he talked about you in his fevered dreams. Do you think that is helpful to him or to his work?"

"I've thought of a way to be a fish and still breathe air," Mia said.

"Have you now?" Despite herself, Elizabeth was curious, then she was immediately distracted when she heard a tapping behind her. There was Louisa at the window, trying to get her attention. Elizabeth waved to her sister, who reluctantly drew the curtain. All the same, if Elizabeth knew her sister, and she did, Louisa would have already arranged breakfast at their table for this unknown guest.

"And I have used logic."

"Really? I seriously doubt it."

"I won't hurt him," Mia said.

Elizabeth shook her head. "Open your eyes. Someone always gets hurt."

Elizabeth reluctantly brought Mia inside, and both sisters studied Mia as she ate. She was ravenous and had the manners of a sailor. She poured warm milk on her oat porridge, a portion enough for three people rather than one, and ate two slices of bread with butter.

"I can't seem to stop eating," Mia said apologetically. Just this morning the thought of food had made her ill and now her stomach was empty.

"You eat a great amount for one woman," Elizabeth said thoughtfully.

"I've come a long way."

"From where?" Louisa wondered.

"New York," Elizabeth was quick to answer.

Mia gazed around as she devoured her breakfast, taking in the rough-hewn kitchen, the stove fed by wood, the pump beside the large black sink, the earthenware dishes for everyday use. Already the room was blazing hot, and it would be far worse later on, when the air turned muggy. While her mouth was full, Mia asked, "Is Nathaniel out walking or is he in the owl's nest?"

The sisters exchanged a fleeting look, with Louisa going quite pale. Perhaps this woman was a faerie or a witch, although her hunger made her appear mortal enough. Mia took more toast for herself without even asking and then spooned on gobs of elderberry jam and wolfed the food down. She was certain she had never tasted anything as delicious as this breakfast, or sat at a more inviting table, with a jug of pink snapdragons set out, and the butter in a glass dish, already melting. This world was slower and smaller, but the details were brilliant, each a spot of shining color in a muted background. She felt heavier, but in a good way, as if her nerves had been calmed now that she was far away from Joel Davis. At last, she had the receipt of fern-seed.

"What do you know of the owl's nest?" Louisa asked. "And how do you know our brother? Are you the woman he spoke about when he was so distressed?"

Elizabeth cut in. "Our mother is resting, and our brother is a hundred and thirty miles away, so once you're done with breakfast, I will walk you home. Surely, you're longing to get back."

"Where is he exactly?" Mia hadn't even stopped to think that Nathaniel might not be at home, writing.

"He's in the western part of Massachusetts," Louisa announced before Elizabeth could hush her.

"I intend to go after him." Mia took what was left of the bread and butter that had been set out and rudely wrapped it in a napkin, which she then stowed in the pocket of her dress. She had never been more famished or more in need of all her strength. She turned to Louisa, who she already knew to be tenderhearted from Nathaniel's descriptions, and whose eyes were filled with concern. "Please, tell me exactly where he is." She was met by a renewed silence, and soon saw that Elizabeth was glaring at her sister, doing her best to ensure that Louisa would say nothing more. "Fine." Mia nodded. "If anything happens to me on my travels to find him, I will blame you both."

Louisa threw her sister a panicked look, fearing

they might be the cause of some catastrophe. And as it was, their guest now took ill. Perhaps the heated conversation had affected her adversely, perhaps she had eaten too much, but Mia now felt sick to her stomach. She excused herself, stepped outside, and was ill near the bushes. The sisters watched her from the threshold.

"Ebe," Louisa pleaded, for her first instinct was always to do good in the world. "What if Nathaniel would want to see her? What if he's desperate to do so?"

Elizabeth's face was grim. She didn't like what she was looking at. A woman on the walkway being sick in their garden beside the twisted vines. "He's been involved romantically in the past, and it has never led to anything that did him the least bit of good."

"If you won't talk to her, then I must," Louisa said, knowing that would get a rise out of her sister.

"I'll handle it." Despite her own sense of impending disaster, Elizabeth went out to speak to Mia. "We discussed this and agreed. You will ruin him."

"I swear if I ever thought I could or would, I would leave immediately. Let me have my chance. Shouldn't I at least have that?"

Elizabeth was no longer convinced this was her battle to fight. She wished someone would give her *her* chance, for anything or anyone, for a single dream. "If you must know, our brother is in Blackwell. He's gone to fish."

Mia took his destination to be further proof of their interwoven fate. "Then he's gone for blue trout," she said with certainty. "I grew up in Blackwell. I know the rivers there."

Elizabeth escorted Mia to the Mannings' stables. Because it was a stifling day, Elizabeth carried an umbrella to keep the sun off her pale, freckled complexion, while Mia didn't seem to care if her skin burned or if her boots were caked with mud. Once they reached the stables, they learned that the fishermen's carriage was not expected back until the start of the following week and there was no other carriage to be had. The clerk suggested that Mia take the new train line, which would go out west via Boston to Albany with a stop before in the Berkshire hills, in the town of Blackwell. This would mean changing trains three times and spending two days on the journey.

"Are you certain you're feeling well enough for such travel?" Elizabeth asked.

"Of course. I'm perfectly fine."

Elizabeth gave her companion a look. Was it possible that Mia had not figured out what was obvious to Elizabeth as soon as Mia began to wolf down her food? "Do you have no idea?" she asked Mia. "Are you that much of a fool? I assume Nathaniel is the father, but even if he is, if you think a fish can breathe that air, you are terribly mistaken. And what becomes of the child of a fish and a sparrow? Where does that child abide?"

Mia sank down on a wooden bench. Her head was pounding, for she immediately knew Elizabeth's statement to be true. She had thought she was ill, or the weather had exhausted her, but that wasn't it at all.

"Perhaps you'll tell Nathaniel about the child," Elizabeth said, "and then of course he'll marry you. He wouldn't think of not taking responsibility, no matter if it will change all that's meant to be. Other men might walk away, they do so every day. Every baby on the hill had a father, but the mothers were the ones held accountable. My brother won't feel that way, and it will change everything. There is one life he's meant to have, and this is not it." They sat side by side, so close that people passing by might have imagined they were sisters.

"My mother ran away in order to have me. She gave up everything and never had a life of her own. I've often wondered what she would have done if she could have lived as she pleased," Mia said. "What would you do if you could make your own choices?"

"I'd run away from here," Elizabeth was quick to say. "I'd go to sea and write a book and have a child that someone else raised so I could be free."

Mia smiled. "In other words, you'd be a man."

"I would. Or a woman in your time," Elizabeth responded.

"There are no promises in my time. It's not everything you think it is."

"I don't need everything," Elizabeth said. "Only something."

When they arrived at the station, Elizabeth bought Mia a ticket, for she had no money of her own. One way, Mia noticed.

"We both know you won't be back," Elizabeth explained.

"Do we?"

Elizabeth gave Mia an onyx-and-silver hairpin, so she could put her long hair up and not stand out. "I don't expect you to return it," she said. She wanted to know about New York and the library; she wanted to imagine what it was like to walk down the street at night and feel that you had every right to do so. She wanted to leave home, even if it meant never seeing the people she loved again. She could have cried right then and there if she'd been another person, if she hadn't been trained to hide her emotions and do the right thing no matter what.

Mia unclasped the pearl necklace she had inherited from Constance. "For you," she told Elizabeth. "To remember me by."

"What makes you think I wish to remember

you?" Elizabeth asked, her voice wary, but the truth was, she was pleased with the gift. The pearls were delicate, with a faint blue tint. She wanted to wear them in the moonlight, as she walked through the grass, as she boarded a boat that would take her far out to sea. She would do none of those things; all the same, the pearls were meant for her. Mia leaned forward unexpectedly and clasped the strand around Elizabeth's throat. She knew from her readings that Elizabeth would not attend Nathaniel's wedding to Sophia, and she smiled to think that perhaps it was because Elizabeth preferred Mia to the wife her brother would later choose.

Elizabeth touched her hand to the pearls and blushed with vanity despite her vow never to have self-indulgent thoughts. When Mia walked along the platform, Elizabeth followed reluctantly, still unsure if she had made the right decision in telling Mia where Nathaniel was. "I'm not certain why I'm helping you," she wondered aloud.

"Because we care about his writing," Mia said.

"What do you know of his writing?" Elizabeth scowled.

"I know it saved me. Do I need to know more?"

"You need to know that it saved him as well."

The train had arrived, and the time had come for Mia to leave. The two women were connected by their love for Nathaniel, and so Elizabeth decided to say more.

"You would never have been happy here. I think you know that. There are no witches anymore, to be sure, but women are judged as if there were. Everything you wear and say and eat is meted out by a rule book. As you plainly see, I am not the one in Blackwell fishing. I am not the one with novels published. You know that's not the world you want."

Women wrote under men's names, or used only initials, hiding their gender, for all they did was considered less important. There were some female academies with high tuition costs for women students, but they were not accepted at colleges or universities, except for Oberlin, which had just begun to admit female students.

"The world will change," Mia said.

Elizabeth shook her head. "Not in time for me or for your daughter if you stay."

Mia looked at Elizabeth, and Elizabeth laughed to see her confusion.

"Girls run in our family. My brother is the one and only treasured boy."

Mia felt the quickening inside her as they stood on the platform in the heat of the day and then she knew. She was not about to hide in the woods invisible and she understood why her mother had done whatever she had not to lose her.

You were mine and mine alone. You were the best thing that ever happened to me.

The train was boarding. Mia threw her

arms around Nathaniel's sister, and as she did Elizabeth felt a sob rise in her throat. Her life was set, and could not be altered, but oh, she wished that it might be. She wished she'd been born a boy, or that she could slip into another time, or that Nathaniel could have all he wanted and still be the writer he was meant to be.

"So now you know," Elizabeth said, taking a step away and blinking back her tears. "A fish may live in the same world as a sparrow, but they cannot marry their lives together, and a hawk cannot marry at all."

Mia understood that Elizabeth considered herself to be the hawk. "You'll do more than most men in your lifetime," Mia told her.

"And will it matter? Or will they only remember what he did?"

Mia could not bring herself to tell Elizabeth that she was right.

"I don't need to see into the future to know that is what will happen," Elizabeth said. "He is my brother and a genius. But in another place and time, I might have been one, too."

Elizabeth surprised herself then. She did not back away when Mia embraced her. "I'll name her after you," Mia said. "To make certain that she's brave."

A conductor guided Mia along, and once on board she was grateful to sink into her seat. She gazed out the window to see that Elizabeth was still on the platform. She waved and Elizabeth waved back, then Mia closed her eyes and leaned her head against the seat as they began to slowly move away from the station. She had come so far and now here she was, headed for the one place in the world she had vowed never to return to. She had to change trains, and she was exhausted, and she felt as if she was going back on her word by heading for Western Massachusetts. All the same, by the end of her journey, when the hills of Berkshire County were in sight, there was nowhere she would rather be.

Nathaniel sat at a table in the rear of the tavern while his uncle went upstairs to nap. It was a sweltering day and there were flies buzzing around spilled pools of ale on the tabletops. Bees hit against the windows, drowsy in the last glints of sunlight. Nathaniel and Robert had been at the river since daybreak and had hiked ten miles or more through damp areas where the swamp cabbage grew and the ferns were as tall as a man. They'd stopped at a fisherman's shanty where several local men were gathered, sharing the stories of that day's catch. One fellow swore he'd caught a blue that was forty-five inches in length, not that anyone believed him. Another said he'd seen the ghost of a little girl at the nearby Eel River, and the men laughed out loud, in utter disbelief. Still another said he'd seen an eel step out of the slow-moving falls of the river and become a woman who'd gone to live in an old fisherman's shanty, another story no one believed.

Berkshire County was filled with tall tales, and Nathaniel loved to hear them, true or not. This was a place where anything could happen, where bears roamed the hills, and children tended the sheep with collie dogs by their sides to protect them. Nathaniel had begun to fill a notebook with words and phrases. He wrote down the local tales, but he also remembered the words that Mia had told him about growing up in this wild place. *Bewilderment, love, judgment, wild rosebushes, the deep heart of nature, the black flower, I wanted more for you than I wanted for myself.*

Nathaniel and his uncle had shared a few drinks with the local men, rough whiskey in tin cups, and that was likely why Robert had been compelled to lie down when they returned to the inn, promptly falling into a deep sleep.

"You'll forgive me," Robert had said when he excused himself. "Fishing is hard work."

"That it is," Nathaniel agreed. It was also curative, as his uncle believed. It had centered Nathaniel's thoughts and allowed words to come back to him, as if they were beads on a strand. The Berkshires reminded him how beautiful this world could be. He felt as if he had woken from a long sleep, as if he was a bear himself, one who'd thought his only purpose was to tell stories, when it now became clear that it was far more important for him to have the ability to love someone.

Nathaniel had mud on his boots and leaves in his hair, though he'd done his best to shake them out before coming into the inn. He'd left his pail by the back door, empty, even though they'd caught several blues, one of which was nearly fourteen inches, a monster that flushed a vivid plum color when plucked from the river. Any other fishermen would have dispatched the trout, smacking it against the rocks, bragging about the catch for months, but Nathaniel and his uncle Robert had set their trout free. That was the secret joy of their fishing trips. They never once kept anything they caught, they simply experienced the marvels all around them.

Nathaniel was himself exhausted; still, words continued to come to him on their own, as if called down by an angel. He took up his pen and pad again, and while sitting at a table in the barroom he made a list of the trees they had seen in the forest: *sugar maple, red maple, black birch, yellow birch, hickory, red oak, beech, white ash, hemlock, pine.* He was falling in love with words all over again, for each told a story in and of itself. He was starting from the very beginning, but he was starting all the same. He didn't have a story, but he had the words to use should he ever have a story to tell. The word *tree* could be anything and everything. An apple tree in a shaft of sunlight. A conifer where crows were nesting. A sapling bent over the river, its roots turning a mossy green. A rosebush outside the inn, the crimson flowers tumbling down. This was how it began, with a world that was as real as a river, even though it was made of nothing more than words.

CHAPTER EIGHT

WEST OF THE MOON

Mia arrived at the small train station in Blackwell, which would be torn down decades before she was born, for the train route had been stopped once the highway was built. It was a white-hot afternoon and before Mia began to walk toward the Jack Straw, she took a moment to sit on a wooden bench on the town green, across from the library. It looked as it had in her time, a brick and shingle building, with leaded glass windows and an oak door. Mia saw the town both as it was and as it would come to be. There was the grocery store, and the sheriff's office, and the town founder's house, which was said to have a garden in which only red plants grew, bittersweet, azalea, and a variety of red lilies that could be found nowhere else in the Commonwealth, along with climbing roses called Crimson Glory. Mia tried to imagine her daughter living in this world, and all she could see were the confines of the Community. *You cannot walk barefoot down the street, or cut your hair short,*

285

or do as you please. You will do as others expect you to do. She crossed the green and stood in the doorway of the library. *But you would always have this, the place where there were a thousand keys to a thousand doors.*

One of the men working at the desk noticed Mia and approached her. "Can I help you, miss?" he asked, for he did not recognize her, and the library was private, a club for men to gather and to expand their minds with readings and discussions. The only public library in the Commonwealth was the Franklin Library, founded in 1790, begun with a donation of Benjamin Franklin's books. The Boston Public Library would not be established until 1848. Most libraries were private, and it would be years until women's reading societies were formed, to include women and girls.

"May I not borrow a book?" Mia asked.

"Is your husband a member?" the librarian asked.

"I have no husband," Mia replied, and when the librarian shook his head, she was stunned. "Are you saying I therefore have no right to read these books?"

"I'm sorry, miss. If the library becomes public, then you will be more than welcome. Until that time, I must ask you to leave."

Walking beyond town, on the dirt road that would someday become Route 17, Mia easily found her way, even without the landmarks—the fence that ran the length of the Community's property, the road signs to Lenox and the Mass Pike, the mailboxes of distant neighbors to whom they weren't allowed to speak. Mia now understood that Joel was well aware that once a girl walked into a library she could never be controlled again.

When she entered the woods, she spied a red fox running through the shady glen, leaping for no reason other than to celebrate the joy of being alive. Such a sighting always meant good luck. See a fox and you'll see your future, that was what Ivy had once told her. There were chokeberries and mulberries in the thickets, and the sky was a luminous blue. Mia hiked through the meadow filled with tall plumy grass and was soon flushed from walking hard and fast. Her skirts caught on thorns, and she'd had to tear the fabric away from the brittle limbs of the bramble bushes. Bees were everywhere, and they rumbled around her as if she were a flower moving through the fields.

Every now and then enormous flocks of sparrows could be seen flying south. In Berkshire County, summer was brief. Nights here were already chilly. The present was always overtaken by the future, spring by summer, and summer by fall. Already, the leaves on some twisted vines in the woods were turning yellow. Mia remembered searching to find the first red leaf of the season.

Here, in the deep woods, there was jewelweed along the damp, muddy banks of streams, as well as patches of cardinal flowers, which bloomed scarlet.

When she came up the hill, Mia lifted her skirt, for the grass was wet with mist. She certainly remembered the Jack Straw Tavern, and how she'd sneaked into the bar, relishing her brief time spent there, when she could feel that she was an ordinary girl. As she drew closer, she spied a tin pail outside the door, and when she reached it, she crouched down to have a look. She saw that it was empty, and that no fish had been caught, and then she was sure Nathaniel was inside, for he'd boasted that he'd never once killed a living creature and never kept his catch when out fishing.

Mia went to the window and peered inside. There he was alone at a table, his dark, beautiful face knotted with absolute concentration as he wrote in a small leather notebook, a plate of food before him left untouched. Her heart lurched as she lightly rapped on the window. At first Nathaniel thought he heard the bumblebees hitting the glass. Then he looked up and his attention was riveted. He thought he was dreaming; perhaps he was asleep on his small metal bed in his room, napping just as his uncle was, and had only dreamed that he had walked downstairs and ordered supper and a whiskey.

Mia waved to him, another dream surely, or so he thought until he pinched his hand and felt the smart under his skin.

When Nathaniel came outside, it was late in the day and the light was silvery and pale. They were beyond words and recriminations. He had been stung by her disappearance, but she had returned, and he was unable to resist her. Without a word, they went inside the Jack Straw and took the back staircase to Nathaniel's room. He bolted the door, then stripped off his black coat. She unbuttoned her dress, until he told her to stop. He would do that for her.

The bed was small, too small for Nathaniel alone it had seemed, but that didn't matter now. Life can be long or short, it is impossible to know, but every once in a while an entire life is spent in one night, the night when the windows are open and you can hear the last of the crickets' call, when there is a chill in the air and the stars are bright, when nothing else matters, when a single kiss lasts longer than a lifetime, when you do not think about the future or the past, or whether or not you are walking through a dream rather than the real world, when everything you have always wanted and everything you are fated to mourn forever are tied together with black thread and then sewn with your own hand, when in the morning, as you wake and see the m the distance, you will understand that v not you've made a mistake, whether or not you will lose all that you have, this is what it means to be human.

As she was placing the book back beneath the mattress, he saw both the name and the title. She'd thought he was asleep, and now she clutched the book to her chest. *You will change everything,* Elizabeth had warned her. *There is no logic in love or in writing,* Mia had insisted, but now she wondered if she had gone too far in tempting fate.

"You must let me see," Nathaniel urged. When Mia refused, there was a darkness in his voice. "It appears to be my book. Is it not?"

"Not yet. Not until you write it. If you saw it now you might be influenced to change it in some way, or to write it as you think it's meant to be written."

But now he knew the title, which he assumed he dare not change. Among the words he'd recently written in his notebook there had been a list of colors. Scarlet had not been among them, but now that he had spied it, he thought it the most beautiful word.

"Did my sister tell you not to show it to me? She's not always correct, even though she believes she is."

Mia had never seen him so shaken. She had ˉd about his black moods and the gloom that often descended upon him, and yet she was unprepared when he stormed out of the room, muttering that he would find some coffee at the bar. As soon as he'd left, Mia thought it was best to conceal the book in a place where he wouldn't think to look. She would stow it in her bag and store that in the fireplace, but as she lifted the book, it fell open on the floor, and then she saw the change had already begun.

The words she knew so well were disappearing. An entire passage she knew by heart, one that concerned what to do with an unwed mother who had broken the Puritans' rules, was gone, replaced by blank white space. *At the very least, they should have put the brand of a hot iron on Hester Prynne's forehead.* More was disappearing as she turned the pages, as if the words were black sparrows flying off the paper, too quickly to be caught. *What do we talk of marks and brands, whether on the bodice of her gown, or the flesh of her forehead? This woman has brought shame upon us all, and ought to die. Is there not law for it? Truly, there is, both in the Scripture and the statute-book. Then let the magistrates, who have made it of no effect, thank themselves if their own wives and daughters go astray!*

Even if Mia was at the fringes of Nathaniel's life, those edges might burn so fiercely they could change everything, and like the butterfly across the world, she would have changed all that he did and thought and wrote as well. Even if she told him how to follow his history, where to meet his wife, at what addresses he should live, the date he was to join Brook Farm, the day he should begin to write his great novel several years from now, she could not make certain he would experience the small details of his life. A dragonfly he spied on a Friday. A bird he noticed in the sky. One meeting in the forest could affect all that he was and would ever be. What would their daughter mean to him, how would she change his vision of the world? A novel was made of personal experience and raw emotion. It was a chart of all that a person was. Even if Mia lived in the cottage, if she saw him once a month, or every six months, it might be enough to change what was meant to be. Elizabeth had been right; it was already happening. Mia went to look in the glass and saw that she was beginning to disappear. Her freckles were gone, her hair was a pale ashy color, her eyes were silver rather than black. That was when she knew, if she waited too long to leave, she would become invisible, both here and in her own world, as if she had walked into the water all those years ago, as if his book had not been on the shelf, there to change her fate.

In the morning, the carriage arrived to take Robert and Nathaniel back to Salem. Their time here was over, and the real world awaited. It had moved on without them, and now it was time to step back inside their lives and pick up their responsibilities and renew their family ties. Robert Manning thought the trip had done his nephew a fair amount of good. Nathaniel seemed in better spirits, and he had stopped talking nonsense about life in the future. The future, after all, was what they made it and what they lived each day.

There were two carriage men rather than the usual one. Robert recognized the regular fellow as the one who'd brought them to the Berkshires a few days earlier, a young man named Tyler, who explained that he was showing the new man the ropes. The new fellow had gone up to Nathaniel's room and brought down his bags while Nathaniel was in the bath. Robert threw a keen glance at the dark figure, who was expressionless as he loaded the baggage into the rear of the carriage.

"He's a bit old to be new, isn't he?" Robert said with a laugh. The man looked somewhat undesirable, in strange clothes with close-clipped gray hair.

"He's working hard," Tyler said. "And he barely says a word. I suppose that's good enough."

Robert's bags and his fishing gear were already on board when his nephew came out of the inn to reclaim his luggage. He'd left Mia in his room in order to explain his situation to his uncle and reclaim his luggage. His hair was wet. There was something wild in his eyes.

"Are you ill?" Robert wanted to know.

"Not at all," Nathaniel said. "Or perhaps I am. If so, it's an illness that affects the heart, one people beg to have, even if there is no cure. Uncle, I think you understand the one thing that would keep me here."

All at once Robert knew. Nathaniel was besotted. "Is it her?" his uncle asked. "The mythological creature?"

Nathaniel laughed. "She's real enough. Believe me."

Robert's keen gaze was drawn toward the second story of the inn, and there, in the window of his nephew's room, he spied a woman with pale red hair. She wore Nathaniel's dressing gown with nothing underneath. Robert felt a wave of sadness, for he understood that he would be returning to Salem alone. He had failed in his mission to wake Nathaniel from his dreams and fantasies and was unable to drag him back to real life. He could quarrel with his nephew, but Nathaniel was stubborn, he always had been, a man who followed his own path and intended to do away with the rules of the past.

Robert stood in the shade of a twisted apple tree and listened to his nephew's explanation of why he wished to stay on in Berkshire County, a tale about needing time to write and think, excuses that didn't ring true. "Be honest, man," Robert said. "Isn't she the reason?"

Nathaniel lifted his eyes to see Mia at the window. He'd been showing her where the bath was, so they'd both been out of his room when his luggage was brought down. Robert laughed when he saw the expression on his nephew's face. He knew a lovestruck man when he saw one. "You answered the question." Robert shook his head. "I'm quite convinced you have no intention of returning to Salem with me."

"Not today. That much is certain."

Robert clapped his nephew on the back. "Take my advice. Do not get married."

"That is an unlikely outcome, as I have no ring," Nathaniel joked wryly.

Nathaniel embraced his uncle, who had indeed been a father to him. He wished he could tell Robert more, but it was best not to, for surely the truth would alarm Robert and make him question Nathaniel's sanity.

"No rash actions," Robert reminded him.

"What I want more than anything is some time, Uncle. I'll stay here and write."

"I'll have them place three more nights on my bill," Robert granted. "Should that be enough?"

It would never be enough, but Nathaniel thanked his uncle. Three nights to do their best to figure out the rest of their lives.

"Just a warning," Robert said. "Love can be dangerous."

Nathaniel softened to his uncle, who always wanted the best for him. "Is there anything worthwhile that is not?"

Nathaniel remained outside to watch the carriage disappear down the road, past a stand of beech trees. When he turned, he noticed that one of the carriage men was still standing there, leaning against the wall of the inn, as if he had all the time in the world.

"They've gone without you," Nathaniel said, confused.

"It doesn't matter to me," the man said brazenly. "I don't work for them. I'll do as I please."

"Will you?" Nathaniel eyed this character with suspicion.

"I've got a farm here," the fellow replied. "The biggest in Berkshire County."

"Do you now?" This man certainly didn't look like the other prosperous farmers in the area.

"She's mine as well," the carriage man said with a grin as he gazed upward.

"I don't know what you mean," Nathaniel answered, but he saw the way the fellow was staring up at the window of his room. Nathaniel had such an intense reaction to this man, mistrust he supposed it was, that when the fellow turned to leave, Nathaniel waited to make certain the stranger was headed off before he went back inside the inn.

"Who were you speaking with?" Mia asked when at last Nathaniel came upstairs. She'd spied him in conversation with a man who stood in the shadows so that she could not make him out.

"Someone who insisted he had the largest farm in Berkshire County when he looked like he'd been sleeping in a barn." Nathaniel sat in the chair beside the bed, his face lined with worry. He didn't like the cold obstinence in the carriage man's tone. He thought of the man Mia had told him about, the one who'd ruined her mother's life and thought he owned everything as far as the eye could see. "Could anyone else travel here, Mia?"

"No, of course not," Mia said. "Not without the book."

"He said you were his, whatever that is supposed to mean."

Alarmed, Mia gazed out the window. *We carry the past with us even when we try to run away. It's never very far away.* It was then she saw a man walking into the woods. She recognized his posture, and the slant of his shoulders, and she certainly knew his walk, for his stride announced his assurance that he owned every bit of the world he was in. And then she knew that when she had come here, he had been close enough to follow her. One step was all it took.

I thought he was a man who would care for me, Ivy had told her one night in the woods, *but he turned out to be the opposite.* She might have been crying, it was too dark to know. Ivy and Mia had been sitting in the grass, and the fireflies were drifting through the forest as if they were globes of light. *He told me a story, and I believed in stories, but everything he said was a lie. He told me he had been terribly mistreated by his family, beaten and uncared for, and that he wanted a new world, where people were guided by rules that helped them through their lives.*

"Whoever he is, he was in our room," Nathaniel said.

"Doing what?" A chill spread through Mia's body.

"He was sent to collect my luggage."

Mia turned to see her bag was no longer hidden in the fireplace but was tossed onto the floor, its contents rifled through. She had stowed her mother's letter and the painting beneath the thin mattress, but the book was missing. She felt sheer panic, for although she had no idea of how Joel intended to use the book, she was certain he would find a way to use it against her. She and Ivy should have made a vow to walk into the future; they should had left the past behind. If you hold on to it, it will only haunt you, it will wrap its arms around you and pull you down. She needed that book in order to return. Nathaniel

298

hadn't yet noticed she was fading, but when Mia peered into the glass, she could see that she was even paler. It was happening to her. The book had changed or it had ceased to exist, and she was becoming invisible.

While Nathaniel went to ask the innkeeper's wife for a packed lunch to take with them when they explored the woods, Mia pulled on her boots and went down the back stairway, used for bringing up coal and wood in the wintertime. She knew Joel, and she was certain that he would be waiting for her. Evil was predictable; it cloaked itself in righteousness, convinced its enemies must be punished. Mia ducked beneath the tree branches, not caring if they tore at her clothes. She saw the stamp of his boots in the damp earth and followed them through the tall stalks of weeds and the banks of wild mint.

He was there waiting. Mia felt as if she'd been holding her breath ever since she discovered that the book was gone. There it was in Joel's hands. He always knew the way to best hurt someone. They glared at one another through the shadows.

"I'm not surprised to discover you're a witch," Joel said flatly. "That was always in your nature. I took one step to follow you and found myself in hell. I said books belonged to the devil, and you've proved me right."

"I want the book," Mia said simply, even

though she felt as if she were a bundle of nerves.

Joel tossed her a filthy look. "I want the painting you stole. You knew it was the deed."

"I did not," Mia told him.

Still, he grinned and said darkly, "I'm not surprised by who you turned out to be, but your mother would be so disappointed in you. She would want nothing to do with you. We should have left you on the town green."

"Don't speak to me about my mother," Mia said in a soft voice.

"And now you're the devil's whore." He was speaking of Nathaniel, nodding to her midsection. "About to have his child I'd guess. At least they know what's right in these times. You'll be in jail if you try to rid yourself of it."

"I wouldn't wish to do so," Mia told him. "But if I did, I should have the right to make that choice."

"Your mother didn't teach you to do as you were told, even though she learned pretty quickly."

"She only stayed because you threatened to take me away."

"I was enough of a father for all those years. My name is on your birth certificate. You're mine and you owe me. It only makes sense for us to help one another. You want the book and I want the deed to my own land. We make a fair and even trade and you promise to take me back with you with whatever witchcraft you've got up your sleeve."

Be careful of who you trust, Ivy had told her once in the woods. *If you want to be smart, something I never was, only trust yourself.*

"If you don't agree to the bargain, I'll take care of that man of yours. I'll break his neck if I have to. I just want what's mine. You listened to me once upon a time, back when I was your father."

Mia felt that chill again, as she had the night she was locked in the barn. It had been summer, but she had been freezing, preoccupied with what would happen if she didn't get away, the public shaming, the brand marking her flesh. "You were never my father," she told him.

"Say what you will. I raised you."

"Give me one more day," Mia boldly asked. "Then I'll do as you say."

"Lovestruck." Joel nodded. He was still a handsome man if you didn't look too closely, if you didn't see what was underneath. "Just like your mother."

Mia did her best to ignore the comment, though she felt herself grow flushed. She remembered the rules about talking back. *Children are not to speak unless spoken to. They must be quiet and polite and never unruly.*

"Fine," Joel said. "Because of your mother, I'll wait until tomorrow."

They agreed that they would meet at daybreak at the farm.

"Today is yours," Joel said. "But when the morning comes, don't make me wait. You'll regret it if you do, and so will that man of yours."

Nathaniel was sitting in a rough wooden chair outside the inn, waiting. He had paced until he'd left a trail in the grass, before realizing it would do no good to worry and fret; he would have to have faith. He was relieved when at last he saw her emerge from the woods, her red hair loose. She had a singular way of walking, different from most women of this time, as if she were free as a bird, and could fly away if she wished. She came to him and sat in his lap, arms looped around his neck.

"This is still the place where I spent my childhood. I vowed to never come back, until I heard that you were here."

"I'm glad you changed your mind," Nathaniel said.

Mia could have cried had she allowed herself to do so. "You changed my mind. Now I want us to have a perfect day," she told him. She really couldn't ask for more. "Can we do that?"

"We can indeed. We've already begun."

They hiked into the woods, where the wild asters were blooming, and the grass was nearly waist high. As they neared the river, Mia heard branches breaking; for a moment she feared it was Joel, out to double-cross her, then they saw two fishermen who waved and wished them good luck, shouting that the trout were running in such great numbers the river itself had turned blue. The orchards of apple trees for which the town would later be famous had sprung from the seedlings Johnny Appleseed had left behind, but there were pine and fir and oak and wild pear laden with fruit, with heaps dropping onto the ground. It was the time of year when bears began to go mad for all the local bounty, devouring the blueberries, and wild walnuts, and the ripening pears, eating all they could before summer's end.

Farther downstream, the deep pools reflected the clouds in the sky. Water ran two ways in this river, down from the mountain. Mia had skated here when she was a girl, fashioning skates of sticks tied to her shoes. It was not a childhood anyone would have chosen, but it was hers all the same. Once, Ivy had followed her to the river. *What do you think you're doing?* Ivy had said, concerned that Mia would get caught breaking the rules.

Having fun, Mia said. *Ever hear of it?*

Ivy grinned, then she tied sticks to her boots as well. Once she was out on the ice, Ivy fell again and again, until Mia came to offer her arm. They skated round on the blue ice until their fingers were freezing through their cheap work gloves.

It was more than fun. It was perfect, or almost.

Don't tell anyone we were here, Ivy had said when they trekked back through the snowy woods, walking lightly over the frost. But Joel had been waiting up for his wife and he'd seen the snow dusted in her hair. The next evening, when Mia saw her mother in the dining hall, she noticed the dark mark on Ivy's arm. Ivy caught her staring and hurriedly pulled down her sleeve, but Mia had seen it. **A** for self-absorbed, **A** for anarchy and for acts of wickedness, as if a cold blue night of fun had been a sin to be placed beside vanity and envy.

When Mia and Nathaniel reached the bank of the river, they lay on their backs to gaze at the wisps of clouds racing through the sky. Mia rested her face against Nathaniel's rough cheek.

Oh, perfect day, the one day they would never forget. Mia ran her fingertips along Nathaniel's features, memorizing him through touch.

"I haven't been honest with you," she said. "I haven't told you how I came to read your book and how it changed my life."

She told him that when she was fifteen and lived just over the hill, on a farm that overlooked Hightop Mountain, she had been so desperate that she had counted out black stones until there were seventy, all glimmering in the sunlight that filtered through the leaves. She knew that there had been drownings in the Last Look River, and she would simply be one more. She told Nathaniel that she had read that people who attempted to take their own lives and failed reported that they regretted their actions as soon as they stepped off the bridge or threw themselves into the sea, but she had been so lost she could not see how that was possible. Then she had found his book, and once she began to read, she understood there was a door that would lead her out of her situation, and that every book was a door, and that there were a thousand lives she might live.

"Mia, I don't know what I could possibly write that would affect you so," Nathaniel said. It was a burden and a huge responsibility, and he didn't know if he was capable of such an undertaking.

Mia held her hand to his face. "You'll write something beautiful and true, and I'll read it and live."

They left their clothes scattered in the grass and went down to the low stony edge of the water. It was the sort of bright, sun-yellow day that felt as if it would last forever. For a few hours, they didn't have to think about what the future would bring.

Nathaniel was the first to step into the shallows. The trout splashed away in a blue blur as he threw himself into the depths with a shout. Mia laughed and applauded his daring. He was perfect. He was still hers for one more day.

"Come in," Nathaniel called. "Be brave!"

She thought of the times she'd been bravest. When she went through the woods to watch the play on the town green on a summer night, when she asked her mother if she could visit the castle and she began to read, when she broke the lock on the barn door and ran down Route 17. You had to lose something to gain something. It was the reason why so many people stayed, long after they knew they should leave. Mia walked into the water. The last time of everything was painful, no matter how beautiful it might be. *The last time I walked with you, slept beside you, loved you, spoke to you, told you the truth, the last time I looked at you.* She would not tell him about their child, and he would not notice. They would see what they wished to see, only one another. The birds were quiet, and all the world seemed still as Mia plunged into the deepest pool. Nathaniel drew her near and she kissed him recklessly, as if the world was about to end, but it wasn't. It was only the story that was over.

On their walk back, Mia asked if they might visit Blackwell, the town she had known so well when she was young.

"Are you certain you won't feel sad as you're reminded of your mother?" Nathaniel asked.

"How can we ever be certain of how or what we'll feel?"

Mia kissed him for being thoughtful, keeping the reason for her request to herself. They walked down the lanes and across pastures that would become Route 17 when all the trees were cut down and tar was laid. Nathaniel put a hand on Mia's arm to stop her before they left the forest. He nodded to a shaded glen. There was a fox, the sign of good luck. They held hands then, their fingers interlaced. Mia was thankful that she knew how to feel one thing and pretend that she was feeling something entirely different. She had learned that in the Community. She knew how to stop herself from crying.

At last they reached the section of the woods where Mia and her mother had stood to watch the play about the drowned girl called the Apparition.

"Shall we turn back?" Nathaniel asked, gauging the sadness in Mia's mood.

"Oh no. We're almost there."

Soon enough they came upon the town center, the place where Joel said they should have left Mia when she was a newborn. Across from where they stood was the library with its brick façade and its turrets.

Mia looked up at Nathaniel, eyes shining. "That's where I found your book."

"By accident," he said. "Perhaps any book would have done as well."

"No. It was meant to be. You were meant to be."

Mia suggested he go on to the library, for she wished to spend some time alone with her memories. She pointed to the far part of the green. "We set up the farmers' market over there and sold apples and tomatoes. I haven't eaten an apple since."

Nathaniel was stunned. "Then you're missing out on something wonderful."

Mia laughed when she saw the concerned look on his face. "I've lived without them," she assured him.

"The Puritans believed that women should be subjugated because Eve ate of the apple, committing the original sin," Nathaniel told her. "You should eat an apple every day to spite the idiots who thought so."

"I'd rather be kissed," Mia said.

Nathaniel was glad to oblige and so he did right there on Main Street, even though several passersby turned to gawk. They then agreed to meet in the center of the green. Mia wandered along Main Street until she was certain that Nathaniel had entered the library, then she headed for her destination. The sheriff's office was exactly where the police station would be when Mia lived here, although it was smaller. It was cool when she went inside. Both the sheriff and his assistant looked up when she entered.

"Can we help you?" the sheriff asked.

"Thank you for asking," Mia said. "Not right now."

The sheriff looked at her, curious. "Are you from around here?"

"Once," Mia said. That much was true. "But not anymore."

When the men turned away, Mia slipped an envelope onto the front desk for them to find later in the day, or perhaps not until tomorrow. That was when they would be needed, out near Hightop Mountain.

Nathaniel was sitting on a bench beneath a huge elm tree that was already gone when Mia was a girl, stricken by Dutch elm disease. His arms were spread out and his face was lifted to the sun. He was so peaceful in that moment, not the haunted man he'd once been. He was here and nowhere else, delighted to open his eyes and see Mia standing before him.

"I have a gift for you," he told her. He took an apple from the pocket of his black coat. "Your first, but not your last."

Mia sat beside him, and he watched her take a bite, delighted by how tentative she was, as if she was accepting an offering from a serpent rather than from the man who loved her. *My Eve,* he thought, *my darling who taught me what I needed to know.* He wondered why the original Eve was not praised for the knowledge she'd brought to humankind, why she wasn't honored instead of disregarded and disgraced.

"How is it?" he asked Mia, who now offered him a bite of his own.

"The best thing I've ever tasted," she admitted. She could tell it was a Look-No-Further, the variety they had grown on the farm, in the orchard where her mother had been working, hauling a woven basket filled with apples through the wildflowers and the weeds, taking her last look at the beautiful world.

That night, they left the window open so they could listen to the crickets' slow call as they lay in one another's arms. They were grateful they could study one another. They did so as if memorizing every feature, knees and elbows, throat and ears, loved and beloved. Mia thought of all the years when she had been certain she would never be able to love anyone, and now here she was. Not only did she have a heart, but it was already breaking.

"Shall I tell you your children's names?" she asked Nathaniel.

She wanted to give him a gift before she left, but when she offered it to him, Nathaniel knew she would not stay. It was a way of saying good-bye, to say what he would experience, and she would not. He nodded and held her close.

"Una and Julian and Rose."

Nathaniel's throat was tight, and he found he could not speak. They were, indeed, beautiful names.

"They will be perfect," Mia told him. "You will love them more than you love your own life."

"Will I?" he managed to say. Nathaniel knew what the endings of stories were like; he'd written them enough times to know that this was theirs.

"You will adore them. You'll write about them, and how fatherhood surprised you and changed you."

"I expect it surprises everyone."

"You're not everyone." His eyes were deep gray now, as dark as she'd ever seen them. As for her, she was still faded, a shadow of herself. Nathaniel could feel her slipping away; she was so light in his arms, she was a ghost of who she'd been and would be so until she returned home. She was glad she would leave before the end and that she wouldn't have to watch him fall in love with someone else. "Your wife will be the right woman for you."

"That's you," Nathaniel insisted, convinced.

"If you love once, you can love again," Mia told him. "I know you will love her." Nathaniel covered his ears so he couldn't hear more, but Mia laughed and pulled his large, beautiful hands away so that he would listen. "I promise, you'll be happy. I've seen your future."

"What about you?" he asked, unsure of what he wished the answer to be. He wanted to be missed; he wanted her for himself. Mia ran a hand through his hair. Elizabeth was right; if she told him the truth, he would never let her go. She would name their daughter after his sister, and she would bring her to visit libraries, just as Constance had brought her to do the same. *Herein are a thousand different doors, and a thousand different lives. Turn the page and you open the door.*

"I'll be happy, too."

By the time Nathaniel fell asleep, it was almost morning. The sky was still dark when Mia left the bed to dress. She spied Nathaniel's notebook on the bureau. He'd made lists of words, a page of colors, another of trees, another with her name written a hundred times, as if she herself were an incantation. Magic was possible, especially once he began to write. She looked until she came upon a page with a single line. *She had not known the weight until she felt the freedom.* It was the line that had disappeared from the book. It was no longer invisible. It was all coming back. Mia knew that every story contained the same things. A beginning, a middle, and an end. What she hadn't known was that the end came before you knew it, it came so fast that all you could do was breathe.

She left Ivy's letter on the desk. Her greatest

treasure would be her greatest gift. He had the words but not the story, so she gave it to him. That was why she had recognized herself in *The Scarlet Letter*. The story would begin with a woman who was not allowed to control her own body or her own fate. It happened all the time. It happened above the burying hill in Salem, a place men knew nothing of, and it happened now in Mia's time. In the story, there would be a man who didn't have the courage to declare himself, and another man who didn't care if he brought a woman to ruin, but there was also a love that couldn't be broken, the love was never invisible, the heart of the story, the love of a mother for her child.

Nathaniel knew she was gone before he opened his eyes. The bed was small, and because he was alone, he had taken up all the space. He wondered how she had ever fit there beside him. He wondered how it had been possible for him not to have heard her leave. Some things were meant to be, that was what his sister always told him, and some were not.

The bedsheets held Mia's scent, a grassy fragrance that made him long for her. There was the letter she'd left for him on the bureau. She'd written a single line on the envelope. *I love you enough to let you go.*

He imagined the future that awaited him. A

wife and three children. A life he was meant to have. Love once, and you can love again. Open your heart, open your eyes, be grateful for what you've had. Nothing was promised in this world, nothing lasted, yet what truly mattered always remained. What was eternal could not be captured, yet it flickered in the dark there beside you, the memory of all that had been.

Nathaniel remembered staring out the window when he was nine. He felt much the same today as he had then, for he was part of the world and still he remained separate from it. That was what it meant to be a writer. He gazed out into the light rising above the treetops. He might have pursued Mia, but he knew it was impossible. He still had the apple core on his desk, with the marks of her small bites.

It would be morning in a matter of moments. The world would fill with daylight, and he would be there to record it. He leaned against the metal bedposts and read the letter, and as soon as he did, he knew it was the story he'd been searching for. A young woman who had been turned away from those closest to her, who only wished to make her own decisions. He imagined the Community to be not unlike the Puritans, the society his own family had sprung from, who believed that it was God's will for women to be subordinate, insisting that Eve's sin was carried by every woman, a burden she would always have to bear, one that spoke of a woman's moral weakness. Nathaniel thought of cruelty and of love; he thought of the choices women make and the choices forced upon them. It was Ivy's letter he read, but it was more than that to him. It was the book he would write.

He closed his eyes so that he might imagine Mia asleep in the grass the first time he saw her. He heard the birds outside his window, swifts and swallows and sparrows, all nesting in the eaves of the Jack Straw Tavern. Nathaniel would think about the novel for years, and then he would write in earnest. He would compose *The Scarlet Letter* like a man possessed, finishing in only a few months. Following the novel's publication, on March 16, 1850, after having been overlooked and thought to be a minor writer, he would be the author of an instant bestseller. One critic said the novel was *a fable of a guilty heart,* and perhaps this was true. It was his burden and his apology all in one. He would take the first copy that was published, come to the library in Blackwell, and sit at the long table to inscribe his dedication before setting the book high up on the shelf.

To Mia, If it was a dream,
it was ours alone and you were mine.

Now he dressed and sat on a wooden chair by the desk. The end of one story is the beginning of another. He had always known that to be true. Soon enough the sky was brightening and the birds in the bushes outside his window began to call as dawn opened across the horizon. It was the next day, the start of the future. He turned away from the window. The whole world was out there, but it was also here in this room. The world was at his fingertips. That was when he began to write.

Mia navigated through the woods, a forest she knew by heart. There were blackberry bushes that were thick with fruit, in the very same place when she was a girl. The women used to pick the berries to make pies, which they sold at the farmers' market. The children always begged for a taste, but Joel hadn't believed in sweets, or in spoiling children, or in playing favorites. He'd only believed in himself.

When Mia walked out of the woods she saw the grand vista that matched the scene in the painting she had folded into her skirt pocket. The watercolor had been handed down through the generations and was a perfect rendering of the mountain and the untouched land that surrounded the peak. Mia went into the old barn, built by the first settlers, used to store hay. It was the same barn where she used to go to read, and she knew all of its hiding places; she tucked the painting beneath a loose board. Then she went outside and waited. She knew he'd appear in his own good time. He'd make her wait, and that was fine. She had been waiting for quite a while.

Joel came up the hill as the light was breaking the sky open. He had the book, but he also carried a rifle under his arm, bought at the back of the grocery store in town. "Just in case," he said when he showed her the gun. "You'd be stupid to trust me, but I'd also be stupid to trust you. You've done something to the book." He tossed it to her. "You've put some sort of spell on it. It's disappearing. Will it still take us back?"

When Mia opened it, half of the words were gone. "The words will return when I leave."

"When *we* leave," Joel reminded her. "I'm not staying here. I'm going back to my farm." He pointed at the ground with the rifle. "Get down, because you're not going anywhere if I don't have the painting."

Mia knelt before him in the grass. This was what he'd done on the day he burned her books, when he locked her in the barn, when he cut off her mother's long black hair.

Sparrows winged overhead. A low whistle sounded, not a bird singing, but a man calling to his dog on a nearby farm. The collie had wandered and now began to trot toward them through the tall grass. He came up to Joel, barking like mad. There were dogs such as these all over the Berkshires, known for their fierce loyalty. This one had taken an immediate dislike to Joel, who raised the gun.

Mia rose to her feet and grabbed the dog by its collar, which was little more than a rope. "Stay here, boy," she said. She wanted nothing to interfere with her plan. She had left her gold earrings, as well as a silver inkwell from the inn, hidden beside the painting. She wanted to make certain when the sheriff came, he would be catching a thief. The note she'd left would likely have been read by now, and it was quite possible Joel would be arrested by the end of the day.

Find him where I have left him in the barn and you will find what this thief has stolen. Be careful. He is dangerous.

"We don't have much time," she told Joel. "The painting is in the barn."

"Don't play with me. Where in the barn?"

"Beneath the loose board at the rear. Where I hid my books."

"Do not move," he warned her.

But once Joel had gone after the painting, Mia let go of the dog, and she ran to the barn door. He'd been wrong to trust her, to think she was still a girl who would do as she was told. She slid the wooden lock shut, shifting her weight against it to fasten it. It was a strong lock, far newer than it had been when Mia escaped. From inside the barn she could hear Joel's shouts. He was so loud and fierce he frightened the blackbirds from the trees. He called out what he would do to her when he escaped, but after she walked down the hill Mia couldn't hear him anymore. She didn't have to listen to him. No one did.

In the year when she was fifteen, she might have drowned, her body dragged back to shore by the same men who had carried her mother's body across the lawn; she might have been invisible, buried behind the wire fence, but that was a lifetime ago. She would have the life she chose, just as her mother had intended for her, just as she intended for her own child.

Mia lifted her eyes to the mountain. The wind had picked up and clouds were moving across the sky. How was it possible for her to have never noticed how beautiful it was here? Years from now Carrie would discover the painting left in an old barn she inherited, and she would become a painter, insisting that she must have already been an artist in another time. The Community would come to be, and Ivy Jacob would find herself there one night when she didn't know where else to go, and Mia would live the first part of her life here and she would always remember that she was loved by someone from the very start. *The best thing that ever happened to me was you,* Ivy had whispered to her that night in the woods when they walked invisible.

Mia wished that her mother could see how beautiful this place had been before it was ruined by shoddy buildings and barns, with wire fencing to keep local people out and the members of the Community in. She wished she could thank Ivy for allowing her to go to the library, for telling her stories in the woods, for wanting more for her. Now Mia wanted her own daughter to know a world where she could go to school, and travel on her own by train, and walk down a city street on a summer evening, and read any book she chose from the shelves of a library.

In no time it would be autumn, the season when Mia always scanned the trees, in search of the first red leaves. At last, she came to the site where the cemetery would be. For now, it was simply a patch of land overrun with mulberries and yarrow, hyssop and wild chives, along with the first of the ferns that would someday take over the area. The fields all around were filled with sunflowers, and the sound of bees was all that Mia could hear. She was grateful for the shade of the huge beech tree, and she leaned her back against its trunk as she sat in the bank of ferns. She thought about the day that she'd believed would be her last day on earth. How lucky she'd been to have walked into a library. How grateful she was to hold the book in her hands.

The world was waking, slowly and then all at once. Birdsongs, the whir of beetles, the wind in the trees. Mia could hear the horses on a nearby farm. The collie dog was racing through the field on his way back home, but when he spotted her, he came toward Mia, a flash of black and white. He was the same breed that could always be found in Blackwell, the kind that had been at the farm, smart, reliable dogs that didn't need much attention and were always loyal. The night she ran away, none of the dogs had barked. They had allowed her to be invisible, and she had started her life over. This would be the third life, the one she would keep, the one she was meant to have.

"Hello there," Mia said when the collie came to greet her.

The dog sniffed, curious, but when he heard his owner whistling on the nearby acreage, he took off through the grass. Mia could see how her mother might have thought she had arrived at a place that was west of the moon. West of the moon was where you journeyed to meet the person you loved, the one you would never forget. Mia wanted to remember everything when she left here. How cold the water was in the river, how long his kisses lasted, how quick the crickets' song was, until it wasn't a song at all, just one great chime of summer's ending. She would always be thankful that she had reached for Nathaniel's book in the library and read it in the barn and that she had stepped into the world he had created out of paper and ink. Luck can be many things, and she carried her luck with her, she carried it in a book.

Once upon a time, she would tell her daughter, I loved you more than anything. I loved you more than life itself. I loved you enough to find whatever awaits us, no matter what it might be, no matter where. We can go as far as we need to, even if it's west of the moon. Sometimes walking away is the bravest thing you can do. When you get there, you'll know where you are.

ACKNOWLEDGMENTS

Endless thanks to Amanda Urban, Ron Bernstein, Marysue Rucci, Libby McGuire, and Dana Trocker.

Thank you to Nicole Dewey.

Thank you, Andy Jiaming Tang.

Thank you to the team at Atria Books.

My deepest gratitude to my friends who saw me through the writing of this book, especially Jill Karp, Diane Ackerman, and Laura Zigman.

Thank you, Nina Rosenberg, for a lifetime of Saturdays.

Thank you to Madeleine Wright for assistance in all matters.

Thank you to the corners in my life, Madison Wolters, Karina van Berkum, and Deborah Revzin. And to David Revzin, honorary.

Many thanks to Megan Marshall for her early reading of this book.

Thank you to Stephen King.

Gratitude to the staff of The Old Manse in Concord and to the staff of The House of the Seven Gables in Salem.

A huge thank you to all of the bookstores who have supported my work from the start.

My heartfelt thanks to the librarians who allowed me to take out as many books as I wanted.

To my readers, eternal gratitude.

To my mother. Now I know the love between us was never invisible, even when I didn't see it. I see it now.

Further Reading:
Nathaniel Hawthorne in His Times, James R. Mellow
The Peabody Sisters, Megan Marshall
The Scarlet Letter, Nathaniel Hawthorne

Center Point Large Print
600 Brooks Road / PO Box 1
Thorndike, ME 04986-0001 USA

(207) 568-3717

US & Canada:
1 800 929-9108
www.centerpointlargeprint.com

The invisible hour
MCN LargeP FIC Hoffma   **31659061880569**

Hoffman, Alice.
EAST BATON ROUGE LIBRARY